COMPOSED

AN ASH PARK NOVEL

MEGHAN O'FLYNN

COMPOSED

Copyright 2020

This is a work of fiction. Names, characters, businesses, places, events and incidents are either the products of the author's imagination or used fictitiously. Any resemblance to actual persons, living or dead, or actual events is purely coincidental. Opinions expressed are those of the characters and do not necessarily reflect those of the author, though she does share some of Petrosky's ideas on rapists. She'll let you guess which ones. No part of this book may be reproduced, stored in a retrieval system, scanned, or transmitted or distributed in any form or by any means electronic, mechanical, photocopied, recorded or otherwise without written consent of the author. All rights reserved. If you want a free book, *compose* your own (or check out the free works I do have available—sign up for my newsletter at meghanoflynn.com to snag those).

Distributed by Pygmalion Publishing, LLC

This book is dedicated to the amazing group who helped me name everything from businesses to people in this novel, the same wonderful folks who keep me steeped in dark jokes and silliness and murderous sloths. I'm honored and humbled to call you my partners in crime.
You sick twisted motherfuckers.

WANT MORE FROM MEGHAN?
There are many more books to choose from!

Learn more about Meghan's novels on
https://meghanoflynn.com

PROLOGUE

The walls are thick with black, the kind of dark that blocks out the world—as it should. Everything feels so loud when it's bright. Creation takes quiet, he knows that now. It takes darkness. And once you pare your craft down to its most fundamental and achingly perfect form, you can release it out into the universe.

But not until it's ready. Finished products are a labor of love, of sweat—of blood.

Finally. Years of musing, of failed attempts, but it's all led here. And he's ready for it, though his hands shake, though his belly feels queasy as if he might vomit. He has already. Twice.

No, I'm ready. And he has an audience waiting.

He looks back down at the sleek magazine in his hand. The pages flip with a plasticky sound, each model practically screaming with the type of confidence acquired through a surgeon's blade. They are but poorly rendered sketches, more Barbie-esque than beautiful—matte and smooth. But those women can't speak.

They're not real—they probably don't exist at all.

He squints at the page in front of him, at her long legs,

blonde hair, creamy skin the color of a frog's belly. He frowns and reaches for the floor beside him. For the blade.

He starts with her upper eyelid.

The first incision goes smoothly, the hiss of steel against flesh—against paper, fair, but it doesn't sound that different from flesh, not really. Or maybe it's that it doesn't feel so different in the wrist. It's hard to tell sometimes what he really means until he writes it down. He's never been great at interacting in the moment, the pressured way his words rush out, half of them not even close to what he wants to say, but just give him a pen.

Or a scalpel.

He traces the gentle slope down to the tear duct and watches as it ruptures, the white of the eye, the glorious blue iris freed from its prison. The room is hot, though when the temperature rose, he isn't sure. Maybe there's something wrong with him. Is he sick? He might be sick.

He moves the blade to the lower lid. And begins again.

Sweat drips from his nose and onto the page—*plip*. He barely notices. In this moment, he's a surgeon; he's a harbinger of perfection. He's a better version of himself.

Hisssssss. The blade pauses as if of its own accord. He sets the tool aside with a clink, but neither that nor the hissing can cover the sound of crying. He ignores it and peels the lower lid away, then swallows hard over a lump that even now rises higher and harder in his throat.

No going back now, no going back.

He tosses the magazine aside, listens to it rustle like the wings of a hundred agitated bats then suddenly cease as if the entire flock has dropped from the sky, just more victims of a world gone mad.

That line, even only in his head, is lovely, but he can't focus on it for long, can't relish it, because from somewhere below him, the cries accelerate, keening and high-pitched and desperate.

He stares at the tiny eyeball in his hand, feels its realness in the pads of his shaking fingers. Sweat drips down his spine. The screaming comes again, cutting the silence.

No, these women staring at him from the pages are not real.

But *she* is.

1

THE RUNNING trail started near the eastern border of Ash Park's downtown strip, but it was nothing like the pretty concrete paths of larger districts; elsewhere, long curves of gray meandered through lines of foliage that brightened in autumn to brilliant hues that somehow smelled of apple cider and hayrides. This path hooked a jagged zipper between bouts of shabby evergreens missing half their needles, scrubby brush, and sickly groves of bare birches—all currently frosted in snow—then looped lazily along the frozen riverbank as if the path itself were so ashamed of its awfulness it would love nothing more than to drown. Edward Petrosky ran a hand over his jowly face, breath pluming in a cloud that should have been good tobacco, and glared at a cigarette butt frozen to the dirt beside the path. The tech companies, the ones who cleared the path in the first place, hired out to keep it free of debris, but there was always an assorted mess of cans and shards of glass that even the most dedicated landscaper couldn't collect, hidden slivers that only shone like diamonds when the sun hit them. Now, the slivers glittered dangerously from the ground beneath the iron bench, inches from their victim's toes, twinkling like tears as if the woman sitting there had let them slip from her eyes in the final moments of her life.

Where the hell is Jackson? His partner had called from her car, but he hadn't seen her as he'd trekked down the path toward the water. The burly rook standing guard behind the bench was staring at him, raising the hairs on Petrosky's neck. The only people here so far were the first responders—rookies with no more business being at this crime scene than a politician belonged in a church. Petrosky leaned toward the bench, jaw clenched, reserving the right to flip the kid off if he didn't stop that shit. But yelling at the guy would raise red flags, especially if it happened in his first moments back on the job.

And there were plenty of other things to worry about. The victim's eyes were half-closed in the exhausted stupor of a person just off a twelve-hour shift, which seemed a small mercy—subdued. Accepting. Excessive mascara held her lashes in unnatural spikes beneath thin curves of blue eyeliner and a darker purple eyeshadow, all of it overdone but painstakingly applied. Long, thick hair fell in a wave of onyx over one bare shoulder, glossy and speckled with ice and the occasional wayward snowflake, all the more striking against her brilliantly yellow sundress. Average weight, but something about the dress was wrong like her body was lopsided beneath, but perhaps it was merely the way she was sitting, and…it appeared the hem was crooked. Might be rigor, though. Her dark flesh, too, was spattered with snow. She'd been dead for some time, grown cold enough for the ice to stick to her skin. Needles prickled between his shoulders—familiarity. Did he know the victim? He racked his brain, but he could not place her. Maybe a working girl, even if the outfit was a strange choice—too prissy, too proper, but the dress wasn't made for a Detroit winter unless you were advertising what was underneath. Even then, walking the streets in that…she would need a coat. But that makeup…

"Name's Ana Patel, twenty-four years old," the rookie flatfoot was saying from his spot behind the bench, forcing Petrosky to glance up. Some asshole with blond hair and a baby face that didn't belong on top of the guy's stocky frame. He probably did CrossFit, or worse, yoga. "Missing fifteen days as of this morning." The kid inhaled and blew out his breath hard and fast, a sigh on crank, probably meant to convey *what a shame*, but Petrosky's fists tightened. Something about the kid's presence bothered him—his face, or maybe the way he'd greeted Petrosky: "So how are you today, Detective? It has to be hard dealing with the worst of the worst cases, right?"

Petrosky turned away from the kid, from the victim, and squinted into the bitter wind. Directly in front of the bench, a clearing in the trees exposed the river, ice glittering dangerously at the shoreline, a thin line of reddish-orange slashing the horizon like a wound. No buildings visible on the other side—just sheets of crusted ice, so the killer wasn't watching now. All alone...he'd left her all alone. *Was this the last thing you saw, honey?* But snow littered the bench on either side of her body, and the ground beneath her bare toes had not been disturbed by a struggle. No cuts on her feet from the glass that he could see. Though dark lines bisected the skin of her ankles and wrists, most likely ligature, her hands and feet appeared unmarked. If she'd been alive when the killer laid her out here, there would be some sign of it, a wound from a final defensive action. And the rookie had said she'd been missing fifteen days; you didn't keep someone for two weeks just to kill them quickly. He felt the truth of that in his bones.

"He took his time," Petrosky muttered, turning back, still ignoring the rook's question, though that didn't stop the punk from staring at him expectantly. Why was he still here? He forced his voice to remain steady. "You got something else you could be doing?"

The kid grunted, half-surprise half-irritation, but at least he backed off and headed up the hill behind the bench—no prints near that snowy stretch, they'd already looked. Along the path, evergreen boughs hung heavy with last week's snow over the barren branches of birch and the occasional poplar. That had to be the way the killer had come. But the only entrance to the path was down a steep set of stairs—no good way to get a body here with a wheelbarrow. He'd still checked for tire marks on his way down.

How'd you do it, fuck-o? Petrosky drew his gaze back up the path, past scrubby bushes that could hide anything, including the piece of evidence they'd need to find this asshole, and...
About damn time, Jackson.

His partner was heading toward him, leather gloves on, cream earmuffs secured against her head, her closely shorn black hair shimmering in the barely-there dawn. Coat the color of an angry bruise, the top button open enough that he could see her black suit beneath—he'd taken to wearing a suit jacket over his T-shirts, but she'd always put his wardrobe to shame. Even her face was more polished, set in the hard, determined lines of a woman who wasn't about to take anyone's shit. Her boots thunk, thunk, thunked against the ground. The noise reverberated through the trees and into his brain; he could almost imagine the sound was from their killer. But it wasn't, couldn't be—that'd be far too easy. So, what did they know? The killer had to be strong enough to carry the body up the walk to this bench and had probably known the path was the one place kept salted year-round by those crazy tech people. People who spent all their time working indoors and believed "everyone could do with some fresh air," according to the press release they'd put out when they paved the path. Stupid hipsters and their community outreach that didn't really help the folks who needed it. Who the hell would run in the winter anyway? Then again, he didn't understand running in the summer either.

And no one had been running last night, at least not by choice—definitely not Ana Patel. *Poor girl.* He forced himself to bend nearer, though his back creaked like an old, rusted car door. The scent of wet earth and the metallic stink of blood bit his nostrils. He could almost imagine she was asleep, her thick foundation covering the death pallor, but her mouth gave it away. Her lips were painted a brilliant bubblegum pink, the outline as perfect as the rest of her makeup, but her mouth was swollen, angry even in death— was that pus? Congealed gore clung to the innermost part of her lower lip beneath her large front teeth. With all the swelling, the blood, he'd have expected to see crooked, cracked, splintered incisors, the result of blunt force trauma to the face, a curb-stomping, maybe, yet each tooth was perfectly aligned with the one beside it. He leaned closer. The sockets where the teeth were rooted…that was the source of the injury, a mess of frozen gore and mutilated jaw. He straightened with a grunt as Jackson stopped at his side.

"We got a crazy dentist, or what?" Petrosky pulled his hat tighter over his ears, the tips of his fingers numb with cold. His partner seemed to be faring better—even with the sun barely over the horizon, icicles still clinging to the underside of the trees, Jackson was squatting as if her joints weren't frozen in the least. Peering at the body as if no time had passed at all since they'd last worked together. He liked her better for it.

"Not sure on the dentist thing, but he's definitely worried about aesthetics," she said. "Looks like he painted her nails." He had. The same neon pink color as her lips. "They would have chipped in the struggle if she'd had them done ahead of time—at some point over the last two weeks at least."

He drew his eyes back to Ana's face, the carefully applied eyeliner, the rouge on her cheekbones. Not a smudge. "He had to be the one who put the makeup on her too; dressed her up after the fact. Maybe we'll get some trace." And the way her hands were crossed, one over the other so politely in her lap—that was a sign of remorse. Was the killer someone she knew?

I hope he came up from behind and blindsided you. I hope he made it fast. But from the terrible state of her mouth, the pus that indicated infection, infection that would have taken a week to fester…the killer had wanted her to suffer.

Petrosky crouched, eye level with the woman on the bench. The woman's half-lidded eyes stared past him, gaze dull, blank, and after fifteen days, finally, blessedly relieved.

2

ANA PATEL'S apartment was in a recently renovated section of Ash Park; their victim was not a working girl, at least not of the streetwalking sort. A recent rash of young professionals to the Ash Park area and nearby Detroit had spurred an equally impressive rash of renovation—old historic homes had been gutted and turned into small apartment buildings, and smaller houses were selling for twice what they'd been worth ten years ago. There were even vacant residential lots amidst the new construction, once marred by the crumbling remains of old Devil's Night fires, now brightened by gardens and orchard trees, their fruit-laden branches heavy come summer with cherries and apples and pears. But today, the skeletal branches clawed at the gray sky as if trying to tear themselves from their frozen roots.

Patel's walk-up was part of an old mansion, six apartments, tops, none more than a thousand square feet. The rubber treads of Petrosky's sneakers squealed against the outdoor stairs as he followed Jackson to the second story, his breath pluming around his face like fog. "You'd think a software designer could afford better digs."

"Maybe she wanted to be close to her job," Jackson said, not nearly as out of breath as he was.

"Maybe." But what was another fifteen minutes if you got an extra thousand square feet and a mortgage—an investment? Despite the recent housing boom, there were plenty of properties with lower price tags. He hauled himself up the last few steps, forcing himself not to wheeze. Three months of abusing his body, of chain-smoking and booze and late nights and waking up screaming, reliving the final moments of his last case, feeling that boy's blood on his hands... He felt as if he'd aged ten years.

But he was ready—Carroll wouldn't have let him come back if he wasn't, and he trusted her more than he trusted himself these days, though he wouldn't admit that to anyone. He just had to get back into it. Maybe he needed more coffee.

The landlord had left the door open for them, and they ducked beneath the yellow crime scene tape. "Where the hell did this come from?" he asked. There was no evidence to suggest Ana Patel had been taken from her apartment—at least not yet. Did someone know something they didn't?

"No idea," Jackson said. "We'll ask. But the place was locked up tight, and the cops who came to the house to follow up on the missing persons call said there were no signs of struggle, which all fits with her leaving the apartment of her own accord and being kidnapped elsewhere."

But where? Petrosky felt along the wall and flicked the light switch. He blinked. The wan morning barely permeated the interior of the living room through the gauzy curtains, and the lamp in the corner was a lazy bastard at best. Plywood bookcases. Plaid couch. A glass coffee table stacked with mystery novels: *The Girls Across the Bay. A Mutual Addiction. A Good Bunch of Men.* He fingered the bookmark—a receipt from Off the Page, a bookstore not more than six blocks from the apartment. Apparently, their victim liked a good mystery, but it hadn't saved her from becoming the victim in her own story. Did that make him the hero? Unlikely. It had been three weeks, and he could still taste the Jack in the back of his throat. He coughed as if to expel the phantom liquor, but it stuck.

Jackson stood at the corner desk, her back to him, sifting through stacks of letters. "Lots of mail from Israel. Looks like she has family there."

His phone buzzed in his pocket, an angry, impotent bee trapped against his chest. "Is she new to the US?"

"I think Michaelson said she's here on a work visa. The rest of her family is still back in Israel."

"Who said?" Petrosky glanced over.

"That cop at the scene, Jason Michaelson. I thought I saw you talking to him when I was walking up."

"The rookie jackass trying to get all personal?"

Jackson shrugged and headed for the back hallway. "Maybe he likes you," she called over her shoulder.

"I doubt that." More likely that CrossFit asshole had killed her and was trying to insert himself into the investigation. But that was a million to one. Petrosky just didn't like the kid—rubbed him the wrong way even if he couldn't put his finger on exactly why.

"Yeah, you're right, no way that kid likes your cantankerous ass. I barely tolerate you, and I'm grown." She vanished through the first doorway.

"There's a lot of love in this room," he called, and he meant it—her harassment said it was business as usual. Maybe she'd forgotten about the way he'd told her to get the fuck out when she'd broken into his place a few months back; all she'd taken was the liquor. And his gun. As if he didn't have another one. He listened to her chuckle, then went back to the desk, peering at another stack of books on the floor beside it—*Shakespeare?*—then at the small photos that adorned the top like pieces of broken glass—like the glittering shards around Patel's feet. The first picture showed their victim with a younger man, maybe a brother: same teardrop eyes, same hollow cheekbone structure. Her face was far thinner without the swelling he'd seen on that trail, but the rest of her was what the fellows called "thicc" or "phat"—small waist, wider through the hips. Smaller in the chest, though, than she had appeared on that bench. Plastic surgery? And...no makeup in the photo—in any of the photos. Telling. Petrosky felt his back tighten, imagining her in that pink lipstick as he raised the photo closer to his face; she and her brother had the same teeth—wide, protruding too far over their bottom lips—but in this picture, her teeth were cockeyed, turned in toward one another making a sharp V beneath her nose.

But on that bench, her teeth had been straight. Bloody, infected as hell, but straight. Maybe the crazy dentist thing wasn't so far off. The skin between his shoulders tingled, electric—it suddenly felt as if someone else was in that apartment with them, some psycho prick ready to shoot one of them... *Ah*. Because the last time they'd been in a victim's home together, someone *had* been trying to kill them.

But Petrosky had shot first. And he still hated himself for it. He'd been cleared for killing the kid, but the hot ache in his belly had not relented.

He set the photo back on the desk and hurried down the hall toward the first doorway—the bedroom. Jackson stood on the far side of the bed, rummaging in the night table.

Petrosky leaned against the doorframe, aiming at nonchalant and getting close to it; just seeing his partner alive and well without a gun pointed at her head made the flesh on his back settle. "The killer moved her teeth," he said. Had the bastard used pliers while she screamed? Must have—and he must have done it soon after he took her judging from the state of the infection. The pus. He grimaced but managed to turn off the visualization when his phone buzzed.

"You and this dentist thing." Her voice came out low, forced, but she didn't sound like she disagreed.

He frowned, studying the tight set of her shoulders. "I'm not saying it's definitely a dentist. I'm just…saying." A killer wouldn't straighten someone's teeth without a reason. If nothing else, it was a signature. Something unique to their suspect.

His phone buzzed again, and this time he drew it to his ear.

"Anything I need to know? Are the optics going to get bad on this?" Chief Carroll's voice was lower than usual, almost husky as if she'd been crying. Had something happened after she left his house this morning?

He glanced at Jackson and said, "I can't help the optics, Chief, but it's not a hate crime—it was a brutal murder, but there's nothing politically motivated, nothing that can even be construed that way." *And she knows that.* Carroll was just checking up on him. Handing over his cell number had been part of his return to work, recommended by the illustrious Dr. McCallum. *You have to trust someone, Petrosky, might as well be someone who cares about you and has the power to stop you if you start to backslide.* That was shrink bullshit if he'd ever heard it, even if the guy was right.

Carroll sighed. "Just find the asshole, okay? Keep me updated." Her voice stayed soft and even. He listened for the click in the receiver; Carroll's breath hissed back. "You sure you're okay out there, Petr—"

He hung up.

Jackson glanced over her shoulder. "You're getting personal calls from the chief now?" "So?" He pocketed the cell.

"It's weird that you're actually answering your phone. You used to take your desk phone off the hook just so she couldn't call you. Made Decantor crazy."

Ah, Decantor. How was that Kardashian-loving shithead?

"Decantor's crazy anyway. Besides, I can't get fired now. I just got back." After three months of feeling like hell—three months of mandated therapy with Dr. McCallum, the department's shrink. But that wasn't why he'd hit answer, nor was it McCallum's shrink-y nonsense; the truth was that he owed her. Carroll was the reason he was still alive.

"She could have fired you before your leave, and you didn't give her your number then."

"Things change."

She met his eyes. "I bet they do." Was she smirking?

He nodded to the bracelet on her wrist, glittering in the light from the bedside lamp. Didn't this place have any overhead lighting? "Diamonds, eh? That doesn't seem like a thing you'd buy for yourself."

She closed the drawer, then bent to look under the bed. "I can buy anything I want, you old bastard."

"But you didn't buy it. You aren't that kind of girl."

"And what kind of girl am I?" she said to the dust bunnies.

"I guess I should ask Decantor."

She laughed. "Well, you just know it all, don't you?"

But he didn't.

3

"She had some issues with her ex, but not like…violent ones." The dark-skinned woman in the chair across from Petrosky had streaks of green in her hair that matched her nails. Ana Patel hadn't had more than a few close friends, this woman being one—"Sam," the "antha" sacrificed to the gods of edginess. What color had the vic's nails been? Pink? *Like her lips, her broken, swollen mouth.* He passed the woman a tissue, and she dabbed her cheeks, the glare of the glass table turning her irises amber.

The company where Ana had worked occupied the entire top floor of the high-rise directly across the street from the entrance to the running path. The owners of C0D3W0RKS operated from out of state, but they were more than willing to allow Petrosky to conduct interviews in their meeting room—their entirely glass meeting room. He felt like a penguin in a tank, right down to the similar body structure. Petrosky could feel the eyes of the other workers boring into his back, could hear the low murmur through the thin walls as if they were collectively wondering whether it was feeding time.

It is, assholes. Sam blew her nose, a wet, hollow honk, and he looked away.

The rest of the loft space boasted long, open tables topped with enormous monitors, probably meant to encourage communication and collaboration, but those wide screens also hid the workers from him; eight pairs of beady eyes vanished every time he turned around. And the colorful beanbags littered about the floor made everything they did here suspect. Jackson was currently in the main room, dealing with the techies and examining Ana's workspace—better her than him. She had younger eyes and more tolerance for man buns.

"I just can't believe this," the woman across from him said, and he dragged his gaze from the wall of glass. "You think this person... I mean, why Ana?"

"That's what we're trying to figure out, ma'am." But so far, information was slim. Her family lived out of the country, and she sent the majority of her paycheck home—probably the reason she had chosen to rent instead of buying a home, that and the temporary work visa. In today's volatile immigration climate, the ol' U-S-of-A could send her packing anytime. Despite a seemingly close familial relationship, her parents and brother in Israel knew very little about Ana's life in the States—no mention of friends or boyfriends. And all they knew about her work was that it was "with computers," which, to be fair, was about as specific as Petrosky would have been himself. His eyes dropped to Sam's fingers—her green nails. "Did Ana wear makeup?"

Sam raised an eyebrow, one corner of her lip twitching up. "Ana? No, no way. She said it itched."

"Not even for special occasions? Nail polish?" If the killer had purchased it, they might be able to trace him—any paper trail was at least a trail.

Sam shook her head. "I never saw her wear anything like that. She wore lip balm in the winter, I guess. Just the cheap stuff you get at the gas station, nothing glossy even." Sam examined her fingernails. Fresh tears sprang into her eyes.

"Tell me about her ex—the issues you mentioned." A boyfriend would explain the element of remorse as well as the care he'd taken in grooming his victim's body. Lots of men believed their woman should play dress-up for them: short skirts, tall boots. Heels sure to sprain the arches of your feet. Not that he'd know that one for sure, but it seemed a valid guess. Though…Ana had been barefoot, hadn't she? Maybe the suspect was strapped for cash—a poorly made sundress, sure, but good shoes didn't come cheap.

"They broke up…maybe three weeks ago?"

The week before she was taken. That was suspicious on its own—nothing triggered rage in an insecure asshole like rejection.

Sam wiped her eyes with a fresh tissue. "She said he annoyed her, calling too often and all that, but I think he was more serious about the relationship than she was. She wasn't ready to settle down." Another tear leaked from her eye and traced a path down her smooth cheek. "But I just can't imagine Ewan doing this. Hurting her."

"Ewan?" The kind of name was Ewan?

Sam nodded. "Ewan Halford." She raised one slender green-tipped hand and pointed through the glass. Petrosky followed her finger, but the man at the receiving end…

"*That's* Ewan?"

As if on cue, the man leaned back in his chair, just far enough for Petrosky to see him between the computer monitors. Man bun city, but his was a mess; kinky brown locks sprang from beneath the hair tie and attacked the tops of his shoulders. Freckles across the bridge of his nose. And Ewan was as thin as Ana had been, maybe even more so, with a spindly little neck, but he had a soft pooch beneath his purple sweatshirt, the cloth more lilac than bruise colored. Only his brown eyes were sharp, the eyes of a hawk behind his blue-framed glasses. But watery. His nose was red too. And Halford…that name…

Petrosky turned back to her. "He's the one who called the police?"

"Yeah." She sniffed as her eyes filled once more. "I feel so stupid. I told him not to call that first day, just figured she was sick, but he was really worried because she wasn't calling him back."

"But if they were broken up, and he was as annoying, as you said, why would she call him at all?"

"They were friends. And she did always call back, didn't want to be rude, I guess." Tears ran off her chin and puddled on the glass tabletop. "She always called back."

Petrosky went through a few more questions, but Sam didn't seem to have any more knowledge about Ana's final hours of freedom than they did—no ideas on who might have harmed her. He left Sam in the conference room and headed across the loft, skirting a bulbous orange beanbag blob topped with a paperback novel. Jackson nodded to him from her spot at Ana's workstation, a Rubik's cube in one gloved hand. When the hell did these people work? He hadn't seen anyone touch a keyboard since they got here, and Ewan was no exception; now, he appraised Petrosky shrewdly as Petrosky approached the man's desk. No, not shrewdly—that was a cold, dead stare.

Ewan sure looked like a dick, but did he have it in him to kill a woman, carry her down that path, pose her for someone else to find? To rearrange her teeth in their sockets? They had to wait on the ME to see whether she'd been sexually assaulted, and an ex-boyfriend was usually a good bet, but this guy? His wrists looked like they might snap if he sneezed into his palms too hard.

"So, you're the boyfriend."

Ewan swallowed hard, and now he averted his gaze, eyes darting this way and that, maybe to see if anyone else had heard, and surely they had; the long shared table thing wasn't much for privacy. Even the separate-but-open desk situation in the precinct's bullpen was better, despite the fact that Jackson usually ended up at Petrosky's desk. Behind Ewan, a dreadlocked man adjusted his earphones and repositioned his hands on an ergonomic keyboard that looked like an emaciated mountain range. Soon, the thin vibration of the man's muffled music and the clacking of the keys were the only sounds from that side of the room.

Petrosky nodded to him approvingly, though the man did not look their way again—it was nice when people minded their own damn business. But the others... At the next table, a blonde with a lip ring had her eyes on her computer, but she was typing far too slowly for her attention to be on her work. No headphones. No headphones, either, for the guy to her left, the most preppy-looking of the bunch: crew cut, no facial jewelry, but his button-down didn't quite hide the neck tattoo that peeked from beneath his collar. His gaze drifted from the screen, to Petrosky, and to the screen once more.

"I *was* the boyfriend," Ewan said, bringing Petrosky back. "I'm not now." The man's eyes stayed glassy, but his mouth was tight. Same with his jaw—Petrosky was shocked that he couldn't hear the guy's teeth squealing. *Those bloody teeth, Ana's mutilated gums.*

Petrosky crossed his arms and leaned his hip against the desk. "You didn't tell anyone you were broken up when you called her disappearance in. From what I heard, you told the call center that you were her man. Currently."

Ewan shook his head but kept his gaze locked on Petrosky as if afraid Petrosky might attack him if he looked away. "I needed them to take me seriously. If I'd said I was her ex-boyfriend, they would have assumed she just didn't want to talk to me."

"You didn't think a missing woman was enough?"

"No, of course not! Even when I said we were together,

you guys told me she hadn't been missing long enough. It wasn't until I told them she was supposed to meet me and didn't show up that they actually came and took a statement."

"And where was she supposed to meet you?" Petrosky hadn't looked at the missing persons file yet, but it was on his to-do list. Maybe this guy could give them a lead on her whereabouts when she was abducted.

"Well...she wasn't actually supposed to meet me."

"So, you lied?" *So much for that.*

"Yeah, wait, I mean no. I guess...kinda." Ewan ran one of those bird-boned hands over his face—*Is that how I look when I do it?* Petrosky frowned. "No one else was worried that she vanished," Ewan said, his voice higher—defensive. "No one else called it in. No one else...cared." His gaze darted past Petrosky, eyes narrowing, but he refocused on Petrosky just as quickly. Petrosky turned. Sam had returned to the main work area and was sliding into her chair beside Ana's station. Staring at them. Jackson was still peering at the papers on Ana's desktop.

Petrosky turned back. "So no one cared about her? No one would miss her? That's what you're telling me?"

"I'm not saying that—"

"What about Sam? She was Ana's best friend, right?"

His jaw hardened again. Jealousy? *Interesting.* "Ana was just...introverted. She hung out at home a lot, read books. She didn't really like to go out, didn't have other people keeping tabs on her, expecting her to be...around."

Didn't have people keeping tabs on her...the way you did? Petrosky's eyes narrowed. "Maybe you wanted her to go out more. Dressed her up all fancy for your very last date."

"Dressed her up?" His brow furrowed. Lips pursed—genuine confusion. "She usually wore like...jeans. Flannel."

"What about a sundress? Pretty yellow thing."

"It's kinda cold, isn't it?"

Yeah, if you're alive. But Ewan's gaze remained steady—no

emotional reaction to the comment on the dress, no excitement or nervousness as Petrosky might have expected from a perp. "Tell me about the night Ana vanished."

He sighed and glanced around the room once more. "Should we go into the conference room?"

"I think we're good right here, hoss." Being in the open clearly made the guy uncomfortable, and in public, something Ewan said might ring untrue to those around them.

Ewan cleared his throat. "Okay. So, I *was* supposed to see her that night. But she called at the last minute to cancel."

Petrosky nodded. "I bet that made you mad."

He crossed his arms over his pooch—his lips were a thin, bloodless line. "Not really." But his voice had risen in pitch and volume despite the blonde with the lip ring openly staring now, not even bothering to pretend like she had a job.

You're next, lady. Petrosky kept his attention on the man in front of him. "Ewan, come on now. I'd be pissed too. A woman you're just trying to be nice to ignores you like you're nothing? What'd you do to deserve that?"

"I..." His shoulders softened. "You're right, I didn't do anything wrong to get blown off. But she said she just wanted to read, and..." His lip trembled. "She used to say that I wasn't competing against other activities that I was competing against her alone time. And she really, really liked her alone time." An almost agitated smile appeared then vanished.

"So she chose nothing over you? She was staying home?"

"Yeah, she said she'd see me in the morning. Here at work. But she never showed up."

And no one had worried? Sam hadn't seen Ana's absence as cause for alarm—she'd told Petrosky as much. "Did Ana make a habit of calling in to work?"

"No, of course not. But she did work from home sometimes. We all do."

No wonder the others hadn't worried right off—it wasn't a visible change in pattern.

"But she said she would see me that morning *at work*," Ewan insisted. "And she never lied, even when it was…hard."

Hard? Huh. He'd have to circle back to that. But if she'd planned to come in, that might help; they still weren't sure where Ana had been taken. No one in the apartment building saw her routinely, and definitely not on the morning in question. And the crime-scene-tape mystery had been solved when they'd interviewed the other residents: teenagers in the next unit had admitted to taping up old Halloween decorations "as a joke" when they found out she was gone. Petrosky had half a mind to haul their sorry asses in. But Ana hadn't been taken there anyway, and she'd walked to work; they couldn't even track a car. Hopefully, the forensics on the body would reveal more—like where she'd been held for two weeks. And by whom.

He blinked at Ewan. "Being the boyfriend, you knew about her routine, right? So what would she have done between waking up in her apartment and showing up at this office?"

"I wasn't really her boyfriend. I mean, we hung out, but it wasn't like that." He scanned the room again—trying to make sure no one was listening?—then leaned closer as if preparing to confide a secret. Petrosky stayed where he was; if Ewan had something to say, the man could come to him. "She…she was gay," Ewan practically whispered. "I think. I mean, maybe she wasn't sure at first, but then she was sure."

She never lied even when it was hard—that's what he'd meant. And that put a crimp in the idea that she'd started dating someone dangerous. Though it was possible for a woman to be a perpetrator, it was a rarity in a case where the victim was brutalized and posed. Shit, was this a hate crime? Or maybe retaliation against a woman who'd rebuffed the killer? Nothing to indicate that, not yet, but…

"Did she have a girlfriend?" Petrosky asked now.

Ewan's eye twitched. "I dunno," he said, but his gaze darted to Sam once more; he shifted uncomfortably in his seat, crossing then recrossing his legs. Petrosky frowned. Looked like they'd have to reinterview Sam to see if she'd been Ana's current love interest, but again, she wasn't likely to be the killer—he doubted she'd have been able to carry Ana's body down that path any more than Ewan. And Ewan still hadn't answered his question.

Petrosky sniffed. "Even if you and Ana weren't in a romantic relationship, you were close. Walk me through her morning, okay? Help me figure out how she crossed paths with a killer."

Ewan slumped back in the chair and swallowed yet again. But he nodded. "Okay, well, let's see... She always got up really early. Liked to get to work by seven, get out by three."

So a masochist, got it. "Fine. So she got up at what? Six?"

"No, no, more like five. She jogged at least two or three times a week—more if the weather was nice. Then she'd go home to shower."

"Jog? In the winter?" Definitely a masochist. And the path... They still weren't sure exactly where she'd been taken, but with the way she was positioned on the trail, it was a good bet that the place had special significance for their killer. Had he seen her running there? Was that where Ana had caught the killer's attention?

"Most of us here walk that path by the river. It's really nice, and the trees block the wind. It's part of our contract."

Their...contract? "Come again?"

"Physical health is a priority or whatever—we get a better deal on our health insurance if we agree to work out. And we have to like...sign off and all that."

So to get better insurance premiums, they freeze their asses off six months out of the year? "Are you stupid?"

Ewan's eyes widened. "What?"

"Haven't you ever heard of a gym? You know, those places with the treadmills *inside* where there's no snow?"

"Do I look like I'd fit in with those guys?" Ewan laughed, but it was dry and without humor, the chuckle of someone who'd been knocked around his whole life. "This, the path... it's close and convenient. Sure, Ana took it more seriously than most of us, but she pushed us—pushed me—to be better." His lower lip trembled again, but he pressed his lips together until they were too tight to move, let alone circulate blood.

"Did she usually wear these?" said a voice behind Petrosky. Jackson, a pair of running shoes in hand—brilliantly pink, the bottoms smudged with dirt.

"Yeah! Those are hers." His eyes filled, but he swiped at them violently with his sleeve, reddening his cheek.

"She like that color?" Petrosky asked. Did the killer know that when he'd painted her mouth, her nails? It would up the chance that the victim and the suspect were acquainted.

Ewan shook his head. "I think they were on sale. She was more of a black and army-green kind of girl. Or orange, I guess, she liked orange."

Another dead end. *Awesome.* "Did she have any other running shoes?" *That she might have been wearing that morning?*

"No, not that I know of. She wasn't really a shopper. Just her boots—that's what she usually wore in the winter. What she wore to walk here. But she always exercised in those sneakers."

If her sneakers were here, she hadn't been taken while out running on the path. So, provided Ewan was right that she'd stayed home the night before the abduction, the killer must have snatched her somewhere between the apartment and this building. "She was a down-to-earth girl, eh?"

Ewan nodded again. "Yeah."

"Did she have any other friends that we don't know about? Anyone she might have seen that night besides you?

Someone she blew you off for that last night you spoke to her?"

Ewan's eyes darted off to his right, to Dreadlocked Man, and back to Petrosky. "Nope."

"You sure, Ewan?"

He sniffed, lip no longer trembling. "She didn't talk about other people with me, okay? She always shut that down, said it wasn't my concern."

That was a strong statement for a woman who was honest *even when it was hard*. Perhaps it was just one more form of honesty—healthy boundaries and all that shit—but it was also apparently an area of her life she kept hidden. Maybe she was hiding a person, someone capable of harming her. Was it possible that the killing was random, that whoever took her had just happened to decide to snatch her up? Sure. They'd had two weeks to buy makeup and a dress, and maybe they'd simply thought the bench was a kick-ass dump site. But that all felt a little too convenient. Petrosky's gut was telling him that while Ana might not have known her kidnapper, the kidnapper sure knew a lot about her. And for an introvert who really loved books and valued her alone time…

He scanned the room, the tapping fingers, the shifty eyes. Hipster after hipster. All of them suspect.

4

"I don't like a single one of those bastards."

"Even the guy with the headphones steadfastly pretending he didn't give a shit you were there?"

"Okay, okay, you got me." He climbed into the passenger side of Jackson's Escalade. How did it still smell like leather? She'd had this thing since they'd met—had it been four years now? He glanced in the back seat as if expecting to see a newly tanned animal hide. He saw wine instead. Merlot.

"Since when do you drink red?" But even as he said it, even though wine wasn't his drink of choice, his mouth watered just a little. Maybe he'd visit Carroll when they got back to the station. She needed an update on the case, right? He pushed the thought aside.

"Since always."

He snorted, glancing at her bracelet again. *Bullshit.* But he'd leave well enough alone for now. Maybe he'd get used to her banging Decantor. Sure, the guy worshipped pop stars the way normal men worshipped pork rinds, but he wasn't a total dick. Unlike Petrosky himself.

"So she was probably taken somewhere between the apartment and work," Jackson said. "She wasn't wearing her running shoes, so we know she wasn't out on the path that day."

"But she was out there often. Maybe that's where he first saw her, or maybe he dumped her there as a way to send a message." Though what that message was remained to be seen. They'd talked to everyone in the building that housed C0D3W0RKS, but those who were regular visitors to the running trail hadn't noticed anyone suspicious—no "weirdos" hanging around, just the steady throngs of working IT people, probably all forced outdoors by the corporate demigods who got their physical activity by surfing in the middle of November. "The time it took to pose her, the risk of getting the body down there…that place has significance for him, or for him and the vic."

"Yeah, agreed." She squinted at the windshield, the pavement and the streetlights now muted by the dreary sky as if the spongelike winter clouds had absorbed the color from the world. Even the thin line of orange horizon he'd noticed at the crime scene had been swallowed up. *What's your deal, you murderous bastard?* Why that path? He let his gaze drift to the window, watching the hulking gray mountains of slush speed past on the far side of the road.

Jackson's fingers tapped against the steering wheel. "The place itself…it's kinda romantic, really, even if it isn't the most perfect trail. The bench is right in front of a break in the trees where you can see the river. I bet it's gorgeous in the summer."

Petrosky thought back to the scene—the river, the skeletal trees, their claws scratching at the wounded sky. The stink of ice and iron. "My money's on someone observing her without being noticed. She seemed pretty intent on keeping to herself." To that, Petrosky could relate. Even Sam had admitted on reinterview that Ana was more than a little reclusive, though Sam had denied having a sexual relationship with their vic.

Jackson kept her eyes on the bleary sky. "But saying she didn't want to get too involved, telling Ewan that she wasn't going to discuss her other relationships... There might have been someone from her past, someone she didn't share with her work friends. Someone dangerous."

Domestic violence? "It's a stretch. Why keep that hidden?" But she'd kept a lot hidden. She'd only recently discovered she was a lesbian if they believed Ewan; she could have a violent man in her past. And it had to be a guy. Petrosky couldn't see a woman doing this—it would have been harder for a woman to carry Patel's corpse down that path, and the posing, the makeup, the sexual undercurrent...the profile just didn't fit. Men were far more likely to have sexual motivations. Female killers, especially serial killers, often had pragmatic motivations, like profit or revenge, and tended to use covert methods like poisoning. And female serial killers didn't go out trolling the way their male counterparts did. *Serial killers*—was he really thinking this was a serial? They only had one body, but the planning, the kidnapping, the posing, the sadism, the teeth...it felt like a serial case, and that thought drove a spike into the center of his chest. *What if she's only the first?*

"Yeah, of course, it's a stretch," Jackson said—what had they been talking about? "I'm just saying we can't discount anything, and her behavior does sound a little more...defensive than I'd expect." She took a hard right into the parking lot. "Hopefully, Woolverton has something so we can stop guessing."

The lot was icy, but still not as cold as the medical examiner's beady eyes. Dr. Woolverton looked up as they entered, but did not move from where he stood behind his stainless steel table. Ana Patel's body lay before him, his thick glasses reflecting the sky-colored sheet that shrouded her corpse from feet to face. A tray of instruments glittered beside the table. And the man was frowning already, though Petrosky had yet to open his mouth.

"What's shakin', Doc?"

"You should know. Your chief called four times, asking me to push you to the front of the line."

Jackson and Petrosky exchanged a glance, and Jackson raised an eyebrow at him like he'd planned it. *Huh.* That was an interesting development. The precinct was neck-deep in homicides, so why would the chief make a call about theirs? *Because she's trying to make your life easier*, a little voice whispered in his head, but another voice, louder, more persistent, roared: *because she doesn't trust you—she thinks you need this so you'll stay sober. And sane.* His chest heated, his shoulders suddenly painful, tight. He stared at Woolverton. Woolverton stared back.

Finally, the smaller man pushed his glasses up the bridge of his nose and drew down the blue sheet.

The fluorescents hit every slash, every pore, lighting up slice after mutilated gouge of destruction. Without the covering of that yellow sundress, it was obvious Patel's brutalized mouth was by far the least of her injuries, though even a glance at that was enough to turn Petrosky's stomach. The sockets where her teeth should have been resting were black, hollow—the teeth barely clinging to her gums. And her breasts were lopsided and strange, pockmarked with small dark holes that might have been needle sticks, deep bruises marring almost every inch around the nipple. A thick line of swollen stitches peeked from the underside of each breast—black and angry.

Oh, honey, what did he do to you?

"Official cause of death is infection—sepsis. But the reason she got that infection..." Woolverton gestured to her right breast, where horrific bruising and congealed blood made it difficult to identify whatever other injury he was supposed to be looking for. "Chicken fat. Your killer injected it into several points around each breast; I think he tried to force larger amounts in through the incisions when that proved insufficient."

Jesus Christ. Heat rose in Petrosky's chest, bile burning the back of his throat.

Woolverton nodded at the table. "As you can see, the tissues are no longer keeping their shape—whatever her chest looked like immediately following the procedure would have soon deteriorated."

"So, adding the chicken fat..." Jackson said. "He was trying to inflate them? A maniac's boob job?"

"I'd say so if I had to guess. But the killer's motivations are more your speed. I can only tell you what I know about the body."

"Which is?" *What else, Woolverton?* Petrosky's stomach was roiling, hot and acidic and sick. He dragged his gaze from Patel's mutilated breasts to the punctures around her gut—had the killer tried to take fat from her belly first? She was thin, maybe too thin to provide enough for his purposes. But Petrosky saw no needle sticks near her hips, and there was definitely extra meat there. *Maybe he likes an hourglass.*

"The cuts are crude, sloppy, and I don't think it's from a struggle," Woolverton continued. "Far too hesitant to be done by a practiced hand."

Jackson nodded, her eyes locked on the body. "So we've got an amateur."

"I'd say yes, but with a few caveats. First, he knows precisely where to inject the fat and how deep to go. And the type of fat, the chicken fat...anyone would know that would cause infection—he probably knew it wouldn't work long-term."

"So a short-term project on an expendable victim," Petrosky said, his voice hollow, eyes still on the minefield that had once been Ana's stomach—the black cave of her belly button, the smaller holes made by the point of a needle.

"This guy knew she wasn't going to survive, and let her suffer as much as possible on her way out."

Woolverton was nodding, his glasses slipping down his hawk nose. "Precisely, especially on the suffering—no signs of painkillers or other drugs in her system, though I did find some additional needle sticks outside of the breast augmentation, as you can see." He gestured to Patel's bruised and pockmarked belly. "Now there are some drugs that process out of the system within a few days, but for them to be gone now, she had to be in agony at the end. With the lack of defensive wounds...maybe she was unconscious—in shock." His nostrils flared, and he gave Petrosky a look that said *we can hope.*

"What about for incapacitation? Anything to indicate how he took her in the first place?" A fully conscious victim being wrestled into a car trunk was loud—that would narrow their search area for the kidnapping site.

"I can't be sure with the initial kidnapping being weeks back, but there's nothing on the toxicology—if he used something to put her out more recently, there's no trace of it. And there are no head wounds outside of the teeth. I noted a puncture in her neck, but again, I can't tell whether it was from a drug or because he was sticking her just to do it—lots of punctures around her belly, too, and I can't imagine him injecting a drug that way. They're all shallow wounds, no damage to the underlying tissue, so it doesn't look like he was trying to suck fat out. And there are so many of them... more like the aggressive stabbings I've seen, just with an instrument less lethal than, say, a blade." Petrosky suppressed a shudder—the sick-o had probably done that for fun. "And she does have abrasions around her wrists and ankles from ligature, as I'm sure you noticed," Woolverton went on. "Bound her arms together, and her feet, but I can't yet be sure what, if anything, she was tied to."

Now the images flooded Petrosky's brain: the smiling girl

from the photos on her desk, bound hand and foot, screaming, blood pouring from her mutilated mouth as a monster approached, needle raised, the tip glinting sharply—deadly.

"I did find some splinters in her feet and in the backs of her thighs," Woolverton said, and Petrosky shifted his focus to the man's face instead of the corpse. *Not a girl, just a corpse—evidence.* "I've already sent those off to your forensics man. And I ran a few additional tests as well. With kidnapping cases, torture, I usually see signs of malnourishment. That was not the case here."

"But her mouth...how could she possibly have eaten?" Jackson asked, stepping closer to the table.

Woolverton's brow furrowed. "There are gouges in the back of her esophagus—I'd say a feeding tube, or he somehow forced her to swallow, pushed the food down with the back of a spoon, or the like."

"So he didn't want her to lose weight," Petrosky said, almost to himself. "He fed her, moved her teeth around..."

"Ah, yes, and the teeth. Traces of metal on the enamel, though there's nothing special about the metal itself. He used some tool, probably pliers, to straighten them out then used epoxy to secure them to one another—creating veneers from her own teeth." He winced. A throbbing ache spread from Petrosky's jaw through his temples.

"Veneers. Breast implants. He was trying to make her perfect," Jackson said. "Or his version of it."

Petrosky stared at the body—the mutilated corpse. "Any signs of sexual abuse?"

"Oh my, yes. But no fluids. Lots of tearing, some older injuries, some newer. Looks like she was abused from the day he took her—raped repeatedly."

Petrosky kept his gaze on her face, on Ana's now-closed eyes. *I'm so sorry, honey.* "So, he's making the perfect woman?"

"Well, he's trying to." Woolverton grabbed the sheet and drew it quickly up over Patel's body, and Petrosky's shoulders softened the moment she was hidden beneath the cloth. "But he's terrible at it; it's like he knows precisely how to do things from a mechanical point of view, but just hasn't had the opportunity to practice on a real person."

So they had a suspect who was either obsessed with medicine—watching videos, buying textbooks—or someone with actual training. A surgical resident, a medical resident kicked out of the program or expelled, even a vet or a taxidermist.

Jackson stepped back from the table, shaking her head. "That's a lot of work just to kill her."

"Obviously, killing her was his endgame," Petrosky said. The killer had made her perfect and used her…until she had nothing left to give.

5

PETROSKY POPPED his neck and watched the sun cast early rays onto the floor of the bullpen. Sleep had come slowly, and when he had finally managed oblivion, he'd dreamed of Jack Daniel's—but in that dream, when he brought it to his lips, it had smelled of iron and tasted of blood. *I should have stayed at the precinct, working.* But Carroll had threatened him with suspension if he didn't go home and get some rest— "take care of himself"—and he'd done it, even though it went against every fiber of his being to listen to her. That's what friends did, right? *No, that's what employees do.* But friend or boss, she'd been wrong—he was just as agitated and exhausted now as he'd been the night before.

It wasn't helping that some asshole was eating a breakfast burrito, the heavy scent of garlic and cumin and chili pepper irritating his nostrils and the already angry lining of his gut. Even Jackson's lotion was bothering him from clear across the desk.

He coughed and choked down more coffee—he needed to think. He'd run sexual offenders, looking for any who might fit the MO, even just dressing his victims up before raping them, or men who attacked prostitutes—women who might have a tendency toward heavy makeup—but none who pinged in the system had any kind of medical background. None appeared controlled enough to do what their man had done. And only two suspects were still free when Patel had been abducted: one had an ankle monitor and was nowhere near their crime scene in the last month, and the other liked his girls thinner—a lot thinner. And younger. Whiter. And perps of this type rarely crossed racial lines when choosing a victim.

So what did they know for sure? The killer had injected Patel with chicken fat, rebuilt her mouth to meet some bullshit ideal, shoved her into a sundress, something she never would have worn on her own—if they believed her ex-boyfriend, who'd said she was a jeans girl—and finally, painted her nails and covered any remaining imperfections with makeup so heavy even her pores vanished along with the waxy pallor of her feverish flesh. Every line perfectly drawn, as if creating a work of art. Was that what he thought he was doing?

Petrosky dropped his precinct coffee on his desk, but he could still smell the acidic bitterness, the plasticky stench of superheated Styrofoam. "I don't think the killer is someone she knew, at least not someone she was dating. He changed almost everything about her."

Jackson frowned, her gaze on the window in the bullpen—the gray sky beyond, clouds pregnant with snow, or, more likely, slushy awful. The bullpen itself was a large L-shaped space, two long rectangles hinged in the middle by a support pillar, making it feel more confined than the loft space at C0D3W0RKS, but the separate desks at least provided some privacy. Except for him—Jackson's chair was directly across from his, facing Petrosky so she could make sure he was actually writing his reports. Over Jackson's shoulder and beyond the pillar, sat Decantor's desk; the broad-shouldered detective was typing away on his computer, probably scouring some Kardashian fan club page—or working a case. Whatever.

Jackson finally turned from the window. "Well, he changed some things, anyway."

"Her teeth. And her breasts." And maybe her belly with all those needle sticks. But Jackson might have a point. "He did make sure to feed her, tried to keep the rest of her body the same size—he didn't want her to get thinner, didn't pull fat from her thighs even though that might have worked better than the chicken fat." Was that how plastic surgeons did it? That'd take some research. "Couldn't he have found someone closer to this ideal? No shortage of curvy women after the Sir-Mix-a-Lot era." But the suffering, the alteration...that was part of his game, wasn't it? Part of the ritual—the fantasy. Maybe he'd chosen her for that reason.

Jackson raised an eyebrow. "What do you know about Sir Mix-a-Lot?"

"I know things, Jackson." He leaned back in the chair, stretching his arms above his head. "I'm just saying, this wasn't about her as a human—he didn't have to know her personally, didn't have to date her. This was all about how she looked. And she was sexually abused from the day he took her, so he was clearly still able to get it up even before he made those changes to her physique. There had to be something he liked."

Jackson glared into her own coffee cup—that shitty precinct coffee—but sipped at it anyway. She grimaced. "With the way he left her lower half alone, he's probably an ass man."

Petrosky nodded. "If only that were rare enough to help us find him." Even searching other rapes with a similar victim profile would give them far too wide a sample size to be useful. And in the end, rape was about power, not sex; with the torture, this suspect was constantly reasserting that power, hurting her over and over, reassuring himself that he was in control. And this wasn't an impulsive power trip. The kidnapping, the assault, the mutilation, the posing: these were the final steps in a well-constructed fantasy.

He sighed, gaze on the desk, on Ana Patel's phone records. Not many numbers besides a local Thai-food delivery place, pizza, a sushi restaurant, and Chinese takeout: her family in Israel, Ewan, and Sam were the only other calls made or received in the two weeks before her abduction. No one had lured her out to wherever she was taken. Someone might have been watching her, but the way she stuck to herself, it was probably a stranger. Which would make catching him far more difficult.

"So if you don't think this was someone she knew…" Jackson began. "You think he was trying to turn her into someone else, or that it's just personal preference?"

"Not sure—maybe both," Petrosky said. "We can look for other missing persons, other murders that fit our victim's profile, but if he'd done this before, posed victims in a public place, mutilated them surgically…we'd have heard about it."

"Maybe. If they happened nearby." Jackson finished her coffee and tossed it into the trash beside his desk. "I'll start with Woolverton's 'too much knowledge for an amateur' idea, hit up the databases for surgeons who have lost their license, any professionals who might have some idea of the procedures but not a lot of hands-on experience." They could still have a guy in his basement watching medical videos all day, but that'd be far harder to track. She pushed herself to standing. "You want to take medical students? See if any of them have related rap sheets, frat boy rape charges that daddy got dismissed?"

"On it." He watched her walk off toward her desk, her new favorite bracelet sparkling in the light from the window on the far side of the bullpen. Decantor was still tapping on his keyboard, though he was no longer alone; his partner, Sloan, was standing beside Decantor's desk now, showing him something in a manila folder. Decantor caught Petrosky's gaze and nodded. Petrosky frowned and turned away, flipping the switch on his old PC. Decantor *might* be involved with Jackson even if she refused to admit it, and maybe he was even nice to her, but that didn't mean Petrosky had to like it. Cops died on duty, and nothing destroyed a person faster than losing those they loved. Shannon, his last partner's widow, had run to Atlanta to forget, taken Evie and Henry away as if they'd forget their father. But no one could escape grief. Petrosky swallowed back bile and pulled the keyboard closer. Jackson wasn't the only one at risk here—they had a killer to catch. Before he did it again.

Petrosky swept his empty cup into the garbage, listening to the staccato clacking of half a dozen keyboards. A search for repeated crimes came up with nothing. On to medical students, but if their suspect had been premed, there was no telling when he'd been kicked out of the program. He'd start with the last five years, schools within four hours of the dump site—of the victim's apartment. This guy *felt* local to him, someone who knew the area well, knew about the path. Maybe their suspect had sat on the bench with someone he'd never get back, someone he was trying to recreate. But Petrosky couldn't just look up all women with certain measurements and ask them if they had a crazy ex. Hell, most of the women in this city probably had at least one crazy ex...what had Jackson called them last week? Fuck-boys? Was that what Decantor was? He suspected that fuck-boys didn't buy diamonds, but he couldn't be certain.

He sighed, punched in the number for the Wayne State University School of Medicine, and listened to it ring.

PREMED DROP-OUT RATES WERE EXORBITANT. Only 17 percent of students who started on the medical path ended up completing med school. But the odds were better once hopefuls started med school itself—only 6 percent didn't complete. Once you put in that much work, you didn't give up too easily; or the premed programs weeded out the ones who couldn't hack it.

The local universities were able to give him names, and narrowing it to males helped some. While they couldn't rule out rape with an object, the odds were on a male killer, a sadist, a narcissist, a psychopath who figured since he couldn't find the woman of his dreams, he'd create her…and force her to be with him. But if that were the case, wouldn't he have done his best to help her survive so she'd stick around for longer? Maybe he got bored quickly.

Petrosky had just printed the last of his three dozen possible med students when his cell buzzed in his pocket. Scott.

He raised it to his ear. Evan Scott was the best forensics guy they had, a genius twentysomething, and the son of George Scott, one of Petrosky's best friends. One of his only friends, though stone-cold-sober George would never understand Petrosky's obsession with the bottle.

"Got a little information, but nothing that will help you, unfortunately," Scott said. "The foundation the killer used is a cheap pancake variety, something you can find online, or at any drugstore, even the grocery stores. Same with the mascara, the eyeshadow. The nail polish. And there's nothing special about the needle marks either—no way to tell where the hypodermics came from."

That meant they had no easy way to trace any of the paraphernalia; it'd be like looking for a specific blue car in Ash Park metro—way too many to pare down. But once they had a suspect list narrowed, they could cross-reference to zero in on their guy. Maybe they'd find an expelled premed student with a list of credit card charges for their specific brand of foundation and mascara. But he doubted it.

Petrosky put his elbows on the desk, resting his heavy head on one hand. "Anything good at the dump site?"

"Nah, the perp wiped it clean—not a single fingerprint on the bench, despite it being a public spot. Even between the metal treads, all I found were traces of ammonia."

Ammonia. Like Windex. That's what the killer used to clean it—he'd made Patel perfect to his standards, and then he'd made the place where he'd dumped her spotless too. Maybe he was one of those obsessive types...but would someone like that really inject chicken fat into Ana Patel's breasts? It seemed a contradiction in terms. They'd have to chat with Dr. McCallum, even if the thought did turn his stomach. Petrosky'd had enough shrinks to last a lifetime over these last few months. Which was one reason he'd ended up talking to Carroll. An accidental connection, it had all happened so fast—

"What about the wood?" he blurted. "The splinters Woolverton found?"

"Haven't gotten to that yet. But I'll call when I have something else, oka—"

A voice at his back cut the goodbye short: "Hey, guy, you busy?"

Petrosky startled and fumbled the phone against his chest as he whirled around. *Acharya*. Dark skin, dark eyes, the thick black hair of a Bollywood star. The journalist stood behind him bearing a cardboard container loaded with four coffee cups from...Rita's Diner. Petrosky's favorite. But Acharya was decidedly not on his list of favorite people. "Who the hell let you in here?"

"Decantor."

Petrosky drew his gaze across the bullpen, where the big man was lowering himself once more into his desk chair. Decantor caught Petrosky's eye and winked. "That Kardashian-loving fuckhead," he muttered.

Acharya set the coffee on Petrosky's desk and paused,

hand still on the lid of the cup as if claiming it despite the fact that it was now on Petrosky's desk and therefore clearly his. "Does anyone not like the Kardashians? They're really successful, kinda the model for—"

"Get lost, Acharya."

Acharya shifted the cardboard cupholder to his other hand and smiled as if Petrosky hadn't spoken. "Real quick: I hear you've got a pretty sensational case. I was thinking that since we've worked so well together in the past, you'd give me an exclusive."

"I don't work with journalists."

Acharya cocked his head. "You know, my book comes out at the end of the year. I've painted you in quite the favorable light."

"So you're a liar in books as well as in articles? Big deal." Petrosky snatched up the cup and glared.

Acharya's smile did not falter. "Good to see you, Detective. And thanks for the pickles. I especially liked the card: 'Best wishes, fuckface,' was it?"

"It was. But Jackson added the best wishes part." And though he'd never say it out loud, those pickles were money well spent—Acharya *had* given them a lead on one of the last cases Petrosky had worked before he went on leave. Before he'd fallen into a hole. *Before I killed a kid.*

6

THE SUN HAD VANISHED, the blackness beyond the precinct window an inescapable void—or maybe that was just his mood.

The makeup was a bust. As Scott had predicted, the brand and color sold thousands of units every month and none sold within a ten-mile radius matched up with anyone on Petrosky's med school lists. Sure, most of the buyers were women, but the credit cards used were often joint accounts attached to male names—and their guy wasn't married, was he? Probably not. And no one single person, male or female, had purchased all of the makeup on the list—some bought the mascara, but not the rouge, some the eyeliner, but not the foundation, some the polish but none of the other items. And a guy smart enough to get into medical school, smart enough not to leave a single trace of himself at the scene…would he really just walk into the store and buy these? More likely, he'd gotten them online, and it was even easier to disguise yourself there.

Petrosky took the last slug of his cold Rita's coffee and tossed the cup into the trash just as Jackson slapped a folder onto his desk.

"I've got two dozen ex-surgeons who look like they could be good for it, but I think we should go have a chat with this guy before we go further. Acclaimed surgeon, some history in forensics, but his license was revoked a few years back—not our guy, but in a unique position to give us insight."

"Fine by me, I'm tired of sitting." He raised his eyes to Decantor's smiling face—his hackles rose. That bastard had let Acharya in just to be a dick. If someone happened to put a wasps' nest in Decantor's desk drawer, Petrosky wouldn't blame them.

THE PLASTIC SURGEON'S HOME, or rather, ex-surgeon, was a Ferndale bungalow fronted by thorny gray rose bushes, their sharp tips brushed in white powder made all the more brilliant by the porch lights. The man who answered the door was thin, but younger than Petrosky had expected, no more than fifty, with deep copper hair that was probably a dye job along with his too-perfect brows.

Dr. Keith Nordstrom appraised them with honey-colored eyes and showed them into a modern living room, the far wall adorned with enormous black-and-white photos: here a three-foot-tall puckered mouth, there a close-up of a woman's eye, there a nude bust, the woman's skin shiny with oil. Every image hung perfectly centered above a series of small square pedestals, each table topped with an award. For surgery? No way this guy was hesitant in his cuts, even if he did seem to meet the perfectionist criteria of their killer.

Petrosky side-eyed Jackson as they sat across from Nordstrom on a black sofa so low to the ground Petrosky's knees creaked as he sank onto the cushion. Jackson set the images of Ana Patel on the black marble coffee table—pictures from Woolverton's office, the stainless steel table glinting sharply, each wound highlighted in stark, horrifying detail.

Nordstrom collected the pictures with long, thin fingers—piano player's hands. Surgeon's hands. He appraised the images, but then his gaze darkened, and his nostrils flared. Angry.

"You okay, Doc?"

"Well, this person has some textbook understanding," Nordstrom said without acknowledging Petrosky's question. "But he's clearly a hack. I can't imagine this person going to medical school." He practically spat the words. "Maybe they read an article about it, or a book, watched a video even, but they don't have any concrete understanding of how the body works." He turned one image for them to see: a close-up of Patel's breast, skin lumpy like there were creatures writhing just beneath her skin. Something shiny and wet had leaked from one puncture wound to the table beneath her. "For instance, this here…you can inject polymer, even fat from someone's own body, but there are steps in between. You have to use a centrifuge to spin off damaged cells and reduce the risk of rejection. If you don't, the body will reabsorb it, attack it, and the fat will distort, just like you have here."

"He didn't use fat from her body anyway," Jackson said. "He used chicken fat."

That hadn't been released to the public. Why tell this guy? Nordstrom didn't need that detail to give them an opinion. Petrosky's shoulders tightened, but Jackson kept her gaze on the doctor.

Nordstrom flipped another photo and grimaced with his mouth only as if his forehead were frozen—at least he still managed to look horrified. "Whatever he used, there is no way this guy is on a plastic surgery track. One week in graduate classes and he would have known the fat would move, that it would start turning to oil; that the body starts to process it out. My guess is that things looked good to him initially because there was a lot of swelling. Once the swelling went down, and he was able to see what he'd actually done to her…" He shrugged.

"So, you think he killed her because of the shame? His own inadequacy?" Jackson asked now, and Petrosky turned to her in surprise. This man was no shrink—who gave a flying fuck what he thought about their suspect's psychology? *Maybe you're just rusty, old man.*

"Absolutely." Nordstrom set the photos back on the table but left the folder open, Patel's bruised right breast on top, the stitches glaring like a mouth. "Seeing the effects of your work, knowing you did a subpar job…I'd say your killer is a perfectionist. Once he could see how awful his results were, she became the embodiment of his failures. And he had to get rid of her."

But he hadn't killed her, at least not intentionally—the infection had. Sure, the suspect would have known she'd die eventually, but medical negligence and slitting someone's throat were the MOs of two different types of killers. And the guy in front of them now sure seemed okay with the idea of murdering a woman for the high crime of healing from a botched surgery in a way that displeased him. The tendons in Petrosky's neck went rigid. He fought to relax his jaw. "I thought you were a plastic surgeon, Doc. You sure know a lot about killers."

"I was in forensics before I went into surgery. That's why you're here, isn't it?" Yeah, Jackson had told him that, and now Nordstrom met Jackson's eyes. She nodded. But her face was placid—calm. Not her usual take-them-by-the-balls demeanor. Did they know each other? Nordstrom's amber eyes gleamed, but he wasn't looking at them; his gaze was on…

Petrosky leaned over the table and slapped the folder closed, hiding Patel's mutilated flesh—the images were suddenly obscene, especially with this guy hovering over Ana like a predator over a kill. He leveled his gaze at the doctor.

Ex-doctor. "If you know so much, if you're so damn good at your job, why'd they take your medical license?"

Nordstrom finally drew his gaze from the coffee table. "I think you know why."

He didn't. Oddly, Jackson had not mentioned that part, and those details usually passed for small talk—maybe she'd changed in the last three months, too. Grown more secretive. Closed-off. To be fair, he probably should have asked her on the way over, but he'd been too busy fantasizing about Decantor and a desk full of wasps. "I'd rather hear it from you," Petrosky said, crossing his arms.

Nordstrom's nostrils flared, but the rest of his face stayed the same—still no movement in his forehead. Botox; had to be. "I wanted to make them perfect—better," he said finally. "Some women didn't want to go big enough or small enough, and it was my job to tell them how to do it right."

But why would offering his expert opinion get him into trouble? Unless... "You did surgeries and made alterations without their permission?"

"I had releases for each procedure—it's not like I did breast augmentation on a woman who was there for a tummy tuck. But my job was to take the paperwork and create art. Like Picasso."

"Picasso is known for mutilated oddities of the human form, that's for sure."

Nordstrom glared at the now-closed folder. "Can I actually see it in person?"

It? "See what?"

"The body." Nordstrom straightened his shoulders—confident.

"What, so you can get your rocks off, you sick bastard?"

"No, because maybe I can...help." He gaped at Jackson, eyes widening. "Am I being accused of something here?"

"Depends," Petrosky snapped. "What'd you do wrong?" He

leaned over the table once more, gaze locked on Nordstrom's frozen forehead muscles—his wide eyes. "Or should I say, what else?"

Jackson raised a hand. "We're just spitballing, and he has an alibi for this, Petrosky. Lay off." But her voice was soft, far softer than it should have been—taking it easy on him? Usually, this was about the time she elbowed him in the ribs. Instead, she picked up the folder and tucked it beneath her arm, then turned to Nordstrom. "We won't need you to examine the body, at least not now."

Or ever. What could this hack find that Woolverton couldn't? Say what you wanted about that medical examiner twerp, he was damn good at what he did. This jackoff couldn't even hold on to a medical license.

Jackson waited until they got into the Escalade to give Petrosky the evil eye. He fired back, "What the hell was that?"

"I know we still have to talk to McCallum, but Nordstrom has a background in both forensics and plastic surgery. He seemed like the guy to ask. And that whole 'seeing the results of his masterpiece falling apart' thing could help us. He had our killer pegged: a perfectionist. Obsessive about his work."

If he's even right. "How did you meet that guy anyway? Some trendy nightclub?" When she scowled at him, he continued, "I just can't figure out why we came here to talk to him—aren't there any still-licensed plastic surgeons who might have given us their insight?"

Her fingers tightened on the wheel. "He used to be friends with Acharya. They went to high school together."

"You called the journalist to get a name?"

"He came to me with it, actually. You were there."

"And you talked to him. Gross."

"He brought coffee." Jackson sighed and relaxed her hands. "What do you know about Picasso, anyway?"

"What? I told you I know things." She stared at him. He

turned to the windshield and watched the streetlights, the sky stretching out to infinity like a black hole swallowing the road at the horizon. It was like they were driving into the maw of a monstrous beast. "Fine. Linda made me watch a movie about him once. But I do know things." Jackson's fingers tapped on the wheel. Her bracelet glittered. "Where can I get a wasp nest?"

"Why would you need a—"

"How do you know the doc again?"

She kept her gaze on the road. "I literally just told you, Petrosky."

The entire episode had been an exercise in weirdness. Even if Acharya had given her the lead, they didn't have to follow up; they ignored Acharya all the time. *Maybe she knows the doc from somewhere else.* He glanced at the bracelet again—fancy. Maybe he didn't need the wasps after all. "Is Nordstrom the guy?"

"What guy?" Her cell buzzed.

"You know, the one you're hiding?" He couldn't see her dating the asshole, but that fuckboy thing...

She pulled her phone from her pocket. "I'm not hiding anyone. It's just not your goddamn business."

He frowned. Jackson was definitely dating someone, and she wouldn't hide it unless it was someone questionable. He'd thought Decantor, but... Was she back with her ex-husband? If so, that child-abandoning bastard was going to get a punch to the dick. If only she were dating someone awesome. Dr. McCallum was a little old for her, but hey, once you hit a certain age, it was all just a number, wasn't it?

The chief's face wandered into his head—he pushed it away. Then it was Linda's face, his ex-wife, the little smile lines around her mouth. Maybe he should call her. She'd tried to help him over the last few months, but he hadn't been able to let her in, hadn't been able to—

"Hey, Petrosky!"

He looked over. "Huh?"

"Bad news." Jackson's jaw had gone hard. "Really fucking bad."

7

I HATE BEING RIGHT. The path was just as cold as it had been the first time, the bench equally shiny in the dark. The floodlight's glare turned the landscape into a scene right out of a horror movie. Scott himself knelt in the brush across from the bench, poking at something in the earth, broad shoulders tight, dark brows furrowed in concentration. He nodded to Petrosky as they approached, then turned back to his work.

"Why'd he kill another one so fast?" Petrosky stepped in front of the body. Yellow sundress, exactly the same as the other, though this one had blood splattered on the front like a wreath of smashed poppies across her abdomen. One of the seams around the arm was loose, gaping, though it was impossible to tell if it was from shoddy workmanship or the result of a struggle. He imagined Patel's bruised flesh, the fat dripping from nipple to armpit. Had this woman suffered the same way? How long had he had her?

He squinted at her mouth—her teeth, at least, looked normal. But that was where the differences stopped. Bare feet. Hands folded in her lap, ligature burns on her wrists, her nails painted the color of bubble gum, the same color as her lips. Long black hair swept over one shoulder. And while this victim was heavier in the chest and thighs than Patel, thicker through the middle, she had a similar build.

Fucking hell. He had hoped it wasn't a serial, but he'd known from the moment he saw Patel on this bench. After so long in the field, he could smell a serial case like the putrid rot of a dead animal stuck in the wall. *Poor girl.* His gut clenched as he said, "He kept Ana for weeks before the infection killed her. It's only been two days since he dumped his last victim." Another woman dead on his watch—another death he could have prevented if he'd solved this thing sooner.

Jackson's face was drawn, all planes and angles in the harsh floodlights. "My guess is he did something he couldn't correct—something that made her suddenly no longer fit his ideal or that made him so ashamed he had to get rid of the evidence of his failure like Nordstrom said."

Or he was escalating—but this was *fast*. "You trust that mutilating motherfucker an awful lot, Jackson."

"Nordstrom found out the consequences of playing god without permission, and he was punished for it—he'll never practice medicine again. He still knows what he's doing, he just wasn't responsible with the knowledge."

Nor was their killer. Petrosky dragged his gaze over the sash of gore across the victim's waist. What was the dress hiding this time?

"Name's Chantal Khatri, twenty-two," an unfamiliar voice said. "She also works in tech, in the building just up the street from Patel."

Who the...? Petrosky looked over at the blond man—square shoulders, wide jaw, all of him silhouetted by the floodlights. Michaelson? Was that his name? The rookie stood behind the bench in the same spot where he'd been the other day, head cocked like a curious puppy, though Petrosky couldn't make out his features in the glare.

"Do you know which company?" Jackson asked. "Same as our first vic?"

Why is she asking this asshat?

"No, this one's called Desygn," Michaelson said. "With a *y*."

Of course with a *y*. That was almost as stupid as C0D3W0RKS. But what did he expect from a group of humans who didn't know what hair was supposed to look like? Blue, green, pink, like a bunch of goddamn Muppets. And what was the connection between their killer and the profession? It didn't feel like a coincidence that both victims had worked in tech, even if that particular block housed almost all the software and tech companies in Ash Park.

"How do you know her name?" Petrosky asked the rook. "Did she have ID on her?" Patel hadn't—was the killer getting sloppy, or was it a clue?

But Michaelson was shaking his head; Petrosky hated that he couldn't see his eyes beyond the floodlights. "We got a missing persons call yesterday night when she didn't show up for dinner with her sister."

"Did you find this body too? Pretty damn convenient."

Michaelson shrugged. "This is my beat, and I've been patrolling down here three times a day since we found Ana Patel; been watching the incoming missing persons calls, too."

Petrosky stared daggers at the man. The air stank of blood—he could feel it cloying in the back of his throat. He stepped back, trying to catch his breath, but a sudden heaviness had invaded his chest. "Who told you to do that?"

"No one, sir. Just thought it might be a good idea. In case."

"Were you expecting more bodies?" Petrosky squinted, but he couldn't get a read on the kid—the floodlights behind the bastard cast his eyes in shadow, deep black pools where his irises should have been.

"I thought there could be—it had the marks of a serial, right?"

"The main mark of a serial is more than one victim—you're clearly psychic." *Or guilty.* But Petrosky had thought the same when he saw Ana Patel's body. Why was he being so hard on the kid? He dropped his gaze—that awful slash of red across the brilliant yellow of her dress, like a belt of horror. Petrosky blinked and knelt in front of the woman's knees before he ripped the kid a new one. He gently lifted the hem of her skirt.

"What are you doing?" Michaelson practically gasped. "You can't touch her, we have to wait for—"

"Shut up, kid." Scott and Woolverton would get their evidence, but right now, Petrosky needed to know what they were dealing with. *What did he do to you, honey?*

Jackson knelt beside him. The yellow fabric caught briefly like it was frozen to the woman's belly, then released, bathing her body in stark white light from the floods behind the bench. And now he could see what it was stuck to: a dozen little holes, wider than a standard needle. A larger gauge hypodermic? Each mark was blue or black in the center, surrounded by congealing blood.

"Liposuction?" Jackson said.

"Looks that way, but your ex-surgeon buddy was right: he's a hack. Probably pushed the syringe too deep, and she bled out, maybe perforated her intestines." Ana Patel's shallow needle wounds could have been practice, the gingerly done prodding of a wannabe surgeon, but Woolverton had compared it to a stabbing—and now it was. The perp might as well have gone at her with an ice pick. Petrosky gestured to the darker black surrounding one of the lower holes, darker than the blood visible near the others, probably leakage from a hole in her bowels. If she hadn't died from the bleeding, she'd have died from sepsis sooner rather than later. At least she hadn't suffered as much as Patel had. Those teeth, Patel's mutilated gums flashed in his mind, and he pushed the image away.

"So she died as the result of his alterations, as Patel did, but probably not because he was actively trying to kill her—looks like he got carried away." He was escalating and quickly. But what had he *planned* to do? What was the point of the mutilation, why work so hard to make them into someone else? "He held Patel for two weeks. What he did with her in that time frame is relevant for our profile."

"What he did with Patel, what he wanted to do to this woman?" Jackson said. "Oh, I dunno, rape them as often as he could. Abuse them. Watch them scream, maybe? He's a psychopath." And maybe a racist psycho, going after women of color. Or was the killer of the same race himself? Killers often attacked within their own racial group, but not always.

Jackson pushed herself to standing and inhaled deeply as if she'd been holding her breath while down next to Khatri's belly. "But you're right that there's something more here. He's so damn careful, perfectionistic in his staging, but he's killing these women accidentally—like he has no self-control."

"Maybe they do something to trigger him, make him lose patience." A little too close to victim-blaming, but in order to find this guy, Petrosky had to think like him. And he doubted the killer believed it was his own fault—those assholes always blamed someone else.

"Either way, this stabbing piece is impulsive. It's at odds with the rest of his profile. Even the fact that they're wearing the exact same dress...that takes planning. And the missing persons was just filed, which means he already had the outfit when he took her last night."

How many outfits does he have? "Maybe it's a role-playing thing, some living-sex-doll bullshit." Petrosky lowered the hem of the sundress—he'd hadn't realized he was still holding it. His knees ached, but he remained crouched there a moment longer. A killer had left his daughter alone too. In the cold. His eyes burned.

"Are we sure it's the same killer and not a copycat?" The rookie again. The guy stepped closer to the bench, boots crunching in the snow. "If he killed this one by stabbing, and the other victim died from infection... I mean, serials don't usually change their MO so much between victims."

"What are you talking about?" Petrosky snapped. "He didn't change—"

"He didn't touch her teeth, and he left her breasts alone."

But they didn't know that, not yet—they hadn't seen the marks on Patel's chest until Woolverton showed them, and Petrosky hadn't lifted the dress high enough to see past this woman's rib cage just now. "The goal is the same," he said slowly, ears pricked for a telltale hitch of guilt, or excitement, but the rook just shook his head and said: "But they aren't lopsided or anything and—"

"What kind of moron are you?"

Jackson kicked him in the ankle, but not hard—barely a love tap. *She's back.* Or he was. "Leave him alone, Petrosky. He's new."

"Doesn't mean he gets to be an idiot." He dropped his gaze to Khatri's lips—that awful bright pink. Her skin was still a rich brown, not yet graying, not yet showing the strokes from the makeup brush. But the eyeliner, the shadow —they were all the same colors that had been used on Patel. "He has a narrow vision of perfection. The alterations are different for each victim, so the goal is the product, not the actions themselves." He wasn't experimenting because he missed medicine, or because he wanted to be a surgeon; he didn't care about practicing technique. The method was secondary.

Petrosky's ears were numb with cold. At least it was warmer down here out of the wind, down by...her knees. Oh god. It wasn't the trees or the bench breaking the wind. *She* was still warm. He stood quickly, the blood rushing to his head, stars of black flashing in his vision.

"I think you're right," Jackson said. "He didn't decide to kill her—the death was an accident. Which means she died before he finished whatever he had planned for her."

And if that was the case…he'd be pissed. Dissatisfied. And looking for another victim.

8

THE DAY BROKE harsh and bright, the sun glinting off the crust of ice that had formed over the powder. Petrosky squinted through the windshield at the line of massive oaks that lorded it over either side of the residential street. No potholes here. No people either, not that he could see, only the tire tracks that cut through the occasional unplowed drive like the ghostly remnants of some archaeological dig. The road felt lonely, but that might have been the knowledge that Chantal Khatri was never coming home. His home still felt abandoned sometimes, like his car, his heart, all of them aching with the absence of his daughter, grief and guilt in equal measure. But the guilt was heightened by the nagging regret over the boy he'd murdered this past fall. Carroll said it was a justified shooting, and maybe it was, but that didn't change that he'd killed a kid the same age his own daughter had been when she'd been murdered. Had the world made that child a monster? Would he have had a chance if Petrosky hadn't pulled the trigger? He listened to the buzz of Jackson's tires, trying to ignore the way her fingers tapped on the wheel—frustrated. Again.

As was he. He'd barely slept—images of the boy with his

bloody lips, of Julie and her gaping throat, of the Jack hidden in the kitchen, assailed him every time he closed his eyes. And it didn't help that they'd made no progress on the case. They had no idea when or where Khatri and Patel had been taken, or where they'd been held. They weren't sure where to look for witnesses. There were no common phone numbers between the two victims in the last six months except the Thai place and the local pizza place. And no one at either restaurant had any criminal history, save one guy with a marijuana charge, the least likely drug to cause homicidal rage unless your victim was a Dorito.

Petrosky sighed, his breath fogging up the side window. The women had a few grocery stores in common, too, but again, the employees hadn't raised any red flags. No one in the medical field worked at any of those places, and no one with a criminal past—the background checks during the hiring process apparently weeded out the same type of characters they were looking for. But he'd go over the workers again once they had a more concrete profile. They also had to do some digging on the women's routines; might be some social media connections, especially with the vics being in the same type of industry, but he needed Scott's help with that one.

"Job's probably a dead end too," Jackson said, snatching her coffeehouse espresso from the cupholder. "Desygn says that Chantal Khatri quit six weeks ago."

Around the same time Patel broke it off with her boyfriend. But even if the two women were lovers, and the killings a carefully planned hate crime made to look like a serial case, Patel's breakup wouldn't have made Khatri quit her job. Petrosky watched the fog on the window dissipate—clear again. Like he'd never been there at all. "What's she been doing since she quit?"

"No idea." Jackson braked suddenly and turned into a

drive, limestone crunching beneath the tires. Petrosky peered out the windshield. He whistled.

The Khatris' home was out of a magazine. Enormous pines flanked the drive, the yard a perfect solid sheet of unmarred snow. The house itself was a two-story brick monstrosity, easily five thousand square feet, with eight windows along the front, the whole thing topped with what looked like copper shingles. Long, low rows of evergreen bushes framed the door.

Petrosky dropped the brass knocker—a lion's head with a ring in its nose. The wind whispered through the trees as if afraid to disturb the pristine landscape, a barely-there hissing amidst the branches.

The man who answered was equally quiet. He invited them into the living room in a small tired voice, face sagging as if it wanted to slip from his bones and puddle on the floor before vanishing beneath the floorboards. The air was thick with the grief of a father less one daughter, a man whose heart would never again be whole. It made Petrosky's chest hurt.

"She didn't really...get along with us." Shayna Khatri, Chantal's sister, had dark hair and reddish-brown skin, but that was where the similarities ended. She was rail thin even in a turtleneck, with pouty lips and a wide nose. Her mother, on the other hand, looked more like Chantal—same build. But she had yet to say a single word, and the father just stared, occasionally dabbing at his eyes with a brilliant purple handkerchief.

"Can you be more specific?" Jackson asked.

"I just mean she had her own thing. Wasn't really into family. Didn't like our traditions, thought we were old-fashioned." Shayna straightened her skirt—long, blue, to the ankle. "But anything I said, anything we fought about...it was all to help her, you know? She had terrible taste in men."

Mrs. Khatri raised a hand to her thin lips as if horrified by her daughter's candor, but she did not disagree.

And dating a serial killer would certainly qualify as bad taste. "Do you know these men she was seeing? Names, or how to get in touch with them?" If their perp was a man Chantal knew, they could narrow the suspect list.

Mr. Khatri lowered his head, revealing the bald spot on his crown. Shayna cast a sidelong glance at her mother and said, "Chantal usually met them at the gym, or clubs—places like that. I'm not sure she got a lot of…names and numbers to call them after."

That didn't ring true; Chantal's phone records boasted hundreds of calls in the previous six months and even more texts. But most of the callers in the days prior to her death had continued texting after she'd been taken—men who clearly hadn't known she was gone. Unless they were trying to cover their tracks. "So she was confident," Petrosky said. "Outgoing? Liked meeting new people?"

Mrs. Khatri raised an eyebrow as if this assessment had never occurred to her. Shayna narrowed her eyes. "I…guess so, yeah."

Outgoing. Lots of friends—male friends. The opposite of Ana Patel, who appeared to be a homebody, who had no phone calls to track. The odds that one of Chantal's one-night stands had also killed Ana, a shut-in lesbian, weren't likely. Better to focus on what the women had in common. Which was what, exactly? That they lived in the same area? Similar job descriptions? Petrosky shifted his weight, the caramel-colored leather like butter beneath his ass—it didn't even squeal.

"Why did she quit her job with Desygn?" Jackson said now.

Mr. Khatri raised his head, eyes wide with surprise. His daughter frowned.

"She quit?" Shayna said finally. "I... We didn't know that. I thought she was still working there."

It had been nearly two months. How was she paying her bills if she wasn't working? The girl hadn't even stopped ordering dinner out—like she wasn't afraid of running low on funds. She had to have a safety net. Had she found a sugar daddy? Petrosky squinted at the Khatris. Her father's face had frozen in a look of perpetual surprise, but her mother...the woman's lips had gone white, her eyes tight, anxious. But not shocked.

"Mrs. Khatri?"

She met his gaze, her lips pressed together in a tight line.

"Were you giving your daughter money for rent?"

Mr. Khatri turned to his wife. Her lip trembled. "She didn't want to work in that place anymore."

"And why was that, Mrs. Khatri?"

"She said she had to be up too early. That she did not like it. Wanted to go back to school."

"It wasn't just that, though," Shayna chimed in. "I mean, I didn't know she quit, but she was convinced she was going to be famous; she was getting social media sponsorships to model plus-sized clothes, even though she wasn't really plus-sized. She wanted to do that instead of working a nine-to-fi—"

Mr. Khatri burst to his feet, sharp words in a language Petrosky didn't speak flying from his lips at breakneck speed. Mrs. Khatri remained sitting, waving her hands, spitting fire back. Shayna just...watched. Jackson rose as if prepared to stop a domestic brawl, but none of them were close to striking the others—just noisy. And confusing.

Petrosky got to his feet as Jackson stepped between the couple. "Okay, okay, enough," she said, and Mr. Khatri quieted, shoulders heaving. "So you paid her bills—fine. You dislike her job choice—understandable. You can argue about that later. Right now, we need your help to find her killer."

Mr. Khatri sat back down at his wife's side and let out a shuddering half sigh, half sob.

"Do you know what she usually did with her days?" Jackson said, easing back down across from them. "Who she saw, where she went?"

"She looked for jobs." Mrs. Khatri shook her head. "She never found another good one. She should have stayed where she was."

"She spent a lot of time at the gym too," Shayna said quietly. "She said it was a good place to...um"—another sidelong glance at her parents—"meet people."

The gym. So Chantal was one of the smart ones who didn't go running in ball-freezing temperatures. Maybe the gym was where she'd met the wrong man.

9

DESYGN, the place Khatri had once worked, seemed like a dead end; all ten employees had alibis, were female, or just weren't strong enough to heft a body down the stairs and up the path to that bench. But they did have a little insight into her patterns. Always late—she never came into work before ten—and she usually went to the gym on Monday late afternoon. That was tomorrow.

Tomorrow, all the regular Monday employees would be there—the folks who knew Khatri. Still, as far as they knew, Patel had never been to a gym in her life. More likely that they'd find the connection in some other common location within the neighborhood. But whatever it was, it was hidden, and the mess at Khatri's apartment wasn't helping; it looked like someone had taken a snowblower to the place. Clothes on the floor, pizza boxes, remnants from the Thai food deliveries they'd seen on her call logs, the leftovers crusty and far too old to have been from the night she was taken. The only place that was remotely neat was the closet—four racks of shoes, at least twenty-five pairs, on the wall just outside the sliding doors, too many to fit inside, all organized by color. Strapless tops and skirts that looked like headbands on the far right. Work blouses and slacks in a tiny section in the middle. But the most prominent section was for workout gear—the entire left side of the closet was biker shorts and yoga pants and tank tops. Scott had said the workout gear was showcased in her social media profiles—perhaps sponsorships, perhaps trying to look good for the men at the gym, perhaps just proud of her physique, but either way, it painted a much different picture from Patel's, who didn't even have social media accounts. No nights on the town either, no drinks with friends.

He slammed the closet door a little too hard, making the shoe rack vibrate. No one at Khatri's job thought she'd frequented the path where she was found—she and Patel didn't have that in common either. And Khatri's credit card history revealed lots of drink purchases at local and not-so-local clubs, but not a single bookstore purchase, the only other regular charge on Patel's card.

Waste of time. But where else to search? "Our victims look similar, but they don't have dick in common."

Jackson raised an eyebrow. "Is that a lesbian joke? Because you definitely should not be—"

"It's just an expression, Jackson, Jesus Christ." But when he glanced her way, her lips were pressed tightly together as if she were trying not to laugh. "Ha-ha, very funny."

"You're taking yourself pretty seriously these days. Maybe you should knock that shit off."

Maybe he should. Would he have been bothered six months ago? He headed for the front door, stepping over a pizza box, the cardboard dark with oil. "Whatever. But you know I'm right. Scott says there aren't any commonalities online—no common friends despite their tech connection." And if Scott couldn't find them, they didn't exist. The icy wind hit him in the face and tightened his shoulders. He turned his collar up against the bitter wind.

Jackson locked the door behind them. "No common

acquaintances at all? That's pretty surprising with them being in the same line of work."

But they had worked at two different companies, and Khatri clearly hadn't taken her work as seriously as Patel. One of Khatri's coworkers believed she'd gotten the degree just to appease her parents, and her mother had said she'd wanted to go back to school, probably looking at a whole different field. Not like she'd be hanging out at engineering conferences. "Our guy...he has to live nearby. The victims lived ten minutes apart and worked on the same block, frequented some of the same restaurants; restaurants everyone in the area goes to or orders from. We can canvass, see if the locals saw anyone shifty hanging around." He stopped at the Escalade and paused with his hand on the door. A voyeur felt more likely than someone the women knew—their killer's criteria seemed to be about physique, not personalities. It was the only common ground between the victims.

Jackson shoved her key into the ignition, and the heat roared on.

He frowned at the haze of fog on the windshield, a mist that felt almost sentient, like the ghosts of their victims were there just out of reach. First-case-back jitters? Maybe. But he didn't even feel like harassing the driver of the Subaru next to them, some blonde woman throbbing her bass so loudly Petrosky's brain ached. Who cared if he could get her to smear her eyeliner when the women in this city were one wrong move from a slow, agonizing death?

Jackson hit the gas, the Subaru vanished behind them, and the pulse in his head eased. "We need to talk to McCallum," he said. The words were sour—maybe he should tell Jackson to go without him. Petrosky was damn tired of his brain being poked and prodded. Of course, he'd killed a kid, so maybe he shouldn't get over that. No one should, regardless of what Carroll believed.

"Already called him—he's squeezing us in tonight after his last appointment."

"He's working Sunday?"

"Psychiatrists, man. Mental health never gets a day off." Jackson peered into the rearview. "And here I thought you hated shrinks."

He watched the last of the fog dissipate in the superheated air from the vents. "McCallum's not a shrink."

"I'd like to hear you tell him that."

"I mean, he's a shrink, but he's not an asshole. Like most of them."

Jackson glanced at him out of the corner of her eye. "Is this your version of occupational bigotry? 'I can't be anti-shrink, I have a shrink friend!'"

"Oh, I can definitely be anti-shrink. I'm just not anti-McCallum."

She rolled her eyes. "I'm sure he'll be thrilled."

"Fine, so we have the gym interviews tomorrow, McCallum later today. For now…" He sighed, his eyes on the icy road. Flakes of white floated down from above like the sky was trying to bury them but was too lazy to make it quick. He ran a hand over his jowly face—smooth, at least. Keeping up appearances, for once, and that had to count for something. "Who's watching the dump site?"

"Michaelson."

"That rookie prick again?"

She raised one gloved hand. "Hey, he's new, but he's motivated. And he doesn't need to do anything but drive by the path and the surrounding streets and radio it in if he sees anything."

Petrosky patted the pack of cigarettes in his pocket, wishing he were in his own car so he could light up. "I don't like him."

"Yeah, I'm sure, because he reminds you of Morrison."

His old partner—a man who'd been as close to a son as

he'd ever have. "That stupid asshole could never be Morrison," Petrosky snapped, loudly enough to make her jaw drop. His chest was on fire, and he wasn't about to start considering why, not now—if he did, he might not survive the day without visiting a bar. He rubbed at his clavicle, then said more quietly: "Sorry, okay? Let's just look at how our killer is choosing these women so we can save the next one instead of coming across her corpse on that bench." But Petrosky doubted the guy would be stupid enough to use the path a third time; he had to know it was being watched. Then again, Michaelson had been patrolling the area, albeit badly, when the perp had dumped the second victim.

"Maybe we should put out a press release," he said now. "I can get up there, let the public know the kind of girl he's after so they can take precautions."

Jackson snorted. "Tell all the dark curvy girls to stay home?"

"I wasn't suggesting that." He shook his head, rubbing harder at his chest. "But it can't hurt, not with a guy like this out there. Right this moment, he's probably out trolling for runners, for—"

"He's not looking for runners, not exactly, it's just that runners or gym rats have a higher likelihood of meeting his physical criteria—muscular legs, thicker thighs."

"A fitness buff." Like the guys at the gym. The skin between his shoulders prickled—*we should head there first.* But Decantor and Sloan were already working the background checks on the gym employees, and if it was someone from the gym, why Patel? He probably would have picked another gym member instead of a random woman off the street. They'd do better interrogating those douchebags once they had a more concrete profile from McCallum anyway. He dropped his arm.

"We can assume the killer's got a place with some privacy," he said. "A house, not an apartment." Even a house in a suburban neighborhood. Just a few years back, Petrosky had worked a case where a sadistic maniac kept women hidden in his basement for years, torturing them, abusing them, impregnating them. Petrosky had found the final victim tethered to a post with her dead friend still chained to the wall beside her.

"Which might help once we narrow the suspect list," Jackson said, bringing him back. "The rest of the things we know about, the makeup, the syringes, all of that can be purchased anywhere." Same with the outfits; it was easy to buy shitty sundresses in bulk—hard to trace too.

"Right," he said, and Jackson glanced his way—was his voice shaking? His lips tasted like whiskey. He coughed. "And this guy doesn't care about the long-term, or at least, a long-term captive isn't his endgame. He's not trying to create a robot to keep her forever." He just needed a place private enough to abuse them for a week or two—then dump them before the neighbors got suspicious.

He turned back to the window, watching his breath on the glass, pretending he couldn't see his old partner's dead glassy eyes just beyond the pane.

THEY CANVASSED THE STREETS—FROM C0D3W0RKS to Patel's apartment, then back down to Desygn, then back to Khatri's apartment building—with the forlorn trudge of an already defeated army. The sidewalks had been doused in salt recently, making their shoes grind against the walk with a gritty *cssssh* that made Petrosky's shoulders tighten. Mounds of dirty slush smothered the curbs like fallen clouds.

The bookstore had been a dead end. No cameras, and while the elderly female owner did remember Patel and seemed genuinely upset that something had happened to her, she was only able to offer a vague description of a man she'd seen outside when the girl had been there: average build, sweatshirt, and a jacket. She hadn't seen his face. And they couldn't be sure he was even there to watch Patel—there were no cameras that might help them confirm or deny whether he'd followed their victim when she left the store. Petrosky squinted at the ice-crusted walk beneath his sneakers, wishing he'd worn boots. Wishing he owned boots. Was their killer out here now, watching? Where had he seen these women? How had he chosen them? But he could have seen them anywhere. The grocery store, the pizza place, just walking around the city. Neither had even owned a car—and because Patel and Khatri didn't frequent the same places, it seemed likely their suspect wasn't choosing his victims from any single location. These were women he saw in his everyday life, who attracted his attention. And he'd stalked them from there.

But abducting them was far more difficult than watching them—you needed privacy to wrestle a woman into your car. Would they find evidence of a struggle, maybe enough DNA to nail him?

They stopped in front of a brick building halfway between Khatri's apartment and her job at Desygn. The man sitting on the sidewalk looked up, pulling the ratty plaid blanket tighter around his shoulders, snowflakes clinging to his eyelashes. Sallow, ashy skin. Hollow cheeks. Thick, curly eyebrows run through with white.

Jackson flashed her badge. "Good afternoon, sir."

The man raised one of those glorious eyebrows—suspicious. Petrosky peeled a ten from his wallet and dropped it into the man's plastic cup. The eyebrow relaxed.

Jackson opened the manila folder she'd tucked beneath her jacket and turned two images to the man on the concrete. "Have you ever seen either of these women?"

Recognition dawned, and Petrosky stiffened—he definitely knew something. The man smiled. "Yeah, that one." He nodded to the picture in Jackson's left hand: Chantal Khatri. "I think I've seen the other one, too, but I can't be sure. It's too dark in the mornings to be positive, but there's a girl who runs sometimes." Now he frowned. "Ain't seen her lately. But the other one, that one"—he pointed again to Khatri—"she comes later, once it's light. Sometimes she has money, sometimes she doesn't, but she always smiles. Most people... act like you aren't there." His nostrils flared—shame or anger at this rudeness? Maybe both.

"When was the last time you saw her?" Jackson asked, holding Chantal's picture closer to the man's face.

He studied the sky briefly, then: "I think it's been...maybe three days?"

Khatri had been down here three days ago, right up the road from where she used to work? What had she been doing? Maybe they'd revisit the Desygn team again.

The man nodded up the street to a place with a green awning. "She was heading up into that building there."

Petrosky followed his gaze, squinting into the icy wind. "The smoothie shop?"

"Yessir."

That made sense. Even if she wasn't working at Desygn, her food purchases hadn't stopped, nor had her gym membership. Same with her clothing and drinks. No wonder her father had been pissed when he'd found out Mommy was footing the bill.

"She go to the smoothie place a lot?" Jackson asked.

"Yes, ma'am." He nodded. "Almost every day."

They certainly hadn't seen credit card purchases from that place every day, but she might have paid cash—how much could a smoothie possibly cost? Unless she was meeting someone who was paying the tab for her.

"Did you see anyone with her three days ago?" Jackson asked, tucking the photos back into the folder. "Maybe even someone out here watching?"

The man's brows furrowed, turning them into a single, angry caterpillar. "Watching?"

"Maybe they were interested in her."

"Well, who wouldn't be interested in her?" He turned to Petrosky as if for confirmation. "She was a pretty girl. Nice, too."

Petrosky sniffed, the wind sharp as blades in his nostrils. "Please answer the question, Mister…"

The man pressed his lips together like he thought they might arrest him if they had his real name. "I'm not sure I should."

Jackson stiffened. There was no need to stonewall if you didn't have anything to say. "Let's not worry about the name," Petrosky said, reeling himself back in so he didn't scare the guy off, and Jackson's posture relaxed. "Let's just worry about who you saw," Petrosky finished.

The man frowned again. His gaze went hard. Then: "I guess there was a guy."

"What'd he look like?" Jackson prodded.

"Well, now, I don't want to make assumptions." He dropped his gaze to his lap. "Lots of cops out here, always takin' in the brown boys, pulling them off the street, and if they start doing that now because of what I say… Hell, y'all might take me in too."

Petrosky crouched down, so he was eye level with the man. "That nice girl who always said hello to you? Someone stabbed her in the guts with a hypodermic needle until she bled out."

The hard look vanished. "She okay?"

"She's dead."

His mouth dropped open, then closed again as if the cold hurt his teeth, and it probably did—Petrosky's own teeth felt frozen to his upper lip. "It's my fault. Maybe." His breath shuddered from his lips in a cloud of white. "Oh, Jesus, help me."

"How about you help us," Petrosky said, pushing himself to standing though his belly had gone hot—that guilt in the man's eyes. He understood it. "Do right by her."

The man's gaze drifted to the smoothie shop and back to Petrosky. "He was brown, but he wasn't black."

"How dark we talkin'?"

"Similar to her color." He nodded to Jackson. "If I had to guess, I'd say he was Indian. The dots, not the feathers."

Jackson grunted softly. Looked like they'd get to play "Is This Racist?" on the way back to the precinct. But he already knew the answer.

"What else?" Jackson said.

"Black hair, real thick."

"What about his face? Big eyes, small nose, what?"

"I couldn't see that, not really. He was standing with his back to me." He gazed off in the direction of the smoothie shop as if trying to make the man materialize, but his head snapped back just as quickly. "Oh, but he had on a black jacket. Like a thick hoodie, maybe like one of those down coats? Black pants. And he was pretty wide in the shoulders, the kinda person you'd expect to go into that smoothie place."

"Like a guy who works out?" A gym rat dressed like an assassin.

"Yeah, like that."

The gym folks were looking better all the time. "Did you see him talk to her?" If he knew her, that should give them a place to start.

"No, she came out of the shop and headed up that way." The man dropped the blanket from one shoulder and pointed, revealing the thin T-shirt beneath. *Damn.* So...the street just past the smoothie shop. It was conceivable she'd have turned up that block—it was a straight shot home from the street behind this one.

"And where did the man go?"

"He...followed her. But I didn't think much about it. People are always out walking here, even in the winter." The man shuddered. He pulled his arm back under the sea of tattered plaid.

"Why don't you walk with us for a minute?" Petrosky said. "Get some lunch. You have to be freezing."

The man shook his head. "Can't. I'll lose my spot. It's a good spot."

"Fair enough." Petrosky slipped another twenty into the man's cup. This time he thought he saw tears sparkle in the man's eyes. He stuck his card in the cup too. "You see anything else, you call me, okay?"

"Okay, yessir." His lip trembled. "I hope you find him."

Yeah, me too.

10

The smoothie shop was like a hippie bat signal: old brick walls, older wooden door, and a new green awning that screamed "vegan heaven"…but no cameras that he could see. No way for anyone inside to see a man on the walk. "From here, Khatri could have gone east one block, then hooked a right back up toward her place," Jackson said, hustling past the shop toward the side street beyond. "Probably where she was going when our witness saw her." She turned the corner and started walking again, but this time she went more slowly, turning her head first right to examine the wall of the shop, then left—the street.

Petrosky hissed frosty air through clenched teeth, his legs on fire despite the cold. He looked over his shoulder. Across the street from the smoothie shop, a wall of tall gothic buildings glowered down at the spot their perp would have been standing. A gargoyle scrutinized them from its perch between two arced panes of glass, both backlit by modern fluorescents—either of those side windows was a good spot for a potential witness. But their suspect seemed too careful to just pull Khatri into his car under those watchful eyes. "He wouldn't have done it in the open. It had to be someplace a little more secluded—at least a spot that wouldn't be visible from the buildings." He hooked a thumb at the gargoyle.

Jackson followed his finger and nodded. Nothing suspicious on the asphalt or the curbs—just snow, all gray, none dyed pink with blood. The sidewalk grew icier as they followed it away from the main strip, but the alley behind the building appeared wet—probably salted—and the back doors for the strip were bathed in shadow. No lights that he could see; no cameras here either. Along the left side of the alley, simple chain link separated the buildings from what was probably residential housing, but the trees and bushes on the other side of the fence were so thick that he couldn't see beyond them. Wheeled trash bins hulked in the middle, the tops obscured by ice-crusted snow. Had the perp kidnapped Khatri back here? It was dark enough, and secluded enough, provided one of the employees from the strip didn't wander outside at the wrong time. But the alley was too small for a car. If he'd taken her here...how had he gotten her out without being seen?

Petrosky squinted into the darkness, then back up the road, the direction Khatri would have taken to get home. If she had indeed been kidnapped that day as their witness suspected—and Petrosky was inclined to believe a man who spent his days scanning for threats to his well-being—they had to be close to the abduction site. But there were no businesses back this way, and the start of residential housing meant more witnesses in the blocks beyond this alley. The killer would have wanted to take her quickly before anyone noticed him following a potential victim down this lonely stretch of road.

They crept into the mouth of the alley, and a claustrophobic tingle shivered up his spine—*Morrison, like the alley where I found Morrison's body*. But there were no cobblestones here, no car. He clung to that and listened to their shoes—it stank of urine and pine, like a car air freshener hanging in a poorly ventilated gas station bathroom. Petrosky scanned the asphalt, then the wall, the brick nearly black, though he couldn't tell if it was from frozen slime mold or the shadows which had engulfed them the moment they'd stepped off the sidewalk. He pulled out his cell and hit the flashlight icon.

No way Khatri would have walked back here herself. If she'd been here, which they had no evidence of, the killer had lured her, perhaps by faking an injury, or he'd grabbed her and dragged her back out of the way of prying eyes; either way, he'd have had to subdue her. He'd have pulled her down as far as he could into the darkness. To keep her hidden.

"Got something." Jackson crouched near the building just behind the trash bins halfway between the two streets. If Petrosky were a kidnapper...that was where he'd do it. If someone had come upon him from either the south or the north, the perp could have run in the opposite direction.

Petrosky stepped up behind his partner and peered at the wall, at the red bricks visible beneath the crust of black. Clean, but not as if they'd been scrubbed by a rag or a brush; more of a round smudge at about head level, where the wall beneath had been uncovered. Had the killer slammed her head against the brick? They still had to talk to the ME about Khatri's body, but from the height, it looked like a good bet. Still too dirty to tell whether they were looking at dried blood or just years of filth, but forensics would test for the things they couldn't see. Petrosky watched as Jackson drew the light down toward the wall at their knees. The grime had definitely been disturbed here. Where it wasn't wiped to the brick, the texture was different, strangely shaped swaths where the otherwise fuzzy-looking surface had been rubbed smooth. And about belly-high...five distinct marks, tiny and circular at the top, each dragging down into a thin, jagged gouge as if someone had been trying to scale the thing. Fingernails. And upturned behind the trash bin, a cup bearing the smoothie shop logo.

This was it, then. This long dark alley was the last thing Khatri had seen as a free woman.

So what had the killer done with her? How had he gotten her out in the middle of the day without someone seeing him?

"I'll call Scott," Jackson said, but Petrosky had already turned away. The darkness was oppressive; it squeezed his chest, weighted his back, wrapped around his throat like a weak but insistent hand.

He swallowed hard and followed the alley. Listened to the *drip, drip, drip* of the water off the roof. The place stank of old snow and new piss and the sharp tinge of pine from the thick row of evergreens that blocked his view of whatever lay beyond the chain link. He raised his light. The walls down here had no marks—they remained blackened with dirt and shadow. The asphalt was filthy but seemingly undisturbed by a struggle. The trees whispered from behind the chain link to his left. He stopped.

An evergreen branch, brittle, cracked, lay on the ground beside the chain link, and another one just a few feet away, the end jagged as if it had been ripped from its host. The foliage directly in front of the discarded branches appeared intact, but just a few feet up the way…a tiny break in the evergreen, barely enough to expose a sliver of white sky from the other side. But their guy wouldn't have needed much space. If Khatri was unconscious, he just had to toss her over the fence and follow after her. Forensics might find traces from him or Khatri—a piece of skin clinging to a sharp branch, a scrap of clothing. But they probably wouldn't find evidence of pine on Khatri's body. He'd taken the time to paint his victims' nails, to do their makeup—he'd surely have cleaned sticky pine sap from their flesh.

Petrosky shoved the tip of his sneaker into the chain link and grabbed the top rail—were his hands sweating? The pads of his fingers felt like they might freeze to it. He heaved himself up and yanked the branches out of the way, pushing his fist, then his arm through the opening. He squinted past his fingers at...

Houses, most of them remnants from a long-gone era, one of the sections of the city that renovation had yet to touch. The home directly in front of him had one wooden shutter hanging loosely from the facade—maybe green once, now black with age and char. This home had burned out long ago. The hole where the back door should have been was a gaping wound. But the driveway was still there, as was the street. Though he could see no tire marks in the snow from here, the perp could have parked in the road, or at most of the houses along this strip.

Then driven Khatri anywhere.

11

Dr. McCallum was a robust man with a friendly smile and a jolly disposition, except when he was berating Petrosky for screwing up his life yet again. Today, the shrink appraised him shrewdly, maybe looking to see if he was wasted as he had been the day Stephanie Carroll dragged him in here by his shirt collar. And though just being here made Petrosky's mouth water, though it brought to mind the way the room had been spinning, the warm, thick feeling in his limbs, the heady haze of the liquor, the steady pressure of Steph's hand, apparently, McCallum liked what he saw now, because he grinned and gestured to the chairs across from him as he lowered himself behind his shiny desk.

"Our guy definitely has a type, a very specific one," Jackson said when they were settled. "Victims are both early twenties, dark hair, dark skin, curvy, with small waists. And he alters them to meet what seem to be very distinct measurements. He inflated Patel's breasts, and we think he used a larger-gauge needle to suck fat from Khatri's midsection... plastic surgery gone wrong." And those teeth. Petrosky suppressed a shudder.

McCallum laced his fingers on the desktop—a signal that

he was about to launch into some hard-core analysis, which was great so long as it wasn't about Petrosky. "Have you considered that he might be trying to recreate a specific person?"

"He might be modeling them after an ex-lover." Petrosky shifted in his seat, trying to get comfortable—he failed. "That slice-and-dice-em doc said the guy was trying to make her perfect; the measurements seem too specific for a more general body-type preference. Don't think he ever dated Patel or Khatri though." If the perp was altering them, they weren't his ideal—he wouldn't have to change his perfect woman. Petrosky hooked one ankle over the opposite knee and finished, "We combed through domestic violence calls in the last three months, looking for arrests who fit the med-school-drop-out profile, or suspects with an arrest for hurting someone who matches the physique of our vics, but...nada."

"And you have a witness who saw your killer, yes? Dark hair, dark skin, Indian descent?"

"We believe so."

McCallum nodded sagely. Did they teach that shit in shrink school? "Interesting that your suspect has similar physical characteristics to the victims, though it's not uncommon in serial cases." True. They already knew that most serials murdered within their own race. "But because of that similarity, you can consider the recreation of either an ex-lover or an abusive family member—someone with a connection to your perp, someone who caused enough pain to make your suspect want to kill them over and over."

Petrosky grimaced. "Figuratively raping and killing his mother, eh?" Seemed far-fetched, even for McCallum, but he wasn't about to argue with the psychiatrist mere days after the doc had signed his return-to-work papers.

"Well, not necessarily—an ex-lover is more likely. Just

spitballing. But many people subconsciously seek romantic partners with characteristics similar to their caregivers."

Spitballing. Hadn't Jackson used that term the other day? And when he glanced up, the doc was looking at his partner, face purposefully blank in that practiced shrink mask. His back tensed. Had Jackson called McCallum to…check up on him? *Am I being paranoid?* He couldn't tell. But he would not give them the satisfaction of losing it. Instead, he forced out, "If it's not one thing, it's your mother."

Jackson snorted. "That joke's stale as hell."

But Petrosky'd had to say something. Bile crept into his throat, burning his gullet. "Tracking down a perp based on what his mother looks like will be nearly impossible, especially since we haven't found other crimes that even remotely match this. We can widen the search for rapists, too, but I don't think that's his main motivation even if it plays a significant role in the torture."

Jackson nodded, her eyes still on the doc. "The pain from the procedures could be part of the thrill. A sadist. Maybe a fetish killer, getting off on something so nasty as the wounds themselves."

McCallum leaned forward, the chair's springs screaming as if begging the doc to just put it out of its misery. "That and notoriety; he's positioning these women in public, overtly challenging authorities, or at least urging us to call him out. I think he'd assume the grandiose nature of his crimes would earn him a little fame."

Petrosky shook his head. He'd considered a press release before, however briefly; now the thought made his stomach turn. "We're not going to give him that." But the press might. If Acharya gave this murderous asshole what he wanted, he'd cut the journalist's balls off. He sighed. So their killer was grandiose, narcissistic, attention-seeking…but carrying a deep wound from a woman who didn't love him the way he thought she should. And some people didn't care what they were known for so long as they got their ten minutes in the spotlight. Khatri's body flashed in his brain—that sash of blood across her middle, garish in the white light—and he blinked it away.

McCallum reached for the file and flipped it open, tapping a page from Woolverton's medical analysis. "He might have a tendency toward sadism, but he feels things, and deeply—more emotional than you'd expect from someone higher on the psychopathic scale. Did you see the latest from Dr. Woolverton?"

The latest? Wait, that paperwork was from Khatri and not Patel? Petrosky and Jackson exchanged a glance. "We've been running around all day," Petrosky said. "Woolverton finished the autopsy already?" Was this Carroll's doing? More importantly, was it for him, because she thought he'd lose his shit if he had to wait a few hours? His hackles rose. Half because he resented it—half because he worried she might be right.

McCallum nodded. "Woolverton found traces of a strong opioid in your second victim's system—a drug called Etorphine. It renders people unconscious almost immediately, but it can also be used for pain relief."

Jackson frowned. "He didn't find that in Patel's system. If the purpose was to dull their pain, why wouldn't he give it to her? With those teeth…she suffered right to the end."

McCallum squinted at the tiny writing. "Perhaps he uses it during the procedures and allows them to suffer in the aftermath. It's also possible that your first victim went into shock and no longer needed it. And the drug has a very short half-life; Patel might have processed it out before she died."

Made sense. Even if he restrained them, there would be more errors, more cuts, if they weren't unconscious—just tied up, they'd…writhe. "So he's not purely into the torture… probably."

McCallum shook his head. "No, I'd say the surgeries are secondary to his goal."

"Which is?" That was the question.

McCallum steepled his fingers and rested them against his thick lips. "The hesitation with the cuts shows he's inexperienced, but he's also nervous, at least when he's with the women. He incapacitates them, drugs them for the pain, but the way he dresses them...it's remorse, but we've all seen that before. This is a more intense variation on that theme. He dolls them up then brings them out to this little secluded place to be with them for a few more moments. If I had to guess, that bench is part of his fantasy, as is the dress he put them in. It's as if he still expects them to reject him, so he finishes that last piece of his fantasy after they've expired." *When they no longer can say no.*

Petrosky squinted. McCallum had a point. The killer could have put the bodies anywhere, and a more trafficked area, even this same area during summer, would give him far more publicity—more chance of discovery by passersby who would surely post images of the corpses on social media.

Jackson was nodding. "That would explain why the entire bench was doused with ammonia and scrubbed down—the killer probably sat there with the bodies, lived the final piece of his fantasy in real time."

"What about the outfit?" Petrosky didn't like the way his own voice sounded—too tight. Strangled.

"Probably something that reminds him of an item worn by the ultimate object of his affection. Anything unusual about it?"

If only. Scott had said the workmanship was shoddy, probably that child labor bullshit, and the material itself was produced overseas and widely distributed. Which meant no good way to trace it.

McCallum closed the file and met Petrosky's gaze. "Your killer will likely be young, probably younger than the typical serial—I'd guess closer to the ages of the victims. Immature. Someone strong, able to lift and transport them without much trouble, as confirmed by your witness. Is he coming in to do a sketch?"

"The witness didn't see his face, but I've got an artist going to meet him, hash out what he did see." That way, the guy didn't have to lose his prime real estate across from the smoothie shop.

McCallum nodded. "As I mentioned earlier, I do believe you're dealing with a man who has a strong element of remorse, someone with empathy even if it's stunted by his own narcissism. Someone who, though he feels guilty about what he's done to these women, will continue to seek other victims as part of a compulsion—he's being driven by something, by this fantasy. He likely feels he has no control over it."

That seemed valid, especially with the way he'd stabbed Khatri—no patience for learning to do it right, no way to go slow. He'd tried to control himself, and he'd lost it. *Like you're going to, old man.*

"Any idea where he might be looking for new victims?" Jackson said. "Do you think he knew these women ahead of time?"

"Hard to say, but once he has them, I think the desire to know them exists. The alterations and the almost provocative way each victim was posed speak to a more adult need—a need to be desired, perhaps a need for companionship. And let's not forget that he kept the first victim alive for weeks until her body gave out. I'd venture that he'd have kept her longer if she had survived, maybe indefinitely."

"Can't get a girlfriend, so he made one, eh? Lonely fellow."

McCallum's face was grave. "Indeed. But this is an escalation, a heightened fantasy—something he's considered for a long time. Your killer's got the patience to stalk them, to keep them in his home. To plan. He doesn't lose control until he's abusing them. But with your latest victim, he didn't have her long enough to satisfy whatever needs he has. He may be more careful in the coming days, but he's going to be looking for another victim."

"We've set up patrols near the area where Khatri was taken, and we've got folks on the path as well, watching the dump site."

"Good." McCallum nodded again, almost imperceptibly, and Petrosky resisted the urge to grab his ears and teach him how to do it properly. "He's patient with the acquisition, but he'll find the right woman sooner rather than later."

So they had no time to lose.

McCallum followed them to the door but put his hand on Petrosky's arm as Jackson walked out into the lot. "How's sobriety treating you?"

Petrosky glanced out the open door, the breeze ruffling his hair. Jackson hadn't even looked back—almost like she knew it was coming. He frowned. "Everything's fine."

"And Linda?"

"I haven't talked to her since...the incident." *The incident.* That was a fine thing to call shooting a teenager in cold blood. He stared at McCallum's hand on his arm until the doctor lowered it.

"Didn't she come to your house?"

"I kicked her out."

"You need support to help you through this."

"Well, there's a reason Linda's my ex-wife, Doc." *Because I'm a royal dick.* "And I've got plenty of support."

"You mean Stephanie Carroll."

Petrosky sniffed.

"She has a family, Ed, a marriage like the one you once had with Linda—and marriages take work. Now, I can find you someone else, additional support, a group, a sponsor who will give it to you straight—"

"Stop, okay? Just stop." There was no one else. Shannon was in Atlanta with his grandkids—she only called if she thought he might do something stupid, and he usually ignored those calls for that reason. And Jackson...she was hiding something. Someone. He was sure of it, and it made him feel disconnected from her—on the outside of her life. As for Linda, George, the girls next door...even if they wanted to help, they didn't get it. Couldn't possibly. Carroll was the only one who understood. The only reason he hadn't found himself staring down the neck of an empty bottle in the last few weeks. *Or worse.* Petrosky turned to the lot, squinting at the lights from the precinct across the way, the forlorn sky above them thick and heavy. "You're telling me not to drag her down with me," he said to the black clouds. "Right?"

"I'm not telling you anything. I'm asking you to consider additional sources of support, a spouse, even an ex-spouse." The doctor's eyes had not left his face. "Find a partner. The way she has."

THE DINER WAS forty minutes outside Ash Park, a greasy spoon with seat fabric dyed a horrid mustard yellow, but the seat didn't squeal the way any self-respecting diner bench should as he planted his ass on it. "The doc says I'm not supposed to talk to you."

Carroll—*not Stephanie, Carroll*—rolled her eyes; the bags beneath seemed darker, heavier than they had last week when she'd met him here. Heavier even than they'd been the other morning at his house. "The powers that be would surely agree with him." She sipped at her water and raised an eyebrow. "Since when do you listen to McCallum?"

"Since always."

"The same way you listen to me, right?"

"Yup." He met her gaze. The silence stretched—not an awkward silence, just a steady, easy quiet. She looked away first.

He cleared his throat. "How's Andre?"

"He's...hanging in there. Things have been a little tense."

Tense. That was how he'd described things with Linda until the day she'd moved out and left divorce papers on the kitchen table. "And how are you?"

"I'm doing the same. Exercising off the tension. Avoiding...temptation." She grabbed a french fry. Carroll didn't order fries unless she was anxious, not that you'd be able to tell by looking at her. Her gaze stayed even, her shoulders straight. Hands steady. "This case...it's a rough one."

He took a bite of his burger, the salt tingling against the roof of his mouth. He'd given up the booze, but the cigs and the grease were here to stay, at least for now.

"I talked to your partner earlier. After meeting with McCallum, she thinks we need to let the city know who this killer is targeting." *Dammit, Jackson.* He'd considered it briefly, but with what McCallum had just told them about this man's quest for fame, the idea should be off the table. "Before you start bitching about it, Edward, she might be right. If we save even one life by letting these women know..."

"That's what he wants."

"He doesn't want the world to know what he looks like."

"And if you release that piece, we'll be inundated with calls about innocent dark-skinned men just trying to take their kids to the movies or go grocery shopping." Not that they didn't get those calls anyway. He stared at his plate, the oil shiny against the glass. The guy was already escalating—would a little fame calm him down, give them a reprieve? He took another bite then said around a mouthful of meat: "I'll do the press conference. Change it up a little for the vultures."

She dropped a fry back onto her plate, mouth gaping.

"What? I can talk to the press. I know everything there is to know about the case." *Except who the killer is.*

Carroll recovered and blinked at him. "I'm not letting you get up there. What are you going to do, call the journalists assholes, then flip off the killer?"

"I was planning on a full moon."

"Keep it in your pants. I've got this."

"No." The word exploded from his lips before he registered his intent to speak. "I mean...let's just wait a little. Get a better read on the killer." His chest suddenly ached, tight and hot.

Carroll leaned back against the bench, and now the seat did squeak, a single, angry outburst that matched his own. "You were willing to do it yourself just a second ago. What's the point in waiting?"

I have a bad feeling. He slugged back his water, though it didn't ease the knot that had formed behind his breastbone. "McCallum thinks he's looking for notoriety—he's probably after another victim right now, and a press conference might speed that timetable."

"All the more reason to make the public aware."

"If it's fame he's after, he could attack a more high-profile target—you don't need to give him one." *Wait, what?* Was that what he was worried about? But...she *did* have the right coloring, the right hair, even if she was a little thicker than the other victims. And older, though he wouldn't say that out loud. The woman had a gun, after all.

"I'm not afraid of him, Edward."

"I'm just saying, this guy is a maniac; you can't disagree with that." Petrosky set his cup on the table, trying to ignore the way it clattered against the wood. "Okay, fine. So what time are you going to do the conference?"

She reached for her fries again, seemingly unfazed, but he knew better. "I'll do it later in the day, prime time. Around six. That'll give you a few extra hours to get your background work done before we alert the killer to the fact that we know more about him than he wants us to. Once we go public, he'll probably go underground—hopefully, the press conference will buy us time."

"Sounds good. I'll be back at the station by five thirty."

"I'm a cop, just like you. I don't need you to be there."

Petrosky nodded, hoping he didn't look like McCallum's dumb ass. His chest burned. "Not to watch you—what if he's in the crowd? Any asshole who likes fame this much—"

"We've got plenty of folks who can watch for him. I'll post lookouts around the venue. But any time you spend there is time you aren't working this case. And no matter what we're doing here tonight, at that precinct, you need to do what I tell you."

He raised an eyebrow. "Yes, ma'am."

She chewed. Grabbed more fried potatoes. At the table behind him, a woman laughed, a sound brighter than the pervasive din of clanging silverware—her amusement felt out of place. "So...how are you?" Carroll asked. "Really?"

I haven't slept in weeks, and every time I hear a car backfire, I see that boy's chest exploding; feel the heat from the gun in my hand. He sipped his coffee—weak and tepid like it had been cut with the tears of whatever asshole decided to use half the normal amount of grounds. The woman behind him laughed again. He bristled.

"Edward, you can tell me. That's how this works, right?"

He set the coffee cup beside his water glass. "You think this is working?"

"As well as it can, given the circumstances." She smiled. "And that damn shrink, trying to get in the way of our fun."

He stared at his half-eaten burger, the droplets of grease on the plate like the splatters of blood that had showered the floor, that had speckled the walls, and Jackson screaming: *What the fuck did you do?* Carroll was staring at him. "I still dream about it," he said finally. "About...him."

She nodded. "When it's a kid, it always sticks with you. I told you, every time I go to my daughter's school, when she has cheerleading practice or a game... Would that kid I shot be playing football? Would he be in the bleachers, his arm around some girl, dreaming about college?"

"More likely, he'd be thinking about what he wanted to do to said girl under the bleachers, or maybe where he could procure a new weapon to raise against another cop, but I take your point."

She reached across the table for his hand. He kept his palms on the wood, so she laid her fingers over the backs of his knuckles—warm, but he could feel her hand shaking. "I know how hard this is. But I also know you'll get through it. That you can handle it."

God, she really did sound like Linda, didn't she? But he hadn't believed Linda, because she hadn't been through it—she had never shot a child. She'd never killed anyone.

But Steph had. *Carroll—Chief Carroll.* Her fingers had gone hot against his knuckles. Sweaty. "Is that why you called Woolverton and told him to give our case priority? Thought you'd make things a little easier for me since I'm so unstable?"

She averted her gaze, which was answer enough, and the burger in his guts soured. "If you were unstable, I wouldn't let you be here—or out there. And I think you know that."

But he *was* unstable. He suddenly felt it deep in his chest, a precarious tightrope-like imbalance, a knowing that though he wanted to be better, though he needed to stay sober, he was one misplaced step away from tumbling to what could very well be his death. And though he never would have believed it possible three months ago, though he never should have let it happen, this woman was his lifeline.

He pulled his hands into his lap anyway. The skin where her fingers had been went cold.

12

Sleep didn't come that night, and the urge to let Jack take the edge off increased with every sleepless hour. Each time he closed his eyes, he saw the bloody shirt of the dead boy or Patel's mutilated corpse on the steel table. Khatri's belly, wounds leaking through her dress. The killer was out there hunting, but Carroll had given Petrosky orders: go home, rest, pick it up tomorrow. But by the time tomorrow broke, his chest was the tightest it had been all night, his eyes sandpapery with exhaustion.

At least he had work to occupy his mind now.

The morning passed quickly, and before he knew it, the sky was shimmering with the waning sun, the icy air kissed with the musty but sharp breath of a long Michigan winter. Their killer was a lonely guy, probably seeking fame, trying to recreate some perfect moment he'd once had with a woman he loved—a woman he'd wanted to love him back. But she hadn't. A mother, a girlfriend, didn't really matter; they knew what she looked like. And what he looked like— maybe. Unless the guy who had followed Khatri wasn't the man who abducted her. They hadn't found evidence of social media groupies, just a few exceptionally underwhelming dick pics, but her public profile meant a higher likelihood that Khatri had more folks than the killer after her.

Petrosky squinted through the hazy afternoon, fingers twitching for a smoke. Of the homes behind the alley where Khatri had been taken, only one was occupied—ten houses up the street from the break in the evergreens, and too far from the burned structure where they believed the killer had crossed. They'd asked anyway. As the kids would say, "hashtag fail."

The smoothie shop was no better. There were no cameras hidden out front, of course there weren't, and the green smoothies Jackson had bought them for lunch made him want to punch every hippie prick square in the jaw. The building across the street—the one with the gargoyles—did have cameras, but their killer had kept well-hidden behind his black down jacket, a scarf, and a pair of oversized sunglasses fit for any pretentious Hollywood actor. There hadn't even been any goddamn sun—the killer had known they'd be looking. Forensics was on it, combing the alley, and the chain link, and the house on the abandoned street behind the alley, but so far, nothing.

God, he hated a savvy criminal. Even the drugs were a dead end. Etorphine was a carefully regulated substance, which made it appear a good place to begin searching, but apparently, it was quite common in veterinary medicine—a vet who'd decided to expand his repertoire to include human subjects had seemed a strong possibility. But there were no hits on a similar physical profile among the actual human or animal docs themselves, nothing on vet school drop-outs either. And it had taken Scott about twelve seconds to order the drug on the dark web. If their guy was internet savvy, they were screwed.

Petrosky grimaced at the clouds, already orange along the horizon line. How had the day gotten away from them so quickly? Less than two hours until Carroll's press conference. He slugged the last of his cold coffee and shoved the cup into the Escalade's cupholder beside his still-full salad-juice.

Jackson glanced at him and pulled into the gym parking lot. Even at four in the afternoon, the time Khatri usually arrived, the place was packed. Didn't anyone have a job anymore? She slid into a spot near the back and cut the engine. "Carroll's going live in ten minutes—let's make this quick in case they have it on the TV. I don't want what she says to color their statements."

The coffee churned in his guts—acidic. *Carroll's doing what now?* He paused with his hand on the Escalade's door handle. "No, that can't be right, she said she's going live at six, to give us extra time to..." *She lied.* Because she knew he'd be watching the lot, worrying about whether their suspect might be there. And if he made Jackson rush over there now, he'd look paranoid—like he was losing it. Maybe he was paranoid. Maybe he was losing it.

Jackson raised an eyebrow, then buttoned her coat against the wind. "Six? When did you talk to her?"

"Last... I dunno, yesterday." When Jackson kept staring, he finished, "She just called to check on the case, Jackson."

"Uh-huh." She sniffed. "Are you guys doing it?"

"Doing what?" Their footsteps made a horrid grinding sound—asphalt and rubber grating against rock salt.

Jackson kept her eyes on the building as they crossed the lot, one hand out as if she might slip on a patch of black ice, which wasn't impossible. "You know, I kinda wish you were doing the chief. Keeping that secret would get me at least an extra week's vacation."

"I don't mix work with pleasure," he muttered. "How's Decantor, by the way?"

"Linda works with us sometimes," Jackson said as if she hadn't heard him, her breath pluming around her face.

"My ex? That's not pleasure." *That's guilt.* Pain, mostly

pain he'd caused. He drew his gaze to the building—glass like an auto showroom, but instead of cars, this place displayed the sweat-slicked bodies of men and women with fake tans and faces that looked like they were in agony or in the throes of orgasm as they pushed through their routines. Where were all the people like him, the fat bastards with cigarette breath and Jack Daniel's in their water bottles? McCallum always told him he should work out, but if it meant going into a place like this, he'd pass.

I should be at that conference. He should, paranoid as it was. Would Michaelson really notice if their guy walked up to watch it? That dumb rookie wouldn't know what to look for. Petrosky should let Jackson take over the interrogation at the gym so he could go back. Better safe than sorry was a cliché, but that didn't mean it was wrong.

But when Jackson frowned at him over her shoulder, he stepped over the curb and onto the walk in front of the gym. He was being ridiculous. *Sounds like you need a shrink, old man.*

Jackson pulled the door handle, and air the scent and texture of a muggy evening in a sweatshop slapped him in the face, followed by musk and bad cologne laced with chlorine. He blinked in the fluorescent lights, trying to clear the spots from his vision as a twentysomething ponytailed douche stepped behind the wide Formica counter near the entrance. A clear bottle of some weird looking milky liquid sat on top along with a square box overflowing with receipts. Tiny pencils lay scattered everywhere, the kind you use to keep score in mini golf.

"Hey, folks, you ready to make an investment in your health?" He had biceps like a lumberjack. His face fell when Jackson flashed her badge.

"We're looking for a guy who might have been seen hanging around here, maybe even looking in the window, or sitting in the parking lot." Starting with the suspect himself

—that was smart. It was possible the killer had never spoken to Khatri, but this guy should have seen him on the property.

He cocked his head. "Like a stalker?"

"Like a killer," she said.

The man's eyes widened. "Whoa. Sorry, I don't remember anyone weird offhand."

Petrosky leaned a hip against the counter. "He's possibly Indian, darker skin, black hair. About Five-seven. Broad shoulders."

The man's eyebrows met in the middle of his forehead. "Sounds a little like Keane, one of our regulars, but he'd never hurt anyone."

"Where can we find this Keane?"

"He's in Portugal visiting family for the month—left... maybe two weeks ago? He'll be back in three days though." He shook his head. "Shit, do you really think he's dangerous? He always seemed so nice."

"If he's out of town, he isn't the man we're looking for," Petrosky said. But they'd verify it.

The man's face relaxed, ponytail bobbing as he nodded. "Okay, okay, that's good."

"Anyone else you can think of?" Jackson asked.

"No one regular. And if anyone had been watching the lot, we'd know about it. We have cameras everywhere out there."

"We'd like a copy of those tapes, if you don't mind," Jackson said. "Might have something you guys weren't looking for."

"Oh, well...I mean, they get recorded over every 24. We don't save them for longer unless someone breaks in, but that's rare—money doesn't even change hands here. And we'd know if a treadmill was gone right away." The guy was smiling. *Why is he smiling? That stupid joke?* But maybe he'd have smiled, too, a few months ago. Something in him still felt hollow—broken. But it was easing. Better now than overnight. The work...it helped.

Jackson already had the folder out. She slid photos of the victims across the counter. "You know these women?"

"Chantal? Of course, man." He squinted at Patel. "I don't know the other one though."

"You know Chantal well?"

"Not really. Just the usual chitchat."

Petrosky scanned the room, looking for anyone who even remotely matched the description of their suspect, but everyone was too light or too dark, too tall or too short, too blond or too bald, or too tattooed. Just a lot of broad shoulders, thick necks, and biceps that looked like they could crush a glass bottle to smithereens. Three of the patrons had spotting partners with them, but they didn't look like friends —two were making notes on a clipboard as the other men grunted through weight reps.

"Who does Chantal usually work with?" Petrosky asked.

The man frowned. "Sorry?"

"Does she have a personal trainer?"

"Oh, no, nothing like that. We all work with all the clients. We write down their problem areas, though, and the exercises we recommend. That way, we all stay on the same page no matter who's working when the clients come in." The man glanced at a particularly buff specimen wearing a tank top that might as well have been made of yarn for all the shiny shaved chest it covered. "Honestly, most people kinda do their own thing once they have a plan, except to get measured once a month."

"And what happens if they don't measure up, so to speak?"

He turned from the floor and back to Petrosky. "I'm not exactly sure what you're asking."

"Is there someone in charge of boot camp if they screw up and gain an inch?"

He laughed. "Man, you really think we run a tight ship here, huh? No, clients are responsible for themselves. There aren't hard-and-fast rules; everyone goes at their own pace."

"You have any trainers who are especially hard on clients? People who might want to take things to the next level?" A trainer who wanted to play god the way Nordstrom had? Who couldn't wait for all that hard work to pay off?

"Not really. I mean, there are always clients who respond well to being pushed, but they tend to push themselves harder than we ever would. Making people feel crappy about themselves is just bad business."

Jackson took the photos back and leaned against the counter beside Petrosky. "Then why measure them at all?"

"Because sometimes people feel stuck. Building muscle means loss of inches, but it makes you gain weight—muscle's just heavier. Measuring helps them to see their progress."

"Who would have access to those measurements?" Jackson asked.

Now Petrosky narrowed his eyes. Was it possible their guy had chosen Khatri based on something so simple as numbers on a sheet of paper? The victims didn't have facial features in common, so clearly, the body type mattered more to him.

The man pursed his lips. "Any of the trainers. Anyone who works here can look in the files, I guess. They aren't locked up or confidential." He gestured to a box on the far right side of the counter, the one with sheets of paper spilling from the top. Petrosky had thought receipts, but...

He reached past Jackson and pulled the box closer. Now he could see the little blue tabs, Rolodex-style separators. "These are the measurements right here?"

"Well, yeah. It's convenient to just have them on the counter. And like I said—"

"So literally anyone could walk in here, snatch a sheet, and leave?"

"I mean..." His brow furrowed. "I guess? But who would want to?"

A killer. He pushed the box back toward Captain Ponytail. "Do me a favor, hoss, and keep these behind the counter for now. Maybe put them in a locker only you have the combo to." Their guy was after more than just the numbers—there were white girls running around with junk in the trunk, too, and dark girls with blonde hair, black hair, even green hair these days. The suspect needed more information than what these files contained. But that didn't mean he couldn't pull the measurements then stalk a list of potential victims.

Petrosky drew his attention back to the room. Three of the men were looking at them now. A redheaded woman with shoulders that put Petrosky's to shame glanced at them in the mirror.

Ponytail was nodding his head. He grabbed the box. "Yeah, I'll put them away."

But Petrosky had a feeling they were too late. Whoever their killer was after next...she'd already been chosen. He peeked through the front wall of glass at the gathering dusk.

13

STEPHANIE CARROLL WATCHED THE ROOM, her gaze swimming as if she were submerged in a dark lake with only moonlight for company—everything was moving, everything but her. Her cheek throbbed, the hard floor beneath her an impenetrable force, smashing her face from below as if trying to buck her off.

She had never been this drunk. Even in her worst years, in the days before recovery, she'd managed to maintain an aura of control. This... No, this wasn't like her, not at all.

Even more disconcerting was that she could not remember drinking. She couldn't even recall taking a shot, let alone putting a bottle to her lips over and over until the room started to spin. And oh god, she'd remember. She'd been sober fifteen years now—okay, thirteen—but still, no, this wasn't right. And her head...

The room spun, spun, spun. She edged her hands beneath her and tried to press herself to seated, but her arms were weights, the pads of her fingers scraping at the angry ground, her spine a useless noodle that she could not straighten. But there were people here—she could feel them watching her, she could see...their eyes.

"Help me. Please help."

She blinked, trying to clear her vision, trying to connect the glaring eyes to the faces attached to them—so many eyes, a hundred people watching as if she were an animal on display. Was she in the hospital? It felt like one of those surgical galleries, seats above the operating room where residents could watch the doctors take a patient apart piece by piece. What were they going to do to her? What had they done already?

The world came to her in barely comprehensible flashes: dark curtains, or was it just her vision making the walls uneven? She couldn't be sure—the walls were wavy, closer then farther as if the entire place were shivering with anticipation. As if it were coming for her. She blinked again, and now she could see the eyes more clearly—not attached to anything at all, just disembodied irises glaring from the far side of the room. Eyes without faces. Pieces of something once alive.

Her belly lurched, and she finally heaved herself off the ground as her abdominal muscles spasmed. Bile, sour and acidic, flooded her mouth, her nose, and she gagged, retching, but then her arms gave way, and her cheek was back on the hard ground, this time in a puddle of her own sick. And... wood. Was she on wood?

She blinked. Watched the room.

Spinning. Spinning. Spinning.

Her head throbbed, the back of her skull brightening with pain, then easing to a subtle ache that pulsed in time to her heart.

Where was she? Why was she—

Her husband. She could suddenly see his face clear as day, his thick glasses, his black beard streaked through with white, his dark eyes. She was supposed to be...

Her anniversary. It was their anniversary. She had told Andre she had to work late, and sometimes that meant she didn't show; that was why they were falling apart, why this anniversary mattered above all others. This was their last shot. Even today, he'd said he felt rejected—she *had* rejected him, so many times, but it wasn't on purpose, not always. The vomit burned in her nostrils. Did he know she'd been taken? Ed should know—he'd certainly miss her, and soon. And while Edward was looking for her, Andre would be waiting for her at—

She jerked to seated, the room trying to tug her back down, but this time she did not let it. She could barely breathe—her dress was far too tight. She had a date. A special date, Andre had said that. Her mouth tasted like acid. Her cheek throbbed.

Spinning. Spinning. Spinning.

I have a special date—

Chin slimy with bile.

But first I have to do that press conference—

Her spine rocked, back and forth, back and forth. Gently she prodded the tender back of her head.

That press conference about the—

Her fingers came away wet.

About the killer.

The killer. The one who'd taken Patel and Khatri. Ed had been right to be worried about her doing the press conference—and she had done it, right? And... Oh god, she'd messaged Edward, the one person who might look for her, who might notice she was gone, that...she was going home. And Andre had said he'd file divorce papers if she didn't show; that he'd take it as a sign. She believed him.

No one else would miss her so soon. No one would be expecting her to call.

She lowered her hand. The killer had stabbed his victims; he'd disfigured them, changed them piece by piece. He'd change her too. And the victims did look a little like her. Back when she was younger—back when she met Andre.

Thunk. Thunk. Thunk.

He's here. The footsteps were slow, methodical, the drumbeat preceding an execution. And...there was another woman here, too, dark-skinned like her, long black hair like her, wearing a black dress *just like hers*, staring her down from across the—

A mirror—not another woman. And in the mirror, she could see the shadowed man at her back just outside the halo of the overhead lights.

Thunk. Thunk.

She was alone here, alone with the monster who'd taken her. Who'd tortured those other women. But the way he stood, so still as if he could see right through her, the way he cocked his head—it was *familiar*. Did she know him?

Thunk.

A hard footstep, so close. She turned, trying to keep her head upright, but her neck felt weak, her head wobbly like a heavy blossom on a too-thin stem. The world wavered, but she forced her eyes to focus: so much blackness, a mere silhouette against the blinding lights. And though she couldn't make out his face, she could see the needle, glinting against those lights, the tip sparkling with malice.

Oh yes, she could see that much.

14

No one from the gym, trainer or client, fit the description of their suspect, and the one guy who kinda did was definitely out of the country. Did anyone in this city meet their description?

Duke snorted, his giant, slobbery face pressed against Petrosky's hip, but even the Great Dane's presence did not take the edge off the sharpness that had settled just beneath his ribs. He exhaled a plume of tobacco smoke and snatched the phone off the bedside table, hoping he'd see a missed call alert from the chief, or from Jackson, someone to tell him they had a goddamn lead that he'd missed, but...nothing.

He crushed his cigarette into the ashtray so violently the glass rocked against the wood.

Carroll had texted after the press conference, said she was going home. Jackson had dropped him off at his place, and though he'd wanted to, he hadn't been able to drive back up to the precinct to make sure the chief hadn't lied to him *again*. Billie'd had his car, driving Duke to the dog park and picking Jane and Candace up from work. By the time she got home with his ride, it was nearly eight. Well past the time

Carroll would have left—she'd surely gone home to her husband by then.

Are things actually going back to normal? He could go back to ignoring her, maybe change his phone number, pretend she hadn't come to his house a few months ago to find him sitting on the floor of his living room with an open bottle of Jack beside him and a gun in his hand. Pretend she hadn't stayed with him that night. And the next. Pretend she hadn't done what Linda had tried to.

Stephanie Carroll had saved his life. But though he was trying his best, though he didn't want her sacrifices to be for nothing, the bottle of Jack called to him from the kitchen cabinet even now at six o'clock in the morning. He shouldn't have kept that bottle—knew he shouldn't have—but maybe he'd kept it to show himself he could resist it. Maybe he'd just wanted an excuse to call Carroll. It was easier to say, "I'm trying to resist the bottle" than "I need to talk." He'd let McCallum try to take that shit apart...if he ever told him.

Petrosky sighed and lit another cigarette. This wasn't about the Jack. He felt...lost. Stressed. Without a soul in the world he could talk to in this moment. Probably the worst combination for an asshole who wanted nothing more than to stay sober.

He heaved himself from the comforter, the dog garrumphing in irritation as Petrosky let his gaze settle on the chair in the corner where he'd thrown his clothes last night. He blinked, and for a moment, he saw Carroll sitting in that same spot in the chair, her face pensive but kind, mint tea in her hand. He hated tea. But he'd drunk it for her. And he'd let her throw away the Jack—most of it. Let her drag him to McCallum's.

Fuck this.

He dressed quickly, Duke watching him from the bed, but the dog stretched when Petrosky sat beside him to tie his sneakers. Duke put his face on Petrosky's shoulder and whined.

"Knock it off; you're not even supposed to be up here."

The dog snorted. Even Duke was laughing at him.

BILLIE WAS ALREADY outside when Petrosky emerged from his house next door, her cheeks pink as she poured salt onto the drive. Duke ran to her, kicking up slush from the lawn, and she grinned at them and straightened. Her dyed hair gleamed in the porch lights, as gray as the winter clouds, with bright blue eyes reminiscent of the sky in a far-off season that Petrosky could barely recall. The cold bit his face. He turned his collar up against the wind and gestured to the bag of salt. "I can take care of that later," he said, but his heart wasn't in it.

"You've got enough to do, Eddie." She set the bag on the ground and scratched Duke's ears, but kept her eyes on Petrosky—were the corners tight with cold, or with suspicion? "Are you okay?"

"Yeah, why wouldn't I be?" he snapped, harsher than he'd intended.

Her gaze stayed as steady as the persistent wind—hard. It had become harder in these last few months—*hadn't it?*—tougher and more frustrated every time she'd come to his house only to be turned away. Eventually, he'd stopped answering the door. Had she been the one who'd called Carroll, or maybe Jackson? He was still too proud to ask.

Billie blinked, breaking the spell. "Just know we're here, Eddie. Candace, Jane...we're all worried about you."

"There's nothing to worry about." Duke ran in a circle around her feet, oblivious to the tension that had crept between Petrosky's shoulders.

"Linda stopped by here the other day when you were at

work. Again. She asked me if I thought you were okay, so I figured I'd ask."

His ex-wife had been here? He hadn't called her in months, not since he'd shot that boy, shot him and watched him bleed out all over the—

The icy air assaulted his nostrils, his lungs. *Nope, not going there, old man, you've got a killer to catch.* "If Linda comes here again, tell her I'm perfectly fine." Linda didn't need to deal with his bullshit too. It was bad enough that Carroll had to. Jackson. All these people he'd drag down with him. And...

He met Billie's eyes, then turned on his heel and stalked toward his car, pretending she wasn't shaking her head, that her lips hadn't gone tight.

Pretending she believed him.

PETROSKY PASSED three liquor stores on the way to the precinct; every neon sign caused his hands to tighten on the steering wheel just a little more. The air outside looked thick and hazy as if his tobacco smoke had billowed from his car to engulf the world. And the morning news radio wasn't helping his mood—they kept playing snippets from the chief's press conference:

> "We will not discuss the awful things done to these women—we do not wish to make a lonely madman famous. But a word to our suspect: you will not win this. Quit while you're ahead, and we'll give you half a line in the morning paper, which is far more attention than you deserve."

Why did she have to say it like that? Sure, McCallum thought the guy was after notoriety, fame, but was making the killer angry really the way to do this? She was poking the bear for no reason. But at least Carroll had gotten the word out—she'd given a description of the suspect, identified what they believed to be his hunting grounds. The phones at the precinct were surely already ringing, especially with a case so sensational, even if those calls usually amounted to a whole lot of useless nothing.

And all it took was one good tip. Just one.

Just one sip of Jack would surely clear your head, old man. Just one, right?

He stopped for coffee instead of liquor, though he'd rather have had the latter, and carried two cups up to the bullpen. The whole thing felt familiar. The frigid morning air, the exhaustion weighting his guts, but more critically, the unease. He did not want to consider why, but the memories came unbidden: the day Morrison died had been a day like this. And he'd found him; he'd found his partner, his boy, wrapped in plastic, that ugly slash across his throat, blood coming out of his mouth—

No, McCallum said Petrosky tended to see connections where he wanted to see them. And they were usually pessimistic—or paranoid. The coffee burned the pads of his fingers through the cups, something Jack would never do.

Jackson looked up as he set the coffee on her desk. "You hear from the chief this morning?" he asked. *That woman can't keep you sober, asshole. It's not her job*, his brain whispered, and then it was McCallum's voice: *I'm asking you to consider additional sources of support; find a partner. The way she has.*

She cocked her head. "Why would I? It's like eight." When he just blinked, she sighed. "It was her anniversary last night, so I don't expect her in for a few hours—at least not if she had a good time." There was a smile in her voice, but Jackson's eyes were cautious, appraising him as she picked up the coffee.

"How'd you know that? About her anniversary?" And why hadn't he? Carroll hadn't said a word. He stood beside Jackson's desk, aiming for nonchalant, then scanned the bullpen as if half expecting to see the chief wandering around with a cup of that nasty mint tea. Sloan and Decantor were already here, typing away at their desks—eight o'clock wasn't that early.

"Flower delivery yesterday." Jackson brought the cup to her mouth but paused with it resting on her bottom lip. "Why? Are you jealous?"

"For fuck's sake, Jackson." He ran a hand over his face—smooth, he'd shaved while he was busy not sleeping, but his skin was dry and wrinkled as used crepe paper. No wonder she wasn't here, why she'd gone straight home last night after the press conference. Who wanted to deal with work during an anniversary celebration? Or deal with…him. He brought his own cup to his lips, trying to ignore the way his hand shook. His fingers stank of tobacco. "What'd Scott end up with from the Khatri scene? He get any results back yet?" Had they only found her body the day before yesterday? It felt like months. Scott was probably still working on it.

But Jackson was already nodding; she reached past her keyboard for a folder—Scott's report on the top. "He found traces of blood on the block wall in the alley near the fingernail marks we saw. It matches Khatri's. Also got a match to Khatri's apartment from some carpet fibers near the base of the wall—she probably braced herself with her sneakers when she was trying to fight him off, not that it did a lot of good." She flipped the top page and squinted at the one beneath. "Also have traces of pine and gravel in the alley that match the property behind the chain link, so he probably came in that way as opposed to following her from her home. He might not have known where she lived, which is why no one else at the apartment saw him. Khatri had a predictable routine, unfortunately for her, so he probably just parked, hopped over into the alley, and walked around to wait for her in front of the smoothie shop."

All of which confirmed that they had the right spot, but it

did nothing to help them identify the killer. "Scott get anything we don't already know? Maybe the killer's DNA?"

"We didn't get that lucky, but he did find some other compounds; he's trying to finish the analysis today. So far, he's identified a few different chemical solvents on the body itself, stuff common in cleaning products, but like the makeup, they're popular enough to be found anywhere." Well, of course, they were; this guy had been careful not to give them a damn thing. "He also found something called Flavacol," Jackson continued. "It's a flavoring common in seasoned salts and the like. I think Scott's trying to weed out a couple other chemical signatures, see if he can find anything unique that might help us narrow down where the killer is keeping our vics, but I'm not sure he's hopeful." And they hadn't found any Flavacol on Patel. If it was a seasoning, he was probably just eating something when he was stalking Khatri, though the thought of their killer watching the vic while munching on chips turned Petrosky's stomach.

"He needs to fucking hurry," he barked. He glanced down at the coffee cup—deformed beneath his fingertips, the wax cracking.

"You're not mad at him," Jackson said, her eyes on his hand.

He loosened his grip. "No, I'm not."

Jackson met his eyes and stood. "Let's go down to Scott's office. He's usually here by now, and maybe he has something else since last night. But be nice, okay?"

Petrosky's chest hurt. He rubbed a sore spot near his clavicle.

"Petrosky!" A low voice—loud and angry.

He turned, and Jackson, too, looked over in surprise. A man entered the bullpen from the stairs—wide shoulders, dark skin, beard run through with white, thick black glasses, hair shorn close to his scalp. Familiar, but Petrosky could not place him.

"Is she here?" the man growled, stalking toward Petrosky's desk like a soldier on a mission. "I've been calling all morning, and she isn't answering."

Petrosky stiffened.

"She has to be here—her car's in the lot." He glared at Petrosky. "Did she stay with you last night? Again?" Jackson's jaw dropped.

"Who?" Petrosky asked. From the corner of his eye, he saw Decantor rising from his seat.

"Stephanie."

The chief. "No, she didn't stay with me." *At least not last night.* And now he recognized the man from the photos on Carroll's desk: her husband, Andre. Petrosky swallowed back bile, but it rose again, hotter, acidic, and not because he was dealing with a guy who surely wanted to punch him in the dick. *Steph's gone?*

Jackson stepped forward, putting herself between Petrosky and the much angrier man. "Are you saying she never came home last night?"

Andre's nostrils flared, and he grimaced, highlighting the bags under his lower eyelids—the red streaks through the whites of his eyes. "She was supposed to meet me at the restaurant. She didn't show." He spat the words as if trying to slap Petrosky with them. "I Ubered home after two hours of drinking at the bar, and I must have fallen asleep, because when I got up…" His breath shuddered from his lips.

"You just fell asleep? You didn't wait for her to get home?" Petrosky snapped. *Shit.* She'd been gone all night.

The man bristled, drawing his shoulders up. "I thought she was with you! I came here to give her these." He snatched a packet from beneath his arm and thrust it at Petrosky—a lawyer's mailing address on the outside.

"You check her office?" Jackson asked.

"Of course, you think I came here first?" But his voice had lost some of its bite. "She really isn't here?"

Jackson shook her head, and Andre lowered his hand, resting the manila envelope against his thigh. Face suddenly uncertain, but not quite worried yet. Confused.

Petrosky was not confused, not in the least. Her car was here—how had he not noticed? And that meant she hadn't left the precinct on her own. She looked like those girls, too, she really did, and the killer had seen that press conference, had to have seen it, and now... "So you just went to bed," Petrosky growled in a voice barely above a whisper—low. Dangerous. "You didn't bother making sure she made it home safe or—"

"This isn't my fault, goddammit!" But it was, because Petrosky would have noticed if she didn't arrive—would have known if she'd been kidnapped. Then again, this man had only lost one person on his watch, and Petrosky had lost—

Decantor stepped beside Petrosky. "Carroll's missing?"

Missing. Maybe dead already. *That maniac has had her all night.* He couldn't breathe—the walls were too close, inching nearer with an expectant energy as if they wanted to be acknowledged before they snapped shut and crushed him. They never should have let her do the press conference, but whose idea was that?

Mine, it was mine. But she wasn't supposed to do it. He was. He should have been the one up there with the cameras in his face.

The man was still staring at him, though his posture had softened—his hands were shaking. "I know you care about her, too, that you have a connection I'll never quite understand."

That was a diplomatic way to put it.

The man's fists clenched at his sides, open, closed, open, closed. Finally, he met Petrosky's gaze. "Please find my wife. If you care about her at all, find her before it's too late."

15

"We don't know for sure it's our guy."

"Don't placate me, Jackson, of course we fucking do." The killer had probably seen Patel at her favorite book store, had seen Khatri at the smoothie shop, maybe at the gym, maybe even on her goddamn social media. And Carroll had become a target because she'd gone public—had her face plastered all over the television on a case the killer was clearly following.

Petrosky and Jackson both leaned in, squinting at the screen in the conference room—the video surveillance. There might not have been a camera in the alley behind the smoothie shop or around Patel's apartment building, but Carroll had been taken from the parking lot in front of the goddamn police station where they could see who was coming and going. Jackson sat beside the IT guy, or surveillance guy, or whatever he was, her elbows on the table. Petrosky stood at her side—electricity raced through his veins, and even standing still to watch the tapes made the nerves in his legs crackle and spit. He should be out there instead, on the street, hunting this maniac. He had to find her.

But how? It wasn't like he hadn't been trying already. He'd failed and failed again.

The camera tech tapped a few buttons on the iPad screen, and the images sped forward—cops running by at hyperspeed, cars entering, then leaving en masse at quitting time. The vehicles in the lot thinned. The sun ducked behind the clouds. The lights came on, casting their sodium glow over the blacktop. Definitely later than when she'd texted and said she was heading home. She'd lied to him. Again. And this time, it might have cost her her life.

"Wait."

The tech hit play. *There she is.* Carroll walked out of the station, down the steps, over the curb, looking left, then right, then left again. Petrosky leaned closer, his heart in his throat, throbbing frantic and sharp like an angry bird trying to claw its way through his Adam's apple. Would she fight back? Were they about to watch her death? But there was no one else that Petrosky could see, no shadowy figure sneaking up on her from a hiding spot behind the building, no stealthy hooded man creeping from around one of the few cars left in the lot. Were they wrong? Carroll drew nearer to her SUV and pulled her keys from her bag. Was she wearing high heels? Yes, and a dress. *Right, her anniversary.* And she appeared thinner than usual like she'd lost weight. Stress? Was that his fault too?

From above, the camera had a clear shot of her ride; he could make out a sticker in the back-passenger window, though from this angle, he couldn't tell exactly what it was, and he hated that it suddenly seemed like something he should know. Carroll turned sideways and edged between her car and the one beside it—

He squinted. Movement. From the car next to hers, a faint shadow in the passenger seat. No one in the driver's seat that he could see, but...was the passenger window down? No one would leave the window down in the dead of winter without a reason.

"Fuck," he whispered.

Carroll reached for the door handle, her back to the car beside her. A gloved hand emerged from the passenger window—a needle. Petrosky barely had time to register it before the tip was in Carroll's back, one deft, highly practiced movement. Maybe he had more experience with needles than they'd thought—maybe he wasn't a hack. Maybe he just liked his work messy.

Maybe he wanted it to hurt more.

The hand retreated back into the car, and Carroll fell to the ground between the vehicles, barely missing hitting her face on the side-view mirror.

"That's gotta be the opioid Woolverton found in Khatri's bloodstream," Jackson said. "Khatri might have knocked it out of his hand in the struggle, which is why she didn't go down right away, but if he shot her up in that alley, he wouldn't have had any issues getting her over the fence."

Jackson's words were hollow, echoing against his eardrums but not penetrating them—he could not take his eyes off the screen. *Come on, Steph, get up and fight.* The chief stayed on the ground. Was she alive?

The car door opened.

Him, that's him. Petrosky forced an inhale—he hadn't realized he'd been holding his breath, but now black dots swam at the edges of his vision as oxygen rushed into his lungs.

Come on, asshole, show me your face. The man was precisely as their friend on the street had described him. Black jacket once again, but this time, he wore a ball cap beneath the hood, probably to obscure his face from the cameras directly above. But he hadn't worn a cap outside the smoothie place... because those cameras were lower. There, he had obscured his face with body positioning, enormous glasses, and a scarf that covered his mouth, his chin. Even now, his hands were covered in black gloves. The only part visible was the back of his neck—dark skin like they'd thought, but... Shit. *He knew exactly where each camera was.* When had he cased their parking lot? Would they see him there if they looked at footage from earlier in the day? The press conference hadn't gone live until yesterday afternoon, a matter of hours before he took Carroll, so unless he'd planned to take her earlier, stalked her months or weeks ahead of time...

Carroll was still a heap on the asphalt. The man grabbed her under the shoulders and heaved her toward the car, but he stumbled, faltered, almost dropped her. Petrosky cocked his head. Their guy was having trouble. Carroll was shorter than him, a little thicker, but even Petrosky would have been able to pick her up with more ease.

"He's definitely not a gym rat," Jackson muttered. "No wonder he uses the drugs."

Or he'd been injured—maybe Khatri had given him hell. And gym rat or no, he'd still managed to get Carroll into his car. The man slammed the door and skirted the back, hurrying around to the driver's side. From the time the kidnapper had stuck his hand out that window to the moment his taillights vanished down the street outside the lot, less than three minutes had elapsed. But at least they had a plate. "I want images from every working surveillance cam from here to twenty miles out."

Jackson shook her head. "Not many out there—no funding for it. You know that."

"At least we know he headed east," said another voice, and Petrosky whirled around—Michaelson, standing in the doorway. What was he doing here?

"How the fuck does that help?"

Michaelson shrugged his burly shoulders. "Well, maybe we can narrow down the—"

"You think this bastard doesn't know we're watching? Doesn't understand the concept of doubling back? He had all the cameras pegged, knew exactly how to hide his face—you think he's that stupid?" Jackson's hand on his arm was a steady pressure, bringing him back before he throat-punched the asshole. Michaelson swallowed hard, eyes wide—scared. Maybe Petrosky should feel bad, but he didn't. The chief was missing—*Stephanie* was missing—maybe being tortured right now, and this guy was wasting their time with dumb shit? Petrosky inhaled deeply through his nose, but the tension in his chest did not relent. "You want to help, track down that car," he barked at the rookie. It would come back stolen—he'd probably dumped it already—but at least it'd give them another place to start looking. And give Michaelson something to do besides vomiting his stupid-ass ideas.

Petrosky turned back to the screen—to the camera tech still sitting at the table, a short, wiry man he'd honestly forgotten existed until this moment. Because the guy was there to do his job and not make a nuisance of himself. Petrosky liked him better for it.

"Rewind to...say, four thirty," Petrosky told him. *You were here, casing the precinct, you murderous fuck, I know you were.*

The tech tapped a few keys, the sky lightening once again. He pressed play, and the tape moved forward, but not as fast as before—slow enough for them to look for the car. For their suspect.

Nothing. The car pulled into the lot for the first time at seven thirty, less than thirty minutes before Carroll had emerged from the precinct. *If I'd just gone back up there, if I'd been there...*

This is my fault.

"When the hell did he case it?" he muttered, more to himself than to anyone else. The cameras were on the light poles, so he might have seen them from the street where they couldn't see him. But they could have had other cameras that weren't visible from the road. To be so damn sure...

"He's been here before," Petrosky said.

Jackson nodded. "Way too confident for someone who's never been near the precinct. And he knew what Carroll's car looked like, parked right next to her—he wouldn't have known that from the press conference."

His phone buzzed, but Petrosky barely noticed, his brain on fire with questions, haphazard pieces of information that didn't combine to form a complete picture. How long had their guy been watching Carroll? Had she been a target all along? No, that didn't make sense; he'd have found women in their thirties or forties to kidnap if his ideal was Carroll's age, Jackson had been right about that. The phone buzzed again, and this time, he pulled it from his pocket, though his brain was racing too quickly for him to read the caller ID. This was why cops shouldn't be involved in the cases of their loved ones. He'd solved Julie's murder, but it had taken him a decade.

And they didn't have a decade to find Carroll. How long had the killer kept Khatri before he started taking her apart? Before he stuck those needles in her guts? Hours? His cell rang again. His hand shook. He didn't want to look at it.

We're already too late. He killed her, and he's already prowling for another—

He blinked at the cell phone screen. It wasn't the flatfoots, or another detective: Scott. He snapped the phone to his ear.

"Hey, I've got something for you."

"Better be something good," Petrosky snapped, but his heart was beating overtime, throbbing frantically in his temples, and the pain in his chest had ballooned into a crushing pressure that threatened to steal what little air he had.

"It is good. Got the analysis back on those splinters we found in Patel's feet. Took a while to identify them because the chemicals used to treat the wood are obsolete—we're looking at wood from the 1800s."

Petrosky straightened, the pressure in his chest easing to

the tightening of a rope around his ribs. "Do you know where it came from?" Jackson stepped closer—*when had she gotten up?*—her eyes on Petrosky's face. He raised a finger and turned away.

Scott cleared his throat. "Well, kinda. From the 1600s to around 1950 or so, they used different varnishes than we do now. And all the oils and resins from that time period are much more susceptible to degrading; the oxidation process starts almost immediately, which makes later analysis difficult. Makes it nearly impossible to break them down into their original component parts."

"But you did it?" *Please say you did it.*

"Who do you think you're talking to?" Scott said, that childish edge creeping back into his voice—a kid with an exemplary report card. "The finish on the wood is a type of shellac, imported from India to the early American colonies beginning in the mid-1700s. It's mostly the secretions of a small beetle called the Laccifer Lacca that eats tree sap and processes it into this hard shell-like material."

"Okay. So the mid-1700s. We'll start pulling properties." But could they narrow the search enough to find Carroll in time? He pushed the thought from his head—*focus on now, don't think about the what-ifs.* But when he blinked, he saw Morrison's face behind his eyelids, his slit throat, teeth bloody, and then it was Patel's bloody lips, her mutilated gums. His ear ached against the cell. He gestured to Jackson and left the conference room, heading up the hall toward the bullpen for his coat.

Scott was still talking. "Well, it became more common as time marched on, so any house from the 1730s to the 1900s might have it."

His throat felt swollen. Hot. "Get to the good news, would you? Spit it out, Scott, we're running out of time." Their footsteps throbbed in time to his heart.

"Here it is: I found a few other components—castor oil,

some resin-type compounds, even a hint of an old dye. So I talked to the curator at the Ash Park historical society, the head of that museum over on Pine."

Petrosky frowned. The place wasn't really a museum, just an old renovated mansion full of shit from the city's earliest days. Who cared about three-hundred-year-old chairs? From the corner of his eye, he saw Decantor turn from his desk, eyebrows raised. *Think about the chairs, don't think about the chief.*

"He said the chemical composition of our wood was specific to a particular builder in the 1800s: a man named Cyrus Spotswood."

Petrosky coughed, trying to clear the lump in his throat, but it stuck. He forced out: "Spotswood? Appropriate last name for a fellow who works with flooring."

"That's what I said. The curator did not get it." Scott laughed, but his voice, too, was tight—and far too high. "Anyway, most of this guy's work, his houses, have been sold or demolished over the years, but there are still four places standing, all within twenty miles of the dump site."

Four. "That should be easier to track." *Please let that be true.*

"It gets better. Two of them have been made into historical sites—they have constant visitors. No way to keep Patel there for two weeks without being detected."

"And the others?"

"One is owned by some tech guru."

Petrosky snatched his coat off the back of his chair and hauled it on. In his peripheral vision, he saw Jackson doing the same. "Sounds like the type of fellow who might be connected to our first two techie victims."

"Well, except he isn't. He lives in Silicon Valley, looks like he just bought the place to renovate it."

"So, it's abandoned?"

"Nope. Over the two weeks your guy had Patel, there

were crews of drywallers and historical specialists in and out."

And then there was one. "Please tell me the last place is a viable option."

"Only if abandoned properties without neighbors are viable." The hiss of papers abraded Petrosky's eardrums as Scott shuffled his notes. "The house used to belong to a Leonard Seol, but it's been abandoned for the last twenty years since he died. No family, no claims against it, nothing that raises any red flags. But if I had to pick one…"

"Thanks, kid. I owe you." Petrosky ran for the stairs.

16

THE ADDRESS SCOTT gave them wasn't a house. It was a mansion, a hulking mass of wood and stone made all the more prominent by the neighboring lots of char and rubble. No cars in the drive, no vehicles on the road, either—no streetlights. This block had been abandoned at some point during the Ford era; with new mansions being erected closer to downtown, the outskirts had become less desirable, especially once it became clear that city funds would be spent on renovations like streetlights and road construction closer to the city center. For their killer, this meant less traffic, and far fewer prying eyes to see him drag his victims in. Fewer ears to hear them screaming.

Petrosky ran up the dirt drive, listening to the hiss of the wind in the trees—to the wet slap of their feet. The haphazard layer of snow on the front lawn appeared undisturbed by human footprints, but it was hard to tell amidst the animal tracks that meandered from the porch to the thickets on either side of the yard. And who knew which entrance the killer had used? The front staircase was gone completely, and the hole where the double entry doors used to be was a dark void hulking at chest level. Petrosky hauled himself through it, arms burning.

Please be alive. Please be alive. Please be alive.

Decantor and Jackson were up and into the house before Petrosky made it to the middle of the foyer. Empty save for piles of debris and animal droppings. Sloan and Michaelson and a few others Petrosky didn't recognize were around the back, probably climbing through a side window, or looking for another entrance.

The wooden floor, softened by rot, muted their footfalls as they fanned out across the ground level. His breath hissed from between his teeth. He paused at the entrance to the dining area, a large space with a domed ceiling and wooden braces cutting the sky, one large triangular section open to the clouds above. No Carroll. No prints. *I'm coming, Steph. Hang on.* But the adjoining sitting room was just as empty, the far wall was open to the side yard, the windows busted out. Old leaves whirled in the icy wind.

"Clear," Jackson said, returning to the foyer.

Decantor was already headed for the stairs.

The wooden treads were spongey and frankly terrifying; they held, though they squealed in protest. If their killer was here, he knew they were in the house.

The landing at the top of the staircase branched out three ways. *Where are you, Steph?*

"Police!" Decantor yelled, blasting through the first door on the left. Petrosky ran right, kicking open a bedroom, a bathroom, another bedroom.

"Steph!" Someone was screaming her name. He peered into another bathroom, the sink long since gone, tiles cracked, plaster walls splintered. "Steph!" Him. It was him shouting, and it sounded as if someone were strangling him. Felt like it too; he couldn't get a full breath.

Jackson stepped beside him in the hallway, lowering her

weapon. "Nothing here." Decantor emerged from the left side of the stairs and shook his head.

"There has to be something," Petrosky snapped. This was where the killer kept Patel—tortured her for two weeks. And he'd only dumped her body last week. Had he really abandoned this place, found another house to keep Khatri so quickly? Petrosky peered at the floor, the tracks made by their shoes. Downstairs had been the same, thick grime and leaves, the only sign of life, their own footprints. The debris should be disturbed if the killer had been here in the last week. Had Scott been wrong?

No, Scott was never wrong. He was one of only four people Petrosky trusted, really trusted. One of them was beside him. And another...maybe she was dead.

No. *No.*

He ran down the stairs two at a time, wheezing, his legs screaming, chest on fire. Maybe the killer had removed a beam from the house, used it in his own place. Maybe the killer had planted the evidence as a ruse, knowing they'd waste time chasing it down. Still, he asked, "This place have a basement?" They hadn't stopped to pull floor plans—they hadn't had time.

"I didn't see an entrance to a cellar," Decantor said. "No doors to an attic either."

Leaves skittered through the foyer like insects scurrying for hidden nests. Lots of these old places had root cellars or coal chutes—they needed to find a hole or a trapdoor in the floor. Those could be in any room, but the location generally made sense; cellars and butler's pantries near the kitchen, coal chutes under living rooms. Petrosky headed for the kitchen, just a few steps off the dining area he'd explored earlier, and knelt, squinting at the ground. So many leaves. Droppings. Trash. But no holes.

He hauled himself to standing and kicked at the ground,

pushing aside debris. In his peripheral vision, he saw Decantor doing the same, his enormous boots making short work of the front section of the kitchen.

"Got something!" Both he and Decantor turned. Sloan, Decantor's short, stocky, and very Irish partner was crouched near the far wall, running his fingers along the ground near the toe of his boot. Decantor clicked on his flashlight as they hustled over. A dark line separated a square of wood from the floor around it, a circular ring pull screwed to the right side that might have been cast in wrought iron. And the wood in the center was clean—too clean. *New.*

Sloan grabbed the ring and pulled. The hinges screamed.

A ladder.

Into the dark, Petrosky yelled Carroll's name.

HE TOOK the ladder rungs two at a time as he had the stairs, listening for the sound of breath, or shuffling, or anything that might indicate another presence in the dark with him, but the blackness was absolute until Jackson followed with her flashlight. "Shit," she whispered.

Petrosky hit the dirt floor and turned, weapon trained on the shadowed far wall where he couldn't see. Was the killer crouching there, hiding with his syringe? Was Carroll? But still, no sounds. No breath save his and Jackson's.

The room was slender but long, made somewhat more expansive by the blackness of the ceiling and the walls as if all sides grew out into nothingness. Was that soot? Had someone tried to burn it? Perhaps the killer had wanted to remove all evidence that he'd been here. He started forward, skirting the first wooden pillar, but paused—thin lines of wear, abrasion, along the bottom of the pillar, wooden shavings at the base, as if rope had begun to saw through the beam. If someone had been tied there, they'd struggled. He knelt and squinted, running his finger along the first indentation—lots of splinters, but some were darker than others. Blood.

This had to be where Patel was held. "We'll need forensics down here," Petrosky said, chest tighter than it had been just moments ago. This was the place, the house where their killer had kept a kidnapped woman for two weeks. So, where was he? Where was Carroll? Did this mean she was already on her way to be dumped on that bench?

He coughed, trying to keep his lungs open, edging forward, scanning the dark room ahead of him, the black walls that looked too soft to be ash. And if someone had tried to burn the place down, that old wooden pillar would have burned before the walls. He reached for the stone—no, cloth. Curtains. Someone had strung fabric along both sides of the space. And when he squinted at the ceiling directly in front of the ladder, he could see a set of nails, black fabric still clinging to their heads, as if there had been a curtain strung in front of the ladder as well. To hide the escape route from his victims? Or to hide them from intruders?

"What is all this shit?" Jackson said behind him. "Was he trying to muffle the noise?"

But he probably wouldn't have had to—they were already underground, with no neighbors anywhere nearby. Petrosky moved toward the back of the room, frowning as the far wall came into focus: a wall that appeared to be watching him.

Literally.

Petrosky raised his cell, switched the flashlight on.

"What the hell?" Jackson breathed.

Hundreds, maybe thousands of disembodied eyes stared back, glossy as if they'd been cut from the pages of magazines.

"He have a thing about eyes too?" Jackson asked. "Is he going to start messing with people's eyeballs next?"

"No," Petrosky said, his gaze locked on a pair of green

eyes with long dark lashes—like Julie's eyes. He leaned closer to the wall, the skin between his shoulders prickling. "He's not worried about the victim's eyes. He likes an audience."

17

She's gone. She's dead. She had to be dead. They always died on him, everyone he cared about. The climb back up the ladder took hours; his throat closed somewhere around the middle mark, and he was dizzy with nerves and oxygen deprivation by the time he hauled himself out of the hole. "You need to be careful, okay?"

Jackson raised an eyebrow. "Why, because you think the killer will come after me? I have too much junk in the trunk, and not enough up top." She patted her shorn black hair.

"He'll fix that...somehow." And he'd be looking now. If the killer had left this place with Carroll in tow, that meant she was dead—which meant the perp would need a replacement. It meant Petrosky had failed.

"I know what you're doing, Petrosky, but we don't know she's dead yet. He could have her somewhere else."

He tried to look at her, tried to meet his partner's eyes, but his head wouldn't turn her way. He stared into the hole. Was that the last room Carroll ever saw? The heat of guilt burned his lower esophagus—or maybe that was bile. "If he's escalating, if he's after another cop for notoriety, you're the closest to his ideal type, and I'm not about to lose you too." His voice had risen with each word—was he yelling?

Probably. Her eyes had widened. Decantor was on the far side of the kitchen, cell pressed against his ear, staring at Petrosky like he'd just announced he'd made a habit of dating horses. "What are you looking at, asshole?" Petrosky growled.

Decantor turned away as Jackson put a hand on his arm. "I'll be careful. Okay? But we're going to find her. We are not giving up."

Petrosky ran a hand over his face. Their guy had been here, the goddamn *killer* had been here. But Leonard Seol or whoever the hell the owner was...their perp wouldn't be using a house that could be traced back to him. He might be a maniac, but he wasn't stupid. They wouldn't find him by looking at the deed.

"Guys?"

They all turned. The CrossFit shithead was back—where had he been while they were investigating the cellar? Had Petrosky even seen the rookie since they'd entered?

"What do you want, Michaelson?"

The kid raised his radio. "I've got something you need to—"

"Is it another of your brilliant theories? You going to tell us again that a guy who spent god knows how long at the precinct watching the place, a guy who managed to keep his prints off everything is somehow dumb enough to get caught because he drove east?"

Michaelson lowered his radio and shook his head. "No, sir. There's a man at the station. He just confessed."

THE INTERROGATION ROOM was thick with fear, a tangy, almost spicy funk. And if the smell hadn't given him away, the look on the man's face would have: tiny, twitchy eyes beneath unkempt brows, a nose that wouldn't stay still; even his ears appeared to be trembling, like a rabbit on meth. And if he was the rabbit, Petrosky was the lion, though his insides were jelly. Maybe he was more like a three-legged cat with mange. Hopefully, that was enough to crack the guy—and find Stephanie Carroll.

He squared his shoulders, trying like hell not to consider what the man's presence in this room meant—*Did he kill her already?*—because if Carroll was alive, panicking wasn't going to help her. He slid into the chair across from Peter Smithwick, but his ass hadn't even hit the seat when the man stammered: "I-I d-did it."

Petrosky narrowed his eyes at Smithwick's hands, splayed on the tabletop—the tips of his fingers were pale, though the rest of his skin was so dark it was almost purple. His pinkies vibrated against the steel. At least he didn't have blood on his hands right now.

"I'll need you to be more specific, Mr. Smithwick. Did what?"

"I hurt people. I r-rape them, I hurt them, p-please just p-put me away." *Rape.* Had he raped Carroll? Smithwick's lips pulled back from his teeth—bright pink gums, and the brilliant white teeth of a predator. But something wasn't sitting right; the man's bared teeth looked less like an angry snarl and more like a terrified grimace. Afraid of jail? Then why turn yourself in?

"At this moment, I'm more worried about the abductions," Petrosky said slowly. He tried to push the word "murder" from his lips, but it wouldn't come.

The man's hands trembled. "I d-did it. All of it."

"Then where is she, Smithwick?"

He kept his gaze on his shaking fingers. "She's g-gone."

Gone. Dead. Petrosky's lungs slammed shut, his belly a molten pool of acid. *Every time I get close to someone, every damn time...* But the man's eye was twitching so hard he was almost winking, and he still refused to look Petrosky's way.

He's lying.

No, I just want him to be lying because then Carroll might be alive. He cleared his throat and forced out: "Where did you put her body, asshole?"

"I-I just... It-it's out there." His gaze darted to the ceiling, lower eyelids twitching just as hard as the rest of his face.

Petrosky's hands balled into fists, but he tried his damnedest to keep his voice even. If he shut the guy down, it would take longer to disprove his statement—they needed him to admit it if he was lying. "Fine, you don't want to say where you left her body; you want to save something for the lawyers to barter with, right? So how about this: Tell me why you did those things to the last victim." Carroll had been very specific about not making their guy famous the way McCallum believed he wanted. She hadn't released any of the gory details to the press.

"I j-just wanted to."

"But why?"

His nostrils flared, face still twitching. "I... They were s-so thin and p-pretty, and I wanted to...d-do things to them."

They were...pretty? The tips of Petrosky's ears went hot, but the writhing in his guts eased. Their perp might be getting off by assaulting these women, but he wouldn't refer to them as pretty—at least not as his main motivation for mutilating them. You injected them with chicken fat to *make* them pretty in your own sick head, but you didn't need to do that if they already were pretty; if you already wanted to "do things to them." And thin wasn't an accurate way to describe their victims either.

"I don't think you're telling me the truth, Mr. Smithwick." And saying it out loud softened the knot between his shoulders, even though he knew that if this guy wasn't their perp, the killer was still out there. But so was Carroll; if she was dead, he'd have posed her on that bench. They'd know if they had another body.

Smithwick's breath panted from his lips, his fists curling on the table. "N-no, you're w-wrong, I'm telling you—"

"If you're the guy we're looking for, then tell me where Carroll is."

"I...d-don't want to."

"Then why show up here?" Petrosky leaned toward the man over the table, and Smithwick reared back. "If you didn't want to tell us dick, then why come to the police station?"

"Reyansh said I should c-come," he blurted.

"Reyansh..." *Acharya?* Petrosky eased himself back into his seat, glancing at the two-way mirror where he knew Jackson was watching. *I told you journalists were assholes.* "How do you know him?"

Smithwick sniffed and glanced at the mirror, then looked down at his hands. "I t-tell him things. About the street I live on. There are lots of p-people who...d-do things they shouldn't."

Tell him things... This guy was a source? But the last time Acharya'd had a lead, he'd brought the man straight to them and demanded an exclusive.

Petrosky narrowed his eyes. Did Acharya not want to be associated with Smithwick, or...did he know this guy was lying, too? Smithwick did seem a little too dark to be their perp. The cameras in front of the smoothie place hadn't captured his face, but they'd been able to see his wrists when they zoomed in. Their suspect was more a dark golden-brown. And McCallum thought their killer might be after victims who looked like him—a similar nationality. Indian. "Smithwick...that Irish?"

The man's lip trembled. He tugged on the top button on his shirt—uneven, secured in the wrong hole. Would their guy miss a button like that, a man so obsessed with appearances? He'd at least clip his eyebrows.

"Where'd you get that last name from, Mr. Smithwick? Your daddy Irish?"

"I-I guess."

"What about your mother? She Indian? They have stricter punishments for rapists over there; maybe we should send your ass that way." He could almost hear Jackson stiffening, but right now, he was trying to piss the suspect off—get him to react. This guy just didn't feel...right.

And he was nervous about something.

"I...n-no, not Indian. But please, man, you g-gotta lock me up."

"Why? Without proof that you hurt Stephanie Carroll, without any evidence at all, we can't just toss you in a cell."

They had a confession—they could do lots of things, even if it was bullshit. But this guy wanted to be in here; he had to have a reason. Petrosky pushed himself to standing and turned toward the door. "I don't have time to waste with you, you goat-fucking piece of shit." He'd have Michaelson follow this prick to be certain, but Petrosky was tired of screwing around. The chief was missing. Maybe dead already. He didn't have *time* for this.

"No! W-wait, I'll t-tell you, okay?" The man's nostrils flared as he leaned forward again, pinkies tapping, tapping, tapping on the steel. "I'm on p-pills. I can't afford 'em. You h-have to lock me up."

"What kind of pills?"

"MPA."

Petrosky dropped his hand from the door. MPA... medroxyprogesterone...something. But he didn't need to know the official name to know what the drug did. After all, he was in the sex offender business. "Chemical castration?"

The man nodded.

"Did you actually hurt anyone this time around?"

The man chewed his cheek.

"Be straight with me, or I swear to god you won't need the chemicals to castrate you another day in your miserable life."

"No," he whispered. His eyes filled. "I d-didn't hurt anyone this t-time, but I don't want to d-do it again. Please p-put me away."

"You been doing anything to self-medicate?"

The man's tone thinned as if he were having trouble drawing air. "I… A little p-pot."

That sounded like a parole violation. Petrosky approached the table once more and said softly: "Do me a favor, Smithwick: toss that chair into the wall when I leave, would ya? And if you see a big blond cop come in here, sock him right in the eye. Resisting officers and refusing the drug test that you will ultimately fail should get you some time inside."

Smithwick's eyes cleared with understanding. His lip stopped trembling. He nodded.

Petrosky hated the guy, and just being in the same room made the animosity gnaw at his chest like a parasite. But helping this asshole stay locked up should keep someone else safe—someone innocent.

Someone like the chief.

And he'd already failed her. He couldn't fail again. Because if he failed this time, if he lost her…

He'd drown in a bottle of Jack, and he wouldn't even try to swim out.

18

THE CAR their killer had used to kidnap Carroll was registered to a Kelly Ann Mathews, a single mother on the west side. The vehicle had been reported stolen two hours after it was used in the Ash Park PD lot.

Figures. Petrosky's ribs were a cage, his heart smashing itself against his breastbone as if panic had solidified into an angry fist. "This is just goddamn perfect."

"Yeah, but at least the Mathews house is close by. If even one person saw his face, and we get a better composite…"

He nodded, mute, a voice in his head screaming: *Don't be dead, please don't be dead.* But every time he begged the universe for a favor, the universe cut him down to size—cut down those he loved.

The passing hours did nothing to bolster his confidence. They knocked on the doors of every neighbor who could have seen Kelly Ann Mathews's drive, and not a single one had noticed a stranger hanging around the block. *Duh.* If a neighbor had seen a strange man getting into Mathews's car, they'd have told Kelly Ann herself, at least. She hadn't noticed until she'd tried to make a liquor store run—a woman after his own heart as much as he wanted that to be untrue. They'd put out an APB on the car, hoping he still had it, but no hits yet.

Petrosky glared out through the bullpen's window, though he did not register what lay beyond the sill. How long before they found the chief on that goddamn park bench, dead? *No, she's alive, she has to be alive.* But where? *Where?* Scott was running forensics on the cellar, and so far, they'd found nothing. And the only other place they knew for certain the killer went was the path, that bench, and by the time Carroll ended up there, she'd be—

He blinked at the clouds, tinted yellow with afternoon. Was it past lunch already? The thought of food made bile rise in his throat. The room spun.

But a little Jack would help. Just a nip, and he'd be fine, he'd take the edge off, no one would ever know—

Jackson slid into the chair beside him and handed him a sheet of paper, still warm from the printer. Their confessor's raggedy face on the top. He scanned it quickly, but Smithwick's earlier crimes weren't even close to what had happened to Patel and Khatri. He had molested three little girls, his nieces, but no penetration, and none of the mutilation tactics—no posing. Straight-up pedophile.

"At least he should be gone for the long haul now," Petrosky said. Smithwick already had two parole violations for unrelated things, and assault on a police officer should keep him locked up for a bit. Plus, Petrosky had gotten to watch Michaelson take one straight to the nose. Missed his eye, but, hey, the bastard had tried.

"Why is the journalist hanging out with pedophiles anyway? Smithwick said Acharya was the one who told him to come down."

Jackson was chewing her cheek, fingernails tapping on his desk. "Acharya said that the guy came to him, that the responsible thing to do was to send him down to the precinct even if he wasn't positive about his guilt."

The words rang true but felt wrong. Had the journalist known it was a waste of time? And Acharya…he was Indian, right? "Acharya didn't even try to use him as a bargaining chip, didn't even—"

Jackson put up her hand. "He was pushing out stories on our serial, trying to find the chief, same as we were. He figured we had more manpower. And he's still at his office now, calling his contacts, all that shit. We're all doing our best." To her credit, she still looked concerned despite the confidence in her tone. But maybe he was seeing what he wanted to.

Petrosky pushed the thought away and pulled the keyboard closer. Acharya clearly wasn't torturing the chief if he was at work, and if he had a way to get the word out, especially if he could use his sources instead of the press, they needed to let him. And Petrosky had a tendency to blame the people closest to him—according to McCallum. If only he'd been more suspicious sooner; it was someone he knew, someone he'd trusted, who had killed his daughter.

Just because you're paranoid doesn't mean they aren't out to get you. He sighed, but to his ear, it sounded like a sob.

"The guy didn't leave anything at the abduction site," he said. "And wherever he has that car, has Carroll, is well-hidden. Even if he kept Patel and Khatri at the mansion, Carroll is getting different treatment. He took her from the goddamn police lot." Unless he'd just managed to get Carroll out of the cellar before they arrived. But that would mean he had inside information—that he'd known they were coming.

Jackson nodded, her eyes far away—bloodshot—her fingernails tapping overtime on the desk. "If the mansion where he kept Patel is any indication, he's holding Carroll at an abandoned property—someplace he won't be disturbed, where no one would think to look."

"Yeah." He rubbed at his chest. Four cups of coffee had somehow slowed his heart—or perhaps his brain had downshifted after interviewing Smithwick. *Dead inside, that's what you are.* But not the chief, not yet. He drew himself up straighter, ignoring the tightness in his back, the screaming tendons at the base of his neck. "That place wasn't just abandoned—it was absolutely isolated. There were no neighbors, and it was too far off the beaten path for squatters. And the cellar where he kept her...it took us twenty minutes to find it, and we were really looking. Even if he did end up with an unexpected visitor, he could lock the room, stay quiet. Unlikely that anyone would just stumble onto it." Unfortunately, too many properties in Ash Park fit the bill, even if they kept it to a ten-mile radius. Ash Park went from metropolitan to ghost town in a matter of blocks.

But the suspect had to be somewhere nearby. He had to be—he was close enough to stalk his victims, close enough to know exactly who he'd take. And he was smart, had known about the cameras in the precinct lot. Although...maybe he'd been there before, not because he had cased it, but because he was a repeat offender. "McCallum said these crimes, the murders, are an escalation of his fantasy. But an escalation of what fantasy precisely?" His chest spasmed, then released—tired, he was just tired, not panicked, not losing another friend. He swallowed hard. "If I'm a killer, fighting these urges...I think I'd test the waters first."

"So the question remains: where would a killer like this start?" Jackson's fingertips tapped harder against the desktop, hard enough to bruise. Her brow furrowed. "We know he likes an audience, but that might be a fetish more than the meat of the fantasy. He might have a rape charge on file, but that would have popped when we ran similars before."

Rape to mutilation and murder didn't sit right in Petrosky's gut either. The rape wasn't their killer's main goal. He definitely used it as a form of torture—repeatedly, Woolverton had said—but he didn't lose control until he started mutilating them. "So...the pain? The procedures themselves?" They had found a few med students who fit their sketch, students who had dropped out—or failed—but none had any criminal history. And he couldn't see someone who had been desensitized to those procedures during coursework escalating to the point where he gored someone with a hypodermic. Gored. His belly churned—*just think about the killer, don't think about her, don't think about what he's doing to her.*

Focus. That was all he needed.

Your killer's got the required patience to stalk them, to keep them in his home. To plan. That's what McCallum had said, and maybe that was the starting point. Stalking definitely felt more on par with what they knew of the suspect's behavior, watching Khatri from across the street from that smoothie shop, maybe dreaming about the procedures he'd do once he finally took her. Maybe he'd dreamed so much, he'd lost his shit when it came time to follow through.

Jackson headed for her desk, and Petrosky typed, ignoring the way his lungs refused to work, ignoring the ache in his chest, pretending the world didn't exist beyond the old PC and the printer. Page after page after page of stalkers. Some had additional convictions, many for firearm crimes, or for actually causing harm to the object of their interest, but most didn't fit the physical profile of their killer. His eyes burned as he stretched his arms above his head, still squinting at the pages. *Which one of you is it?* His bones felt heavy—weighted. They'd have to pull Michaelson in, Decantor and Sloan too; if they split up, they could cover this list in—

"Petrosky." Jackson stopped beside his desk but didn't sit. She rested a hand on the desktop beside his paperwork.

He straightened his pile of assholes. "Lots of stalkers out there, but only a few of them meet our guy's physical description. I'm thinking we've got someone local, someone who knows the area well and probably works or lives nearby

—that way, he'd be able to watch potential victims closely. Get to know their habits. Which I guess we already knew." He held up his pages. "These are my best..."

Jackson hadn't moved. He glanced at her hand; her fingers were a tight ball against the top of his desk. He dropped the sheets. "What is it?" His lungs were far too small, his heart a prisoner beneath its cage of bone. "Is it..." He couldn't say it, couldn't make his mouth form the words.

She dropped her gaze. "They found her," she said softly. "They found the chief."

19

The ride to the hospital was one of the longest of Petrosky's life. Would they be identifying a body? She was still breathing when they'd found her, but a lot could happen in an hour. It wasn't even three o'clock, but it felt like midnight, his body worn and heavy as if he'd been up for a week.

He stared at the sky as Jackson filled him in, her fingers tapping like mad on the steering wheel. Carroll was found in the park, like the others, but not near the bench—he'd left her down near the water about 100 feet up the path. "Thank god Michaelson was there running that path again," she said. "Got to her before she froze...or bled out."

Michaelson? Again? "Every crime scene, we've got that guy. I want him checked out."

Jackson's fingers paused above the wheel. "What?"

"Michaelson. I want his alibi, I want his address, I want his mother's maiden na—"

"He doesn't even come close to our guy's physical description. He wasn't the man in the parking lot. We watched our suspect drag Carroll into the car."

He frowned as Jackson wheeled into the parking structure and killed the engine. "Maybe there are two of them," Petrosky said, climbing out—icy air bit at his face despite the walls of concrete. "And Michaelson sure knows the layout of our parking lot. He's there at *every single scene*, Jackson, why the hell doesn't that bother you?"

"Everyone's on every scene, everyone that can be. It's a serial. It's sensational. Even Acharya's on his way to the hospital, just waiting to get five minutes with the chief."

"Are you kidding?"

"He's got a police scanner." She shrugged. "They aren't illegal."

"Being a dick should be."

Jackson stepped through the automatic doors, their mechanical hiss the sharp collective inhale of the thousand frantic loved ones who'd come before. "If being a dick was illegal, you'd never see sunlight again." But she didn't smile. His lips felt numb.

Inside, the hospital was intensely bright, searing his eyeballs like the sun through a magnifying glass. They hurried through the lobby to the music of scuffling shoes, beeping monitors, and the droning of a bored-sounding voice over the intercom, which did nothing to soothe Petrosky's shattered nerves. *Please be alive, please, Steph.* Maybe this was all a bad dream. He'd surely wake up soon. *As if I'd get that lucky.*

The third floor was already packed with cops. Decantor turned when he saw Petrosky and headed their way, his face drawn—not a good sign. *Shit.* No, this was real. She was here, maybe alive, maybe not, and he couldn't breathe, his heart was a block of stone in his chest, and he couldn't—

"She's okay," Decantor said, his voice low. He squeezed Jackson's shoulder and dropped his arm. "It looks like she'll live."

"Did he..." *Rape her.* Petrosky's mouth was stuffed with

cotton, though his rib cage had loosened just enough to allow his heart to resume its beating.

Decantor shook his head. "No signs of sexual assault, but she's got some major trauma around her abdomen—deep lacerations to the skin from above her hips up to her lower rib cage. He took off a few good chunks of meat."

The room spun, the bile in his esophagus burning, acidic. "Can we see her?" As much as he wanted to let her rest, to heal, they had to find this guy. She must have seen his face, right? And Petrosky needed to see *her* face. *Maybe they're lying to me, maybe she's dead, and they just don't want to say it while I have a gun.*

"They took her back to surgery," Decantor said. "They'll come find us when she's moved to recovery. I impressed upon them the importance of speaking to her sooner rather than later."

Petrosky nodded, throat too tight to speak. *She's alive, they're going to fix her up, but she's alive.*

"Do we know anything else?" Jackson asked Decantor. "I know Michaelson found her near the path, but…"

"Yeah, actually." The big man nodded. "You better come with me."

He blinked. Did they have the killer in custody? Or… had they found another body? No, Jackson would have mentioned that. Though even if she had, Petrosky doubted he'd have absorbed the news.

They followed Decantor as he threaded through the uniforms and plainclothes to a door marked "JANITOR."

Focus, Petrosky. Focus. "If you've got a cleaning job to do, there's no way in hell I'm helping."

Decantor grabbed the handle. "Needed a place to keep this safe until you got here. Scott's on his way to pick it up, but you might as well take a look before he sweeps it off to his lab."

The janitor's closet was far bigger than Petrosky would have expected, more than enough room for the three of them even with the two long rows of shelving...and the other detective standing in the middle. Sloan, Decantor's partner—dark hair, dark eyes—had his hands crossed in front of him. Holding...a plastic bag?

Petrosky squinted. "We doing a chain of custody thing, or what?"

"Yeah, Sloan rode with Michaelson. He was there when they found her." He gestured to the bag, and Sloan raised his arm, holding the plastic to the light. "This was lying under the trees next to her."

Petrosky frowned—torn black fabric, pieces of what looked like thick nylon shredded to ribbons.

"That a shaper?" Jackson asked.

Petrosky cocked his head. "A what?"

"You know, a shaper. You wear it under your clothes, and it kinda smooths things out." She met his eyes. "Does she always wear one?"

"How would I know? And why would anyone need that?" He put his hand on his gut, but he could not take his eyes off the bag. When Carroll was walking to her car...he'd seen the difference in the video. He'd wondered if she'd lost weight. "Does it make you look thinner than you are?"

She nodded. "That's kinda the point."

Sloan lowered the bag as if it were suddenly too heavy to hold.

"He's angry," Petrosky said, his voice hollow.

"Well, yeah, he's a crazy man," Jackson shot back.

"No, about this shaper thing. That's why she's alive. It was enough to make him lose his shit." He locked his gaze on the pile of useless fabric wrapped in plastic—he couldn't draw his attention away, as if that piece of cloth held the secret to their killer. "The other women, he kept them, right? Raped them. Here, he peeled that shaper thing off, and all of a sudden, he doesn't want her?"

Jackson eyed the bag as if she, too, were mesmerized by it. "I mean, we knew he was seeking out women with a certain body type, same coloring and all that. But all of his victims had things he tried to change."

"But maybe he hadn't planned on changing anything that much. He's awfully angry about a few inches—didn't even try the needle in the gut the way he did with Khatri." Instead, he'd taken a blade to her belly.

"Hey, but like you said, that might have kept her alive." Decantor was staring at the bag too. "He didn't pierce anything internal when he carved off her love handles."

Jackson's brow was furrowed—thoughtful. "She wasn't perfectly on par with his standards, sure, but the others weren't exact to his specifications either, and he still managed to rape them."

"He might have issues with women in authority, needs them submissive," Sloan offered, his Irish lilt a low vibration against the closet walls. "And the chief sure as hell isn't submissive."

Petrosky almost smiled, then remembered where they were, why they were standing in that damn closet, and his gut clenched. But still... *Who gets this angry over a few inches?* Was it because he couldn't get it up? Or was there a deeper message they were missing? The other victims were killed accidentally—perforations, infection. But here...he hadn't waited to dump her. He hadn't even posed her. "This is well outside his norm," Petrosky said. "He didn't dress her, didn't paint her nails, nothing. Even with the incisions, slicing off her love handles, she still wasn't good enough for him—he was furious at her, even went so far as to leave that shaper. He hated her for pretending she was a different size."

"Oh god," said a voice at Petrosky's back. "So that's why he did it."

Jackson and Petrosky both whirled around. A tall black man in green scrubs stood in the doorway, a surgical mask hanging around his neck. And was that blood on his sleeve?

"Did what?" Jackson asked.

The doctor's eyes were grave. "He carved LIAR into the flesh of her stomach."

20

"None of these fit."

Jackson had the photos from his earlier search spread out on the cafeteria table: forty-three tiny stalkers all in a row along with the sketch they'd gotten from the witness who'd seen Khatri in front of the smoothie shop. Which was absolutely useless. The guy had been clear that he hadn't caught the suspect's face, but Petrosky had hoped for more than a sketch of the man turned away from them, for more than an ear and the vague outline of a cheekbone. "They might fit the physical profile, but their victims aren't right. Only a handful even come close to ours, and a few of those perps"—she tapped a key on her laptop—"are in lockup." She slammed the computer shut. "He has such a rigid view of human attractiveness that he can't handle anything that deviates. He's not going to stalk a little twig of a woman one day, then suddenly start obsessing over a totally different body type."

"Maybe. Or maybe he always had stalker tendencies but didn't lose his shit until he met a specific woman…a woman like our victims."

"Or a family member, right? That's what McCallum said."

"He's not obsessed with his mother," Petrosky grumbled.

She shook her head. "That's not what I meant. McCallum said he had a fucked-up attachment history, and lots of people look for romantic partners that have something in common with their parents."

Petrosky frowned but forced his voice to soften—tired, he was so goddamn tired. "Speak for yourself, Jackson." He raised an eyebrow. "Does your daddy look like Decantor?"

She ignored the question. "I'm desperately trying to figure out another way to isolate what we need. We've got eyes on the house where he kept Patel, and on the path, and patrols down along the strip where both Patel and Khatri worked, where he would have seen them."

Petrosky sighed. "We'll show these photos to Carroll when she wakes up." That would be the fastest way to vet them. Witness reports were often wrong, but he had a feeling Carroll wouldn't miss a beat. At least he hoped not. She was the only one who'd—hopefully—seen their killer's face and lived to tell about it. "But this guy...he started up so suddenly, and now he's moving so damn *fast*." Their perp might have a history of being a stalker or a rapist, might be sadistic, might like fetishes or violent sex, but they'd looked for related crimes; there were no killings like this in any database that he could find, no other rapists in the system with this very specific history. Either he'd hid the previous victims, which was bullshit given the way he was seeking attention now, or he had never killed anyone before. That's why he was prone to losing control like a fifteen-year-old boy during his first sexual experience.

But the question remained: Why now? Even if he'd raped before, even if he'd stalked, why start killing? Something had happened—a stressor. And from the looks of the victims, a female stressor. Could be divorce. Being cheated on. The death of a loved one. *Anything*. And the scope of his obsession was apparently narrower than they'd thought—even if he planned to change those measurements by mutilating the victim, a few inches off, and he couldn't complete his abuse cycle. Got so frustrated he'd tossed Carroll out bleeding in the snow. It was surprising he hadn't waited for her to bleed out before he dumped the body, but that was the fury—the loss of control. Maybe that impulsive move would finally help them catch him.

"This measurement thing," Petrosky said now. "How can he gauge those very specific measurements from afar, and in winter clothing? A few inches isn't a lot of wiggle room."

Jackson pursed her lips, thoughtful. "I guess I can tell by looking at an outfit if it'll fit me. It's a skill—takes practice, but it's doable." She squinted at the cafeteria table; at the mugshots. "He's...dressing them. In a specific size and a specific garment. Both Patel and Khatri were wearing that yellow sundress."

But not the chief. Because...it hadn't fit her. "That dress matters," Petrosky said, "that dress in that specific size. Scott already looked at the fabric and ran it for trace—nothing there. The material is made in China, and with the shoddy workmanship, he probably ordered them from overseas."

Jackson's bracelet glinted in the overhead lights—the bright cafeteria fluorescents. The din around them rose then faded. "What if he didn't?"

"What if he didn't what?"

"Order them." She met his gaze. "What if he made them?"

Shit. She was right. Why hadn't they looked at that before? "So we've got a measuring man. A tailor or something? Quilter? Fabric...architect? He has to be doing it himself, I can't imagine he'd hire that out." Their guy was careful; ordering a shipment of dresses online was one thing, but showing your face to have them custom made here was another.

"I doubt he's a tailor—the seams were crooked, not what I'd expect from a professional. Can't hurt to look, though." She pulled out her cell. "We'll see what kinds of tailors we have in the area on the off chance he had someone else make them. If he did it himself, he should have been able to adjust the seam for Carroll."

That was a good point. Carroll's body lying in the parking lot flashed in his head, then that shredded nylon, the bench, the icy water… Was the riverbank still stained red with her blood? He rubbed at a spot above his clavicle, chest aching, burning. "You think he has another hostage yet?"

Jackson lowered the cell, her eyes cast down at the pictures. "Haven't gotten a missing persons call, but…" She shrugged.

It didn't mean shit. No one had called Carroll in as missing until her husband had shown up at the station. Speaking of, where was Carroll's husband? They hadn't seen Andre in the waiting area; if Petrosky's wife were injured, traumatized, he would have been right there waiting for her to wake up regardless of whatever problems were happening at home. But Petrosky had a job to do, and coddling the victim's family wasn't in his job description.

He looked at the clock: nearly four. "How long you think she'll be in surgery?" Their killer could be shooting chicken fat into someone else right now, some other innocent woman.

"Even if she got out now, it'd be another hour before we could talk to her…probably longer."

He grimaced. He couldn't even believe he was considering this, but— "Call your boy."

"Who? Decantor?"

He cocked his head. "I meant the journalist—Acharya's downstairs, right?" *Is she actually banging Decantor?* She was probably screwing with him. "Let's see how fast he can put out a description on the car the killer was driving, and the information on the clothing; lots of seamstresses for hire out there, off the books, and if I were a crazy asshole murderer, I wouldn't go to a professional tailor's shop. I'd find a housewife with a side business—harder to track." And that would explain why he didn't alter the garments to fit as he went... unless their killer simply believed his victim should fit the dress and not the other way around.

"Fine. And I'll tell Acharya he's got first dibs on the story once we're ready to share more." She drew the cell to her ear and glanced his way. She lowered the phone again. "Why are you looking at me like that?"

He shrugged. "It's just weird how you figured 'your boy' meant Decantor."

"What are you—"

"Did you know he likes merlot?" The pressure in his chest eased ever so slightly.

"What?"

"Like that bottle in your car the other day." He inhaled deeply. *Everything's fine, pretend everything's fine, just like you always do.*

She pursed her lips. "Keep your mind on your business."

"You didn't say I was wrong." *And everything is fine, Carroll is alive, Jackson is alive, and we'll stop him before he does it again.*

"Because you never are, right?"

Are what? Oh, yeah. And was that an admission? But she was already standing, heading away from the table with the phone pressed against her ear. And just as well. Their guy was already hunting for someone new to fulfill his fantasy—had to be. And he wouldn't stop until he had her under his knife.

21

IT TOOK that journalist prick one hour to write a story and put it out to the masses. Scott came by to pick up the shaper from Sloan, and thirty minutes later, Carroll was out of surgery, but it sounded like it might be a while before she woke up—he understood. Anesthesia hit hard, at least from what he remembered going under the knife for his heart. It had been hours before he was lucid enough to talk, let alone form a complete sentence.

He rested his heavy head in his hands, elbows cold against the Formica table in the hospital cafeteria. Jackson's fingers clacked against the keys on her laptop, her voice a low drone, cheek pressed against her cell. When she finally repocketed the phone, she shook her head. "No one's missing, but we've already got a hit from Acharya's article. On the material from the dress." Guy was smart to include a photo of it, though Petrosky hated to admit it. "Turns out that while it's manufactured overseas, and is usually sold direct, a couple of local stores carry it. The owner of that big fabric store up on Queens remembers shipping an order for that same material about four and a half months ago."

He straightened, suddenly lighter. Four months? Their

killer had been planning for a long time—if he was accumulating items to carry out his plan four months ago, how long had he been living this fantasy behind his eyelids? No wonder he'd lost control in the middle of the procedures. "We have an address?"

"We have a PO Box. The order came through their website, all of it paid through some online service. Got Scott on it now, but he says it looks like it might be dark web, or at least a fake IP."

"The money's real enough, though." He twisted in the seat and peeled his jacket off the back of his chair.

"Real but cloaked. But we can head to the PO Box, see if anyone saw him. He had to pick up his material delivery in person, so we might get additional footage from the surveillance cams."

Petrosky blinked, but his eyelids felt heavy. The voices of the other diners swelled in the background, a morose drone steeped in pain and worry. His ass was glued to the chair.

She put a hand on his arm. "There's nothing you can do here, Petrosky. The best way we can help Carroll is to find the guy who did this to her. If she finds out you waited around instead of following up on this…"

She'll kick my ass. He heaved himself to his feet, body aching. "Let's go."

THE PO BOX was located in a strip faced with gaudy blue cinderblocks, between a dry cleaner and a Thai food restaurant that would have looked promising if they'd spelled the word "checken" right. He wasn't sure if the misspelling was intentional, like "krab" instead of "crab," and he didn't want to find out. Worst case, it was that vegan "meat," and he was not about to risk that shit.

The cinderblocks from the outside of the building extended to the interior, but the blocks in the lobby had long ago lost their painted sheen. Across ancient linoleum stood a chest-high counter topped by plexiglass with little holes drilled through it as if the man sitting behind it was an old turtle in a terrarium.

The man tried to straighten his bent spine when Jackson flashed her badge, cocking his head, but realization didn't dawn in his eyes until he'd pulled down the enormous glasses from the top of his head. "Who're you after today, detectives?"

Petrosky leaned his forearms against the countertop. "You get a lot of police traffic, do you, Mr...?"

"Whalen." His mouth tensed, edges turned down as if he'd smelled something bad, then released. "And I suppose we do—lots of people buying things online these days, things they shouldn't. It's in the contract that they can't have drugs and what-have-you delivered here, but..." He shrugged one thin shoulder.

Ah, the power of the darknet. Anything you wanted, right to your door.

Jackson nodded and slipped a couple sheets of paper from her jacket: a surveillance image from the building across from the smoothie shop, then the ear-partial-cheek sketch from their homeless witness. "We need to look at the box for this man. We believe he's using 506."

Whalen frowned at the sketch, surely confused as to why they were showing him images with almost no identifying characteristics, but he reached beneath the counter and heaved a cracked binder onto the Formica before him. "I've got an Ernest Frost in 506."

Same name given to the fabric store. And no one by that name anywhere in the Ash Park area—they'd checked.

"How often does he show up to collect his mail?" Jackson asked.

"Oh, now that I can't tell you. I've only seen him a few times."

Made sense. He wouldn't have psycho supplies coming in every day. Petrosky pressed his bulk against the counter, squinting through the plexiglass, but spots and smudges obscured his view. "Do you think you can give us a description? Maybe sit for a sketch?"

"Now, son, my eyes ain't what they used to be." Whalen scratched the bridge of his nose beneath those enormous coke bottles he called glasses.

"Do you wear those glasses all the time?"

"Nah, they hurt my head a bit. I put 'em on for reading."

Well, there went that. Petrosky raised his arm and knocked on the plexiglass wall just beneath the air holes. "Lots of security here."

"Well, like I said, this business ain't what it used to be. And the street around us, well...let's just say I'm not taking any chances. Gangbangers coming in here looking for someone else's stash—stuff they mailed in."

Petrosky scanned the ceiling, the corners, the pockmarked walls. No cameras that he could see. "What about other types of security?"

"Nothing in here, but I have a camera to catch 'em before they walk in. That way, if someone's pounding on the front door before I open, I can tell whether I want to let 'em know I'm here."

"We'll need to see those videos, Mr. Whalen." Petrosky leveled his gaze at the man, waiting for him to say "sorry, I tape over them every month" or "I don't tape them at all, just use them to watch the feed in real time," but Whalen reached beneath the counter once more, and a buzzing cut the air, then a heavy clunk—the door to the right of the plexiglass. Whalen waved them through.

Composed

THE OFFICE WAS BARELY big enough for one, so Petrosky took a seat at the desk while Jackson stepped out to follow up with the hospital. Was Carroll awake yet? Was she okay? He pushed those thoughts aside. This was his job right here, right now; this was where he needed to be.

Whalen stood behind Petrosky, leaning over to push buttons, the air between them sticky—far too close to be comfortable. To Whalen's credit, he kept years' worth of videos, all organized by day. The fabric store had sent the package on August third, and the delivery had been logged at the PO Box three days later. The pickup was that same afternoon. Petrosky watched as a grainy Ernest Frost walked up the sidewalk in front of the brazenly blue building, scanning the world around him like a nervous meerkat. Petrosky could almost make out the silhouette of the suspect's nose, which would have been a great addition to the ear and cheek sketch they had already, but the angle of the camera wasn't going to show his face unless he looked straight up. There did seem to be a fuzziness, maybe shadow, along the lower part of his face—did he have a beard? It was hard to tell.

And something wasn't right. Their witness had identified the man as strong, a bodybuilder type, which fit with the video taken across from the smoothie shop. But this man was even more slight than he'd appeared in the cameras in front of the precinct. Petrosky had suspected the man was weak, not a gym rat at all, but any broadness through the shoulders must have been his coat—and in August, the puffy down had been replaced with a light hooded sweatshirt. From this angle, sweatshirt open, plain white T-shirt beneath, the guy was smaller than average—thin. Provided that Whalen was correct.

"You're sure this is him?" Petrosky asked as they watched the suspect approach the front door and vanish into the interior.

Whalen nodded. "I recognize the hoodie more than the face, but I'm almost positive."

Almost but not totally—because they couldn't see his face. But if he came out with an armful of yellow sundress fabric, they'd know for sure. Two minutes passed. Three. The suspect reemerged with a black package hugged against his chest, cradling it like a newborn baby. And...was he pressing his face against it? Smelling it, he was smelling it. And then he was gone, up the sidewalk and out of range of Whalen's cameras.

Petrosky's hackles rose. This scrawny fuck? This was the guy who'd taken the chief? The guy who'd carried those women up the path to pose their bodies? Maybe if he threw them over his shoulder, but shit. How had he managed? Did he have a partner?

Tap, tap, tap. He turned. Jackson stood in the doorway, peering around Whalen's hunched form, her face drawn. But...smiling. He stood so fast he knocked into poor Mr. Whalen, and the man's glasses fell askew.

"Is she okay?" Petrosky asked, his words a tight wheeze. "She awake?"

Jackson grinned wider. And nodded.

22

Petrosky stood at the foot of Carroll's bed, his legs weak with relief. But the air was still so damn thin—were others having issues breathing?

It didn't appear so. Carroll was propped up in the hospital bed, IVs sticking out of her left arm like a human pincushion, but her chest rose and fell steadily—normally. Her husband, Andre, sat in the chair at her bedside, clutching her hand with his long thin fingers as if trying to keep her with him, and surely that was the case in more ways than one. Petrosky kept his gaze on Steph—*the chief*—and edged toward the opposite side of the bed from where Andre had taken up residence.

"I don't remember being knocked out, not really," Carroll said. "I remember walking out of the precinct and heading toward my car, but…" Her eyes filled, but she blinked, and the water vanished, replaced with the fiery glare of a woman ready to detach a pair of testicles and mount them on her mantel. His guts twisted into a hard knot beneath his ribs. She wasn't just angry—she was scared.

"What's the next thing you remember?" he said quickly before the ache in his throat prevented him from speaking.

She swallowed hard. "I woke up in a room. Black walls. Everything was moving, so I was drugged with...something." She raised her eyes to Petrosky, and this look he definitely recognized, the look of a million other victims—shame. *Tell me it wasn't my fault.* But she'd looked at him like that in his house, too, when she told him about her own history; her alcoholism. When she was trying to help him. *That's all this is —she's trying to help us find him.*

He tried to clear his throat, to force his tongue to work, but Jackson was faster: "Woolverton found traces of an opioid in Khatri's system, too," she said. "One needle stick and you were out within seconds. There was nothing you could have done."

Carroll's face relaxed.

"Do you remember him using the drug, any other syringes later on?" Jackson's face stayed placid, steady, but he could see the tightness across her shoulders.

Carroll shook her head. "No other needles until the very end when he moved me to the river, but that drug didn't hit me the same. Maybe he gave me something weaker because I already had one ankle tied to the couch leg, but it definitely wasn't what he gave me the first time. And..." She hissed an inhale through her teeth, then: "I was awake for the rest." She closed her eyes for a beat longer than a blink, and Petrosky's chest filled with molten iron, burning his throat, searing his brain. *I'll fucking kill him.* He had hoped she'd say that the bastard had put her out, mutilated her while she slept, that she'd just woken up less two love handles. But she'd been awake. Suffering. And when she licked her cracked lips, he could almost hear her screaming.

His chest was on fire, and he inhaled to cool it—*just think*. The pain...their killer got off on the pain. If he had injected her with a second type of drug later, maybe something that slowed bleeding, the toxicology reports could identify it. Hopefully, that was something they could track, even if they had come up empty on the other drug. Petrosky met Carroll's eyes—the dark bags beneath them. He could hear his teeth squealing together and tried to relax his jaw.

"I remember thinking there were more people there," Carroll said, "but...they were just eyes. Like someone had cut them out of magazines."

"So were the walls black or covered in eyes?" her husband asked, but Petrosky already knew the answer because he'd been in that cellar—curtained walls on either side, and the far wall covered in magazine irises. How had the killer gotten her out before they arrived? Had he driven around for hours before dumping her at the river, her blood soaking into the back seat of his stolen car? *Lost her, I almost lost her, and then what would I—*

Carroll's lids dropped closed, her lips pursed. Finally, she said, "One wall had the eyes. The others were all black." Again, the cellar flashed in his brain, the long low ceiling, the narrow walls that felt like they might close in...all those eyes. But how had they missed him?

"And there was a mirror," Carroll continued. "One of those big rectangular ones that you put on the back of a door, just kinda propped against the wall."

A mirror? He frowned. There hadn't been a mirror in the cellar, he was certain. Had the suspect taken it with him? But why move it? Unless it was part of the fantasy. Petrosky's head throbbed. He blinked hard, trying to focus his eyes, but the bleariness stuck. *Please remember something, give us something that will help us find this asshole.*

Carroll finally dropped her head and winced, hand on her belly. "It was like...being in a cave. A huge cave. I guess if I had to compare it to something...it was almost like an amphitheater, but not quite that large. And no seats like you'd see in a real theater. Just a big loft space."

Her eyes went vacant, looking past Petrosky as if there was something fascinating but utterly horrible creeping up the wall at his back. Was she seeing the killer's face right now? Seeing him coming closer, feeling him hacking at her belly? And...she'd mentioned a big loft space. But there was no mistaking the cellar for a loft.

"Were there support beams in the room?" Jackson asked. "Wooden posts, metal braces along the ceiling?"

"No beams at all. Just the wood on the floor and the black walls."

Petrosky and Jackson exchanged a glance. So he'd recreated his cellar room in another location, but who knew where that other place might be? Had she been kept in an abandoned warehouse? Maybe an upper floor in one of the vacant high-rise buildings downtown. Maybe that's what the curtains were for: to block out the windows so she would never know they existed. At least they knew the eyes were part of the killer's fantasy.

"Anything else about the room?" he said, hating the way his voice sounded—strangled. "You thought it was underground, but do you recall a ladder, maybe stairs—"

"I've told you everything I can remember about the room. It was all black." And if there were curtains covering the walls of the place Carroll had been held, she couldn't see a ladder or a staircase; the ladder in the cellar had been hidden behind a wall of black too. *That's why he does it—in case they live, they can't tell anyone where they were held.* But then why change locations?

"It wasn't just the walls, though," Carroll said now. "The lights were low, too. It was really hard to see—my vision wasn't cooperating fully, blurry like I'd been hit in the head, but I don't have a concussion; I asked. And even when he and I were face-to-face..." She sighed. Petrosky forced a breath through clenched teeth as Carroll closed her eyes. Andre squeezed her hand tighter. When she spoke again, her voice was far away. "He must have been standing in the shadows, waiting for me to come to." Her lids remained closed, as if the act of opening her eyes, seeing the sterile hospital tray, the sickly pale sheets, was too much to bear. "All of a sudden, he was just there with a needle in his hand—a really small needle, not like a regular hypodermic. I thought he might try to...well, do what he did to Khatri, but he just set it down on this..." Her eyes snapped open. "Wait. There was a table. By the couch, against the wall on one side, you know? Not the one with the eyes, one of the black side walls."

Was the furniture arrangement part of his fantasy? Maybe not—there had been no furniture in the cellar. Just that wall of eyes. Petrosky watched Carroll's shoulders: rigid despite the nasty wound on her abdomen, hard like the muscles in her jaw—he'd never seen her look more fierce. It relaxed the tightness in his own belly, just a little. She might be scared, but she was ready. She'd get through this like she'd gotten through the rest of the bullshit life had thrown her way.

She licked her chapped lips again—that had to hurt. Didn't they have lip balm here? But she probably couldn't even feel it with the painkillers in her system. Andre had no such anesthetic—his chin was trembling, eyes glassy. Was he crying? And...his beard. He'd shaved it.

"What happened next, after you saw him enter the room?" Jackson prodded. At least one of them was still on task.

Carroll's eyes narrowed. "He seemed like his arm was sore; I remember him wincing when he moved a certain way." Was that why it had been harder for him to take Carroll? Why he'd struggled? Hopefully, Khatri had done it, maybe injured him in that alley. But it sure hadn't stopped him. He'd still managed to walk Carroll down that path. Managed to pose Khatri.

And he'd manage to do it again. Soon.

"Oh, and he gave me food—cookies," Carroll continued, and Petrosky squinted at her. "From the table. He said I needed to eat them. And I...did. I worried they might be poisoned, but I did it anyway." She shook her head. "I know all the things you're supposed to say, but they all just fell out of my head." She shuddered and dropped her gaze to her hands. Probably berating herself. If there was one thing he'd learned about her in the last couple months, it was that she was damn good at dressing herself down.

But he wasn't going to placate her—she hated that more than anything, including the nasty voice in her head. And he'd rather listen to his own nasty voice all night than have someone sweeten up a shit situation for him. "You know this is part of the process," he said instead. "That stress changes the way we react. And nothing you said was going to make this bastard let you go. I think you know that."

Her husband drew his eyes up to meet Petrosky's. Rage, maybe jealousy, but understanding too. Petrosky turned back to Carroll, who was already shaking her head.

"I didn't have a chance to say anything anyway. He gave me this...script. Like a movie script. He said we needed to practice."

Petrosky frowned. *What did he make you do, Steph?* But he dared not ask that question, at least not that way. Andre's lips were already tight, his gaze worried, his knuckles clenched, all of his attention focused on Carroll. *Chief Carroll.*

"I read it." Her face twisted in disgust. "Pretended like I... cared about him." She shuddered, and her husband clenched her hand tighter, his jaw set with rage. "It was a love scene, some Nicholas Sparks kind of shit, but it wasn't quality—it was riddled with misspellings, but there were red pen marks on it, corrections, almost the kind of editing you might do for an assignment. And he was terrible, too, a terrible actor, I mean. Over-animated. It was like watching Jim Carrey on meth." She forced a smile, and Petrosky smiled back though it made his face hurt.

"What was the play about?" Jackson said. "Outside of being corny romance?"

"Wasn't even romance. More like a terrible porno. These

people meet in a grocery store in the frozen food section, and he notices her because of her nipples. And the two of them get so turned on by one another that they go..." She swallowed hard. "They go have sex in the bathroom."

"But it stopped before you got there?" Petrosky barely managed to force the words out, and again Andre looked up at him, agitated—maybe suspicious. What had she told her husband about them? The truth?

"Actually, he didn't have me read that scene," she said, and Petrosky turned away from Andre though he could feel the man's gaze boring into his head. "There were three scenes that I saw, and he read the first one, the grocery store porno, to me; my eyes weren't really working right, maybe from the drugs. Then he read the second scene the same way—that one took place at some vegan restaurant."

"Fucking vegans."

One corner of her mouth turned up. She loved burgers as much as the next person. But when she spoke again, her voice was lower—softer. "Then he had me read; we rehearsed the beginning sequence in scene three, what he called 'the seduction sequence,' six or seven times—we stopped running lines before the characters had sex. He treated the whole thing like he was a producer, focused on the writing, the way the words were said as if there's a right way to say 'I've waited my whole life for you' without sounding corny. If I talked too fast, he made me do it over. Then he said it was time for a dress rehearsal." Her face contorted; she pulled her hand from her husband's, wrapping both arms around her belly. "I'm going to be sick."

Jackson snatched the kidney-shaped plastic tub from the end table and edged it beneath Carroll's face as she retched. Petrosky looked away. Maybe the surgical painkillers were wearing off, but it was probably the trauma. *Goddammit.* Andre's chin was still trembling, but his nostrils flared as he watched his wife, his fists clamped against his knees. If they found this fucker, they wouldn't have to put him on trial—three minutes with her husband, hell, with any of them, and he'd never be able to hurt anyone again. Or take a leak without assistance.

The heaving subsided, and Jackson passed her a glass of water. Carroll finally looked up and met Petrosky's eyes. "He told me to get undressed. And I did. I didn't even argue. And then..." She coughed as if trying to expel the memory, as if she could force the terror and pain from her lips and out into the air where they could do no more harm. It did not appear to work. She sipped at the water with a shaking hand. "He saw the undergarments, and he got upset. Said his leading lady didn't need that."

"The shaper?"

She nodded. "And then he... I didn't even see the knife."

I can't listen to this anymore—the flesh of his stomach was burning as if he'd been cut.

"It wasn't a kitchen knife, I don't think, more like a butterfly knife. His character carried one in one of the earlier scenes. Used it to cut off the woman's dress in the bathroom. Which is completely ridiculous as a premise—what woman would let some random guy cut off her dress in a public place?"

"Well, clearly, that's the most upsetting thing about the situation," Petrosky said. "His lack of attention to details and the insane amount of plot holes."

Andre was glaring at him. But Carroll smiled, and it actually looked genuine if not tight with pain.

"What did he look like, Steph?"

"I think he was younger; it was hard to tell with the lights that low."

"But if you had to guess—" *Steph, you called her Steph.*

"Twenty-five, maybe, but mostly because he said he thought I'd be more committed to the part because I was older. But he could have meant that I was older than the other...victims." *The perfect leading lady and the press conference was her casting call. Shit.*

Her lip trembled. "God, this really does screw you up, doesn't it?" She passed the water to her husband and folded her hands in her lap once more. "Anyway, that's when he cut me. First, he cut the shaper off, said he was going to try real hard to make the dress fit, but he didn't think he could."

That's why that damn dress mattered—it was a costume. It had all been about this stupid play.

"I tried not to look at it, because all I could think of were the photos of the other women—the things he did to them. But it was the same color. That awful yellow." Her eyes filled, and though it must have hurt like hell, she straightened, shoulders rigid once more.

"I felt the blade going in, felt the...wet. But I rolled a little and I...I kicked him in the face, with the leg that wasn't tied up. But I was still so woozy, you know? And then he grabbed the needle, and when I went to kick him again, he stabbed it into my calf. The room went fuzzy pretty quickly—I could barely see at all. And I remember sweating, shaking. Not sure how long I sat there, but the next thing I remember, I was on the ground. By the water. And it was cold. God, it was *so cold*." She shivered. Her eyes stayed dry.

Jackson nodded. Petrosky held Carroll's gaze and wished he could hold her for real.

23

THEY LEFT Carroll with a sketch artist and set up camp in the hospital cafeteria to wait. Petrosky wanted to see this bastard's mug the moment it materialized on the page.

"So the rape," he said. "It isn't just about rape, about power. This is about his scene. They play it out, then the dress rehearsal, then have sex when the script calls for it, probably at the end of each scene."

"And it sounds like the play is written specifically to make someone love him—to force them to act that way. Screams abandonment issues, just like McCallum said."

"Yeah, and you don't write a scene like that just to act out banging your mom." But people had done weirder. Maybe not grosser, but weirder. And it didn't sound like the scene Carroll had read was their killer's final act. "I bet he's an exceptionally frustrated playwright at the moment. He probably has someone else in mind already."

How long did they have? Every time he dumped a body, he'd taken a new victim within hours. And what happened when he finished the last act? Was there some final endgame? Death by cop? *Please let it be that one.* His trigger finger twitched just thinking about it, and this time, the images from the recent shooting stayed buried. He wouldn't feel bad about taking this shot, not at all.

Jackson's face was grim. "We've got Michaelson, Sloan, and Decantor out there canvassing the streets around the path, and a uniform at each of the tech companies, just in case."

But they'd vetted the employees, at least the ones at the corporations where their victims worked. So what were they left with? He wasn't sure. They had a maniac trying to direct his own movie—someone trying to make his leading lady adore him. Clearly, their killer was someone who had a difficult past with the opposite sex, but who didn't? And it didn't take much to push a maniac over the edge. The steady buzz of the cafeteria filled his ears, half from the angry fluorescent lights, half from the other diners. He still had the list of stalkers, but they'd wait for Carroll's sketch before they chased down any new leads—better to put the sketch out and see what came back. And in the meantime… "Wherever Carroll was kept must be nearby. And she used the word amphitheater—it has to be exceptionally large."

Jackson's brow furrowed. "An old theater would be a perfect place to hold her. If he fancies himself a playwright, he'd love acting it out on a real stage. But just because he used a theater for Carroll doesn't mean he'll use it for the next victim—three scenes that she knew of, right?" And three settings. He'd thought the same. And they'd only found Patel's DNA in that basement cellar—Scott had called just a few minutes ago. The killer had kept both Carroll and Khatri somewhere else.

So, where's the setting for scene four? "He might reuse this one. Carroll messed with his plans. He didn't get to complete his fantasy in that location." But that was risky at best, and their guy wasn't an idiot. They could compile a list of old theaters, see if there was evidence to suggest he'd been there—DNA. But if they were wrong, if he'd moved on to another scene...they had no idea where that might take place. *Maybe on that damn bench.* He ran a hand over his face—prickly. Rough. "No matter where he's keeping them, it'll be somewhere quiet, abandoned. That's one constant between victims. No matter what else he is, he's cautious enough not to get caught."

"Right. We can start canvassing tomorrow morning. McCallum will have your head if you don't get some rest. As will the chief, injured or no."

Oh, fuck McCallum. He ignored her and said, "What about failed playwrights, failed writers; is there any way to find out who's been rejected professionally? Maybe that's what pushed him over the edge."

"We can put in a few requests, but we don't have any idea where he might have pitched this brilliant script. At any agency or publishing house unfortunate enough to receive his work, that shit is sitting in the slush pile or the trash."

He raised an eyebrow. "The what pile?"

"It's what agents call all the works they have to sift through. I think. It's something like that."

"How do you know so much about failing at writing?" When she dropped her eyes to her laptop, he said: "Let me guess: Decantor's trying to sell a book about how to be a royal doofus with a Kardashian obsession and still manage to survive in law enforcement?"

She made a note on her laptop—*click-clackity-click*. "I'll pull the local theater groups, look at auditions; he's a writer, sure, but he clearly fancies himself an actor as well, terrible or not. Maybe his goal has to do with acting in the movie and not so much writing it; he definitely gets into character when he rapes his victims." She grimaced. "And with the room Carroll described...he likes feeling official."

Petrosky nodded. "There should be casting-call records, and if he's signed with any acting agency, we'll have a name pretty quickly once we get Carroll's sketch. I'm sure there are lots of Indian actors, but our guy doesn't have those "The Rock" kind of muscles. Maybe the little guys are easier to weed out."

"The Rock isn't Indian."

Petrosky frowned. "Who said he was?"

Jackson's cell buzzed. She glanced at it and stood. "They're done."

The hallway back to the chief's room felt longer somehow, every step sending electrical currents through his chest that felt as if they might zap his pacemaker. A few steps and he'd finally get to see the bastard who'd hurt his friend—who'd killed two innocent women. Who was surely preparing to hurt someone else.

Carroll was still sitting, but her eyelids sagged; even the set of her shoulders appeared looser as if she were slowly melting into the bed. The pillow behind her back was cockeyed. The thin man at her bedside still had his pencil on the page, hand working back and forth.

"They just gave her some pain meds."

Petrosky turned. Carroll's husband stood in the shadowed corner by the bathroom, his arms crossed; too dark there for Petrosky to read his expression. Perhaps that was how Carroll had perceived her attacker, a figure in the gloom. Andre sniffed. "She wouldn't let them give her anything until she finished the sketch for you, so it better be worth it." But Petrosky heard what he meant: *You better make it worth it. You better catch him.*

And they would. Petrosky approached the bed, Jackson at his side, and the artist turned the sketch their way.

Jackson stiffened. Petrosky stared.

"What is it?" Carroll. Her words were slurred, just the

tiniest bit, like she'd forgotten how to form the letter *T*. Petrosky looked back at the sketch, sure this time he'd see something else, someone else.

He didn't.

The man staring back at him was Acharya.

24

"I WANT eyes on that journalist prick," Petrosky said as he followed Jackson down the hall toward the cafeteria—again. "And tomorrow morning, he comes in to answer our questions whether he likes it or not."

"I'm sure he'll answer whatever questions you have," Jackson said over one tense shoulder. "But that sketch is not Acharya. It doesn't look anything like—"

"Are you serious?" Three orderlies huddled around the nurses' station glanced up. Petrosky gave them the evil eye, then continued, more softly, "It's not perfect, but sketches never are. Something always gets lost in translation." She whirled on him, and he put up a hand. "And before you say it, this is not an all-brown-guys-look-alike thing."

Still, she glared, her fingers wrinkling one corner of the sketch she held clenched in her fist. At least the orderlies had dispersed. "You just want it to be him because you know where to find him—it'd be easy to stop him. But there's no way."

"Think about it, Jackson: he's a writer who has insight into what we're doing. He knows our parking lot; he's been there enough times. And he sent us a fake confession—he had to know that pedophile asshole was lying through his teeth, and he still sent him down to waste our time."

She shrugged. "Maybe Acharya wanted that guy off the streets as much as we do." But she didn't look convinced.

"Maybe he wanted him off the streets, but Acharya didn't need the asshat to confess to a murder he didn't commit to accomplish that. Acharya had to know that every moment we wasted with Smithwick was time we weren't looking for Carroll's kidnapper. Maybe he did it to give himself a window to dump her. The timeline certainly fits." Her jaw dropped, but he continued, "The guy just happens to show up to confess right when we found the killer's hidey-hole? When we were all occupied there, including Michaelson, the guy who's been stalking that park bench his entire shift? Giving us a false lead sure kept us occupied for a few more minutes, long enough to dump Carroll at the trail. Which is exactly what happened."

But Jackson was shaking her head. "It's... No, it's ridiculous."

"What's his mother look like?" He squinted; the fluorescent lights felt suddenly brighter, burning his eyeballs. The air buzzed.

"His mother? I thought you just said—"

"Does Carroll know him?" He was bait and switching her. Why was he doing that? Was he…interrogating his partner? "Think, Jackson. Has Carroll ever seen Acharya at the station? Would she know him?"

Her brow furrowed. "I… Shit, I don't think they've ever met. I can't really remember."

"Then it's not a matter of familiarity; she didn't accidentally assign her sketch Acharya's features."

"She could have seen his photo online. He writes a ton of articles, and I know she's read a few."

"They stick the photos at the end, with the byline. Does anyone ever read that shit?"

"It's not a match." Jackson waved the sketch in his face, her shoulders rigid, the paper snapping. "That's what you're not seeing! The skin, the hair, those are too common to be definitive. His nose is pretty middle-of-the-road, nothing remarkable there either."

"His mouth, though... it's spot-on."

"He has a normal face," she said, meeting his gaze. "You're seeing Acharya because you want to see Acharya."

He snatched the sketch from her hand and held it up, the way she'd done to him. "Why *don't* you want to see Acharya?"

"The age isn't right—didn't McCallum say he thought our guy was younger? Closer to the ages of our victims?"

"That's just a guess. And he's certainly close to Carroll's age."

"But Carroll confirmed it—she said she thought he was twenty-five, and Acharya's in his forties."

"You're the one who told me black don't crack." Somewhere behind him, an elevator binged, bringing with it the sounds of the hall—people talking. Steel wheels on linoleum.

"My lovely skin aside, he's not a medical student, Petrosky. Or a vet."

Which *still* wasn't an answer to his question—why didn't she want to look at him? "Neither is our killer; he might have a little knowledge about plastic surgery, but we don't have any confirmation that our suspect has ever been a part of any medical community." He stepped closer, voice low. "But Acharya is a researcher. Someone who could look up how to do these procedures, maybe even talk to experts in the..." *Shit.* "Didn't you say Acharya was the one who introduced you to that plastic surgeon with the rap sheet?"

"Yeah, but that has nothing—"

"Of course it does!" *What is wrong with her?* "Acharya's inserting himself into the investigation, has been from the very start. Every time I turn around, that bastard is there. If I was a killer, that's what I'd—"

"He told me about the plastic surgeon because he was trying to help me."

"And why would he do that? He's a bloodsucker, he doesn't give a shit about anything but the story. And he was at the hospital before we were—how'd he know, Jackson? From that damn police scanner? We knew before the scanner did, and he still managed to get there before us. Almost like he had inside—"

"I called him, okay?"

"Why would you…"

She looked away, toward her arm. His eyes dropped to the bracelet on her wrist.

Oh shit, anyone but him. "He's the guy, isn't he?"

Jackson sighed.

"Oh….oh god." He shook his head as if trying to dislodge the image. "Jesus Christ, you could have banged anyone, and you picked a *journalist?*"

"He's a good guy, Petrosky, and you don't have a leg to stand on here, you're the one—"

"Nope, no more, I'm not doing this." He was pouting like a five-year-old, but he didn't care. He wanted to gag. Nothing mattered but the goddamn killer. And if she wasn't impartial, if she wouldn't help him investigate that asshole, he'd do it alone. Even if he wasn't really impartial either. "I'll call a lift home." He glanced back over his shoulder, met her eyes, and shook his head. "Jesus Christ."

25

THE BEDROOM WAS DARK, Duke's giant slobbery head against his hip, the laptop open in front of him, the screen painting everything, including the dog, in that cold blue haze of death. Ominous. The flesh prickled between Petrosky's shoulder blades.

He still hadn't recovered from the previous night's shitty sleep, or today's absolute shitshow of activity—the news of Carroll's abduction, the house, her return, the PO Box, the hospital...had it really all taken place in one day? But it wasn't just the timing. Petrosky felt off-balance as if someone had smashed his equilibrium with a journalist-sized mallet. And the research he'd been doing had not helped to ease his mind.

Goddamn Acharya. Every line he read made him more suspicious. Though he hadn't found any nasty romantic breakups on social media, they could still exist—not everyone aired their dirty laundry publicly, Petrosky included. But Acharya had a far more interesting point of reference than a bad-tempered ex. The journalist had immigrated to the US as a child because his mother was a writer— and a pretty famous one at that, the author of thirteen books on economics, of all the things. She wasn't known for fiction or screenwriting, but that didn't mean her boy wasn't trying to follow in her writing footsteps.

He leaned closer to the laptop screen, earning a hearty grunt from his Great Dane. Acharya's mother, Kareena, was pretty, with tiny lines around her eyes, far too few for a woman her age—*plastic surgery?*—and thick black hair, though, cut shorter than on the women the killer had chosen. And she was *so thin* in her author headshots, at least through the upper body. Petrosky clicked through a few other photos until he found one from a book signing. *Aha*. Thicker in the hips than he might have guessed, but still not as curvy as the dead women.

He resisted the urge to throw the laptop at the wall. Was Jackson involved with a murderer? Maybe she really was next. But she'd refused to even entertain the idea. At least she was safe—he'd sent Sloan to watch her house since his shift was over, to look out for her and Lance; promised that Irish bastard a steak dinner and a case of Guinness if he kept it quiet. And Carroll would approve the overtime...maybe. If she didn't, he'd pay the guy out of his own pocket. Petrosky didn't care about the money, and he sure didn't give a shit if Jackson hated him when she found out—tonight, she and her son were safe. And, just as critically this evening, she was out of the way. Otherwise occupied.

Where she couldn't watch him.

He closed the laptop, and Duke snuffled as if he were considering nudging Petrosky in a bid to change his mind. The dog apparently thought better of it; he rolled away.

"You're fickle, old boy."

The dog grunted again as Petrosky heaved himself from the bed. No rest for the wicked. He headed for the door.

ACHARYA'S APARTMENT was all the way out in Farmington Hills, and Petrosky had it on good authority that the journalist was working at his office—writing, no doubt, the story of the month, the police chief who was going to guarantee a killer didn't get famous only to get taken herself, thereby making the opposite true. Convenient. Doubly convenient if you were the killer *and* the reporter who got to break the story.

Outside Acharya's apartment building, the sodium lights glared down from above like the eyes of an angry god. But maybe that was the guilt. Petrosky paused, his gaze on the glass-fronted building, considering. Nope, not guilt. Annoyance. While a well-lit street was great if you were in law enforcement, it was less fantastic when you were working outside the law. His fist tightened around the stick he'd hidden beneath his jacket, a little thicker than his middle finger, but heavy—enough to do the job.

"Yip! Yip!"

He turned. A woman with a little floof of a dog, a dog too small for Duke to even consider it a snack, walked by carrying a plastic bag—a bag of shit? Tiny shit. He stooped to tie his shoe, his back to the door, so she didn't think he was watching her, and waited. A keypad beeped. The door buzzed.

One one thousand. Two one thousand.

He stood at the end of two, took three loping steps in quick succession, and squinted through the glass front door at the woman and her little shit dog, both now heading for the elevators. Then he slipped his stick between the doorframe and the door as it eased closed. *Three one thousand, four.* If the woman saw him walking into the lobby after her, she'd surely call the police. Plus, he didn't want to scare her; she had enough to worry about already. Like carrying around a bag of fresh crap.

Five one thousand.

The lobby was empty. He took his stick with him when he closed the door behind him.

The stairwell was dark, the blackness here thick as felt after the glaring brightness outside and the harsh yellow in the lobby. The door to the second floor passed, his shoes a steady throbbing that beat in time to his heart. He was certain he'd get to the third floor and the door wouldn't open to admit him, but the handle turned, and it creaked open without issue. The hallway was clear, the pine green of the walls making the walk to Acharya's door practically reek of evergreen. It brought to mind the thick woody scene on the trail where they'd found the bodies, the icy dank of the river water.

His chest hurt. His eyes burned. *Carroll—he fucking left her there to die.*

Petrosky paused at number 368. No one else in the hall, no sounds from beyond the other doors; no sounds behind Acharya's door either, but he already knew there wouldn't be. He pulled out his Swiss Army knife and made quick work of the lock—the guy was too cocky to even set the deadbolt—and slipped inside.

Dark. It whispered from every corner, the haunting unreality of unseen things. And wafting from that blackness, a smell—cinnamon? Something spicy and sweet. He listened for one more moment, hearing the darkness like the voice of a lover. And flicked the light.

The foyer was normal, if not bland: utilitarian and sparse in a mossy gray hue that reminded Petrosky of molded putty. *Where would you keep it, sick-o?* He wasn't sure what he was looking for, exactly, but he was certain he'd know it when he found it.

The bedroom was painted in that same greeny gray, the furnishings just as spare: a bed, a nightstand, mirrored closet doors. Petrosky frowned at the bed—sharply made, the edges of the comforter tucked neatly beneath the mattress. He couldn't recall the last time he'd made his own bed. Was that a thing that people did?

The pine nightstand held a cup of water atop a glass coaster, three hard-cover novels stacked neatly beside it. Murder mysteries, like the ones at Patel's home. The titles weren't familiar, but that didn't mean it wasn't a connection. Had he bought them from the same bookseller? Did Khatri read? They hadn't found evidence of it at her place, though, and that wasn't how the killer knew Carroll.

His heart spasmed, and the acid in his guts edged up his esophagus. *Don't puke, old man—terrible time for a heart attack, too.*

The closet held nothing but clothes. Whatever demons Acharya was hiding weren't in the bedroom where Jackson was allowed. *Oh god.* Had Jackson been in this room? In his *bed? Gross, Jackson.* It was like picturing his sister with a goblin. If he had a sister. He glared at the bed on his way out.

The living room boasted an L-shaped sofa and a glass coffee table, neither of which was hiding a damn thing. The office was more of the same: a desk of steel and glass, and a modern chair that looked like its goal in life was to give you sciatica, but no file cabinets or any other good hiding places unless the guy could fit the damning evidence inside a laptop cord or a spare cell charger. Surely, Jackson would have spent time here too. And in the living room. If Acharya was hiding something in these rooms, she'd have noticed. Unless he'd moved it.

Did you know I was coming, asshole? He didn't think Acharya knew about Carroll's sketch, not yet, but the journalist had to expect it, and he'd surely guess Petrosky was going to be all over his ass. Jackson's voice rang in his ears: *It's not a match though, that's what you're not seeing!* But no, the sketch was close enough to rouse suspicion, or it should have been—unless you were fucking the suspect. And he'd had this feeling before Carroll was taken, this… unease. He couldn't afford to be wrong again.

He paused in the hall. No more rooms to search, none except… His eyes grazed the stainless steel appliances. Jackson didn't cook. She hated to cook. He'd never seen her in a kitchen that he could remember.

He headed that direction, taking in the gas stove—the black granite. *Pretty fancy, Acharya.* But there wasn't a single bowl of fruit, no plates in the sink. Did the asshole cook, or was this all for show?

He opened the fridge: mineral water. One shelf held yogurt and berries and two apples. The drawers were empty. The freezer contained vodka and a bag of peas.

The microwave was clean but empty. Then he yanked the handle of the oven.

Jackpot. Acharya knew someone would suspect eventually, but even for a criminal, this was a stupid place to hide things. Petrosky snatched up the single folder and brought it to the countertop, flipping the cover open. He frowned.

Photos. But they weren't pictures of their victims, nothing crime-scene related, no images of the sundress their suspect had recreated with that yellow fabric. These looked like promotional images, glossy headshots, like the ones the actors signed backstage for their die-hard fans.

He squinted at the pictures, his heart in his throat. *What the hell, Acharya?*

Three actresses from *Cats*. One from *Phantom of the Opera*. All leading ladies, no men. Had he been looking for other victims, trying to decide who would be next? These women weren't all Indian, they weren't all curvy, but they had similar skin tones and wore copious amounts of makeup. *Stage* makeup? Scott had known it was pancake makeup, but they hadn't made the link to the theater until Carroll. Acharya wouldn't have known…unless he was their guy.

He pulled out his cell and snapped his own pictures of the evidence. Then he stacked the photos as they had been and returned them to their precarious position in the oven. Petrosky might not be able to use them if it was discovered that he'd broken in, but at least he'd have enough on his phone to show Jackson. And then he could get her away from Acharya before he lost another woman he cared about to a monster.

26

He should have gone home—Petrosky knew he should have gone home. But though his eyes burned through the haze of tobacco smoke in his old Caprice, though his chest felt heavy and tight, though the acidic burn in his guts was trying to digest his stomach from the inside out, he drove to the office—Acharya's office.

The building was little more than a glorified three-story townhouse, but unlike Acharya's apartment, the press offices had security; he wasn't going to get in without the man knowing.

He approached the burly fellow behind the counter, a man who absolutely did look like The Rock, and asked for Acharya, making sure to flip his jacket just enough to give the guy a glimpse of his badge. The guard spoke into the phone in hushed sentences, then waved Petrosky toward the elevators. Top floor. Acharya was standing in front of the doors when they slid open, bags under his eyes, the top button of his shirt undone.

"Detective." Acharya turned without waiting for a response and headed through the maze of desks. The third story was an expansive loft full of cubicles with tiny workstations, the chairs even more uncomfortable looking than the one Acharya had at his place. This was where he'd elected to work instead of at home on his couch?

Petrosky gestured to Acharya's bare flesh just beneath his collar. "You trying to seduce me, or what?"

"You're the one who came out in the middle of the night looking for me." He chuckled and lowered himself into his chair, ankle resting on the opposite knee. Bare feet? Acharya tapped his knuckles on the desk, but not the way Jackson did it—as if knocking on a door. Still...had she gotten the habit from him? "To what do I owe the honor, Detective?" It was meant sarcastically, but the guy didn't look like he was joking, nor did he look agitated by Petrosky's presence. He just looked exhausted. Though anyone would be if they had to work a full-time job and still find time to stalk, kidnap, and carve up innocent women.

"I think you know why I'm here."

His knuckles stopped tapping. "She told you?"

Carroll? "Told me what?" *About you moonlighting as a killer?*

"That we're...you know. Together."

Petrosky's nose wrinkled with distaste. He might hate the guy, but did this asshole really think he was here in the middle of the night to berate him about dating his partner? There was plenty of time for that when the sun was out. And many more creative means for harassment. "This isn't about Jackson."

Now Acharya's brow furrowed. Genuine confusion...or maybe he was a good actor. The journalist put both feet on the floor and leaned forward in his seat. "Are you ready to give me an exclusive?"

"Actually, I was hoping you'd give me one." Petrosky pulled the sketch from the folder he had tucked beneath his arm and extended it to Acharya. The man stared at it blandly. Had Jackson told him about the sketch already? No, she couldn't be that stupid, no matter how good a lay he was.

"Who's this?" Acharya asked.

"Looks like you, I'd say."

"Maybe a little." Acharya passed the photo back. "You're here because Carroll gave you a sketch that you think looks like me? I sure hope you have something else, Petrosky."

"See, here's where I get a little...contemplative, right? Maybe I've had too much therapy."

Acharya chuckled, not worried in the least. "Or not enough therapy."

"Trust me, if that were the case, I'd have tossed you through the window by now."

Acharya met his eyes and closed his mouth. Maybe he believed it. He should.

"So our suspect—he's a planner. A stalker. McCallum thinks he's got some mommy issues, a real Freudian shit-fest. A guy after fame, who got so angry when Carroll said she'd repress his identity that he came after the chief herself to make sure he made it to the front page."

"Sounds like any of a hundred psychopaths or narcissistic killers I've written about."

"Ah, but you might have more in common with this one than you think." Petrosky leaned closer, close enough to smell the thick musk of the man's sweat—a little spicy, like his apartment. *What the hell is that smell?* "Your mom...she had a little plastic surgery in her day, didn't she?" No way the lack of fine lines was natural, no matter what Jackson said.

Acharya's eyes narrowed. "What's that got to do with anything?"

"Just seems coincidental, that's all. Our guy, running around turning victims into his vision of the perfect woman through artificial means, injecting chicken fat into their chests." He looked down at the sketch once more, then drew his eyes slowly back to Acharya.

The journalist was shaking his head. "My mother wanted

to do a little freshening up after my dad left, and somehow that's my fault?"

"Freshening up? So you think she needed it?"

"What are you—"

"Was she old? Used up? Needed to get her measurements *just perfect*?"

Acharya crossed his arms. "My mother did what she wanted to make herself feel good. It has nothing to do with this case. If every man with a mother or a friend who's had plastic surgery is suspect—"

"But you can surely see why it's suspicious. Right?"

Acharya blinked. The silence stretched.

"What about ex-girlfriends, Acharya? You have any that look like Mommy?"

Acharya yawned. Petrosky watched his face, the veins spiderwebbing his bloodshot eyeballs, his bored expression. Usually, being interrogated was enough to keep suspects awake, but the guilty ones sometimes fell asleep in the interrogation room when Petrosky went out to grab a coffee. All their nights worrying about being caught, and finally, it was all over—they slept like babies, drooling on his stainless steel table, their wrists cuffed to the side.

Petrosky popped his neck and waited for Acharya to meet his eyes before he said, "You know, I think I've got an idea for your next book: *Staying Woke While Killing Women*. Or something. I'll admit, the title is a little long."

Acharya raised an eyebrow…and smirked. Fucking *smirked*. "That's not really what woke means."

"Is this funny to you?" Maybe it was—Acharya was still unaware that Petrosky had seen the glossy photos of those women. But Petrosky couldn't tell him…yet. He needed a reason, any reason, to get a warrant.

"Of course it's not funny." Acharya rested his hands on his knees, his fingers like claws. "But the fact that you're here harassing me when you should be out combing the streets…" His nostrils flared.

"I'd like you to come with me, Acharya."

"Where?"

"To answer a few questions. Officially. You've been inserting yourself into this investigation from day one, and our sketch looks exactly like you."

"Well, not exactly." The journalist frowned. "Is this really about Jackson? She said you were going to be pissed, but I didn't think you'd accuse me—"

"Do you have an alibi, Acharya? For even one of the crimes?"

The man met Petrosky's gaze. And shook his head. "I research alone, usually from my apartment. And that's all I've been doing since the first body showed up. This is the first time I've been at my office in three days." He set his jaw.

Petrosky stared at him. Acharya stared back. Then Acharya pushed himself to standing and snatched his laptop from the desk. "I'll come with you. I'll answer your questions. I know you can't arrest me, you don't have shit, but this killer…he'll do it again, and soon. You and I both know it. Better that I'm alibied in your station than out there when it happens. Plus, I'll get to see my girlfriend." He winked.

It took everything in Petrosky's power not to punch him.

27

JACKSON WAS SCOWLING AT HIM, and he hadn't even made it to his desk. "Where the hell have you been?"

Chain-smoking in my car after berating your stupid-ass boyfriend. But it was better than staring at his ceiling, seeing that kid's chest explode, feeling the weight of his gun, drooling over the Jack under the kitchen cabinet. He was exhausted, but this was the most *him* he'd felt in months. "Out."

"Yeah, no shit." She plopped into her seat at his desk, tossing a quick wave over her shoulder at Decantor. *Dammit, why couldn't she have picked Decantor?* He might die in the line of duty, like they all might, but at least he wasn't a murderer. Or a journalist. Petrosky almost wasn't sure which one was worse.

Jackson slid a folder onto the desktop. "Got the toxicology back on Carroll. Whatever he shot her up with that second time, it wasn't Etorphine—there wasn't enough in her system, and the doc said that drug wouldn't affect her like she described. But no traces of anything else; whatever he gave her before he dumped her on that trail either vanishes at hyper-speed, or it's something naturally occurring in the body."

Well, that doesn't help.

"I ran down what actors guilds I could find last night—agents too," she continued. "None of them recall meeting someone matching our suspect's description." She tapped her fingers on the table, and he remembered Acharya and his damn knock-knock-knocking on the desktop. Was the guy sleeping in the interrogation room now? "We know the perp's local," Jackson said, drawing his eyes back to her face. "If he's doing plays or acting or anything like that, I can't see him having an agent in a place like, say, New York."

"Right." If he were that good an actor, he'd be starring on the silver screen, and women would be lining up to act with him. He wouldn't have to kidnap anyone.

Jackson was staring at him. "You still think it's Acharya."

"I do." He sniffed.

"Because of the sketch."

"Have we gotten any other leads? Did anyone else happen to show up with information on your boyfriend's doppelgänger?" They'd released the sketch to the Ash Park PD last night, but so far, nada. It'd hit the rest of the world for the morning news, all those journalists writing their version of the story, a fact that was probably pissing Acharya all the way off since he'd missed his exclusive on it...if anyone had told him.

She shook her head. "Nothing yet. But I'm not sure our guy would be so visible, that he'd—"

"Of course he would. He wants to be famous. If you don't trust me, you at least need to trust McCallum." He planted his elbows on the desk. "I talked to Scott about the makeup this morning...again. He said it was pancake makeup, but there's virtually no difference between that and stage makeup." Which Acharya had known. Petrosky had also asked Scott if there was any way to tell who had recently watched online videos on how to apply said makeup, but the kid had laughed and told him he'd have better luck spitting into the wind and seeing what came back. Acharya hadn't watched any according to his—freely given—laptop browsing history, but with his career with the press, he didn't need a tutorial.

"We already knew about the makeup. Why would you talk to him again?"

"It's just strange, isn't it? Well before we learn our killer is into plays, Acharya's already printed up a million pictures of women from the stage."

Jackson cocked her head. "Acharya did what?"

"He's got pictures of women all over his place—and all play actors. Maybe studying makeup techniques." His voice was pressured, forced. "And Acharya had that information, knew about the makeup, well before we knew about the acting angle—the theater angle. If he didn't do anything wrong—"

She put up a hand. "How do you know this?"

"What?" His heart was beating frantically, much too fast. He took a breath to slow it before he blew his stent.

"How do you know about the pictures of women in stage makeup?"

He stared her down. She stared right back, as Acharya had. "I peeked through the windows," he said.

"He's on the third floor. You couldn't have seen that by peeking through a window." She crossed her arms and leaned back, as far away from him as she could get without standing up. "You broke into his apartment."

"I don't know what you're talking about."

"Goddammit, you—"

"I plead the fifth." He coughed.

She leaned closer, more slowly, her eyes narrowed. Studying him. "You did…something to him, didn't you?"

"Something like—"

"Did you handcuff him to a pole in his underwear? What?"

"Nah." He shook his head. "He's in a cell."

"*What?*"

"Kidding. He's in the best interrogation room money can buy."

She slammed her palms on the desktop, earning them another glance from Decantor, but the big man was good enough to turn away and mind his business. "You can't hold him; you have nothing on him because he didn't—"

Petrosky put his hands up in surrender. "Hey, hey, hey, your lover boy *wanted* to come down to the station. Said he'd rather be locked up here when the killer snatches another woman off the street." It wasn't the worst way to weed him out, but Petrosky hoped that Michaelson, or whoever was out there patrolling, would catch a break before their killer posed yet another dead body.

"So, you're going to leave him in the interrogation room while you follow the leads he handed you?"

"The leads he *handed me*? He didn't give me shit—he hid it. I still wouldn't know about those photos if I hadn't broken in. And if he knows I have them, we won't get to use them later." *Against him.*

"Well, yeah, and we shouldn't. You're in the wrong here, you—"

"He hid it from you, too, don't forget that part. I can't believe you're not furious. He let you call him, let you give him leads, let you tell him where to show up, tell him what we knew, and he didn't bother to reciprocate. What kind of relationship is that?" He whipped out his cell and turned the screen so she could see it—the photos he'd snapped at Acharya's place. "Look at all this. Either he's a part of it, or—"

"Or he had a hunch that the suspect was into the theater." But her eyes had clouded.

"Let's say you're right that he had a hunch—again, why

hide it? We found out about the theater-screenwriting element because the chief woke up. What if she hadn't?" Even saying it made bile rise in his throat. He swallowed hard. "He kept it to himself when we were waiting for Carroll to open her goddamn eyes, and all that time, we could have been looking for our guy—we would have had a better idea where to start. Even if Acharya hates *me*, why not tell *you*?"

She looked past him, her gaze far away as if suddenly mesmerized by the dawn breaking through the bullpen window. "I don't know."

Petrosky reached into his drawer and laid another folder in front of Jackson on top of hers: old theaters he'd researched this morning while he was busy ignoring Acharya. He'd even spent the two hours before dawn exploring the abandoned theaters in the area, while Acharya rested in interrogation, but there were no signs that anyone had been there recently—just leaves or animal droppings, the occasional squatter. And no trap doors. "The abandoned theaters are a no-go, and most of the theaters are active—too busy for our killer to keep a victim there for any length of time." But he could have turned any room in his house into a theater, complete with a gawking gallery of pasted magazine eyeballs, as he had in that cellar. Even Acharya's living room might have worked with the right curtains. But that didn't feel right either—too public. Too many neighbors. Whoever their guy was had a special place for each of his leading ladies. A place no one would hear them scream.

"When was the last time you were at Acharya's apartment?" he asked.

Her gaze stayed on the bullpen window. Her wrist was bare—she'd taken off her bracelet. *Trouble in killer journalist paradise?* "It's been over a week."

"Your choice, or his?" Had he hidden those photos recently, or was it part of an ongoing obsession?

She said nothing.

"Come on, Jackson. This is important." *Isn't it?*

"His." It came out a whisper. "We were both busy, as usual, but he hasn't invited me over. Usually...he does."

And the look in her eyes made his stomach sink. "We have to investigate this, Jackson. He didn't say shit about those photos, even under interrogation. Either he thinks we're on to him and knows I can't use what I found in court, or he's hiding this information so he can be the one to break the story—which means he cares more about his career than these women."

Jackson's nostrils were still flaring, her jaw hard. Angry at him, or disgusted by Acharya? Either way, the journalist was about to feel the wrath of one angry woman.

Finally, she shook her head and pressed her fingertips to her temples. "We've got enough to hold him?"

"The sketch is enough."

"No, it isn't." She dropped her hands to shuffle the files on the desktop. "We should show Acharya's picture to Carroll. We should have done that last night before we left."

"She was sleeping, recovering from surgery." *And traumatized because of what that monster did to her.*

"Even still."

He sighed. "Fine. But Acharya hasn't given us an alibi, and that'd help us more than a witness statement. Carroll already admitted that it was dark and that her vision was blurry from the drugs."

Jackson pursed her lips. Finally, she nodded. "We'll leave him here. See what we can come up with in the meantime; I am not about to let another woman die because we're babysitting the wrong guy at our precinct." But the tightness at the corners of her eyes told him she really wanted to prove him wrong—for Acharya to be innocent. "Carroll said the guy who attacked her was young," she said now. "McCallum guessed he would be, too—impulsive. And if our guy is that young, the people who know him probably are."

"So?" He frowned.

"This generation doesn't watch the news, Petrosky. They don't read articles about local crimes."

"Neither do I."

"I'm just saying, twentysomethings are dealing with climate change and not local crime. They're numb to it, more worried about school shooters than a serial killer."

"Fine, so where would we find his people? Where the hell would they be?"

"Where any new-age hipster spends their time."

"The goddamn coffee shop?"

She shook her head. "Running up student loans they'll never get out from under. Remember what Carroll said? That there was red pen all over the script, that it looked like an assignment." She pushed herself to standing. "Maybe it was."

He nodded. "Lead the way. We can stop by the hospital, too, show Carroll a picture of Acharya's giant melon." Because as much as he hated Acharya right now, he wanted it to be someone else, too, if only to wipe that haunted look off Jackson's face.

28

By lunchtime, Acharya was resting in a cell—at his request—his laptop locked up tight in Jackson's desk. Was the journalist hoping for another woman to go missing to exonerate him? Was Jackson hoping the same? Petrosky didn't think so, but his partner wasn't about to waste time on the theory that Acharya was guilty either, especially since Carroll had shaken her head when they showed her Acharya's headshot. He wasn't sure he believed in the man's innocence, not entirely, but the evidence wasn't stacking up against Acharya as he'd hoped.

On to plan B. Or plan M. Whatever step they were on. It had only been a week since they'd found Patel's mutilated corpse on that bench, but it felt as if they'd been on this case a year. So much for easing back into work.

Jackson had already compiled a list of actors and agents, investigating them as he had done with the smaller theaters and playhouses, but he had little hope it would pan out. Their guy sucked at acting, Carroll had said so; no real agent would have signed him. And failed authors were a dime a dozen. But they didn't need just any author—they needed someone working on a play.

Composed

Petrosky scratched his nose, the heat in Jackson's car making his nostrils dry and harsh, desert-like. There were eight different screenwriting groups that met around Ash Park metro, and three of them met later that day.

They'd already emailed their suspect's sketch to the administration, but it couldn't hurt to look in person, even if all they did was observe the drama students as they wandered out of their classes. School seemed the most likely place for someone hauling around a marked-up script... unless writers marked up their own work. Which he couldn't be sure of.

Jackson turned down the street toward the university—calm now, though that could change. He was still prepared for a good face-punching. "We'll stop by the screenwriting groups after dinner," she said.

"It'll have to be an early dinner."

"Yeah, well, it was an early morning," she said, cutting her eyes at him. "For some of us, anyway." She hooked the Escalade into a spot near the curb. "Did you get any rest last night?"

"I slept an hour or two in my car." But he hadn't. And though the exhaustion weighed on his chest, it didn't feel terrible—almost normal. Like he was getting back to his old self.

She cut the engine. "McCallum's going to kick your ass."

Maybe. But he hadn't thought about Jack Daniel's once in the last day or so, had he? *Put that in your pipe and smoke it, McCallum.* "I'm just trying to help you clear your luvva." The frigid wind slapped him in the face, and he wrapped his coat tighter against it.

"My luvva? Don't call him that," she said, slamming her car door harder than necessary. "It feels like I'm talking to my father about sex."

"The word luvva makes you think of your father? Is that why you call Acharya 'Daddy'?"

"I don't... Jesus Christ, Petrosky, what the hell is wrong with you?"

"I'm not the one fucking a journalist, Jackson." But he was too relieved about her probably not fucking a killer to be as snarky as he'd like.

She rolled her eyes, but halfheartedly, and she didn't even bother jabbing him with her elbow when he stepped up beside her. She was probably thinking about that killer thing too. And when she spoke again, her voice was strained. "I'm sorry for what I said, too. About you being into it with the chief. That wasn't the time."

He sniffed. "I'm not into it with her."

"You don't have to expl—"

"I know." And he wasn't going to. No one else knew Carroll was his sponsor, no one else knew about her history except McCallum—not even her husband. It wasn't his secret to tell. "I just wanted you to know that she and I are absolutely not...together. Like she'd put up with me."

"Well, that's true," Jackson scoffed. But she didn't sound convinced. He wasn't sure he cared.

The campus was a dirty gray slush pile this time of year, the concrete walks salted and wet-looking in the hazy afternoon light. The classes were spread out more than he'd have liked, but most of the acting classes were located in the building beside the amphitheater. Petrosky had already taken photos of the theater itself and texted them to the chief—it was not the place where she'd been held, same as all the other auditorium photos he'd shown her.

The hallway smelled of strong coffee and old pencil shavings and that sweet vape smoke that always made him a little nauseous—cookies were for eating, not for smoking. He strained his ears, but the building was steeped in the pressured hush reserved for students and board meetings. Then, a door at the end of the hall creaked open, and the world erupted in a cacophony of boots and bags and chatty young adults shuffling for the exits.

Petrosky nodded at a slim woman with blonde hair halfway down her back and the shaped eyebrows of a fashionista. "She looks like an actress." Would she know their suspect? If their killer went to this school, they didn't want him to know they were interrogating his classmates, or he'd simply disappear. And then take his aggression out on someone else.

She was heading up the hall toward them, eyes on her cell, thumbs on the screen. "Excuse me," Jackson said.

The woman looked up, and Jackson flashed her the sketch —Carroll's sketch of the suspect. "Does this man look familiar?"

The young woman frowned at the photo. "Not really. I mean, there are so many people on campus, I hardly notice anymore. But I don't think I've seen him in my classes."

"Do you take a lot of the acting classes?" Jackson asked. "Film, theater, screenwriting?"

"Oh, no, I'm a business major." She laughed, showing straight white teeth. "This is an elective; an easy A for me."

So much for first impressions. If this was her only theater-type class, she wasn't likely to know their suspect even if he did go to the school. "What about someone who's a little more serious about acting and screenwriting?" Jackson said.

The woman scanned the crowd that was still filing from the room. "Oh...him." She raised a hand, waving at a man with hair black as night and eyeglasses to match. Black polish on his fingernails. He raised his dark eyebrows and approached, slowly, suspiciously, scrutinizing Petrosky and Jackson in turn as if trying to figure out what he might be walking into.

"Brent, hey."

Brent blinked rapidly. "I...um...hey."

"These guys were asking who the best student in the class was, so of course, I thought of you." She flashed him that straight white smile. The brain seemed to drain from Brent's ears in an instant, but she headed off quickly enough for him to regain some of his composure.

Jackson showed him the picture of their suspect. "We're looking for this man. He might be a student, or a teacher, a guest lecturer. He might even be someone who's auditioned for a play."

The man was still staring after the pretty blonde, but now he turned his attention to the sketch and frowned. "You know...he does look familiar, but I'm not sure where I've seen him. Maybe the coffeehouse?"

"The coffeehouse?" Petrosky said. *I knew it.*

"Yeah, lots of us go over there to write."

Hipsters and their bullshit.

Jackson slid the photo back into the folder and tucked it under her arm. "Do you know his name?"

Brent shook his head.

"Ever talk to him?" Petrosky asked. "Maybe know where we can find him outside of the coffee place?" *I hate the goddamn coffeehouse.* "Class schedules, or—"

"Oh no, nothing like that. When I'm writing, I don't really...pay attention to anyone else, you know? I do remember he typed really fast. And he would kinda...wave his hands around a little. Like he was acting the parts out as he went."

So an actor, maybe, but definitely a screenwriter. "What was he wearing? Any identifying marks?"

"Wearing black. But that's not...you know. Weird."

Petrosky scanned the guy—black from his hair to his nails to his boots. *Some help you are.*

Jackson was pulling something from her coat: another photo. "Is this the man you saw?"

Petrosky squinted. Acharya.

Brent frowned. "No, I don't think so. This guy...he was a little thinner in the face, you know? Smaller lips, too."

Jackson glanced Petrosky's way, almost defiant. He scowled and pretended not to see the way her shoulders sagged with relief.

29

―――――

The coffeehouse was packed, but the baristas weren't busy; the patrons had apparently snagged their coffees already and were busy taking advantage of the Wi-Fi that came free with the purchase of a double-tall-mocha-fucking-coconut-milk whatever-the-hell.

The woman who approached them had three earrings in her nose, one on either side and one in the middle like a bull, making her nostrils appear like an upside-down three-leaf clover. She had a blue jay tattooed on her wrist, and her navy wrap-around sweater would have looked at home on someone four sizes bigger—Petrosky could have worn it without issue. Her eyes widened when she saw the sketch of their killer.

"Yeah, he's in here sometimes. Double espresso with a shot of sugar-free caramel. Usually sits in the back with his laptop."

"Do you know his name?"

She bit her lip. "Actually, that's kind of a running joke. Every time he's in here, he uses a different name for his order. Sometimes William, sometimes Edgar. Sometimes Viva."

"Viva?"

"He said like 'vivacious.'"

Petrosky raised an eyebrow. "And did he live up to that?"

"Nah. He was really quiet, kinda awkward."

People like this guy ruined it for the rest of the socially awkward quiet folks. Petrosky wasn't exactly shy, but he sure didn't like other people enough to chat them up. "When was the last time you saw him?"

She frowned. "You know, it's been a bit. A few weeks at least."

"Cash or credit?"

"I... Cash." She chewed on her lip like it was a piece of bubble gum. "What's going on?"

"I need you to do me a favor, okay?" Petrosky slid his card across the countertop. "If this guy shows up, give him his order like usual; don't let him know anything's wrong. And call me right away." He set a copy of the sketch on the counter and pushed that her way as well. "Stick this in the office. Make sure anyone who works here knows not to approach him."

She swallowed hard. "Is he dangerous?"

Jackson nodded. "More dangerous than you know."

"You still want to keep him in holding?" Decantor's voice was quiet, almost like he was whispering into the phone.

"Hey, he still wants to stay, right?"

Jackson watched Petrosky as he hung up his cell, her fingers tapping crazily against the wheel. "Your boy's fine," he said. "I hear he's working at your desk right now."

The tapping paused, then resumed more ferociously than before. "Well, whatever works for him, I guess."

Yeah, until Decantor kicked him out, and, so help him, if

the journalist got bored at Jackson's desk and went through his stuff...

He turned to the window—snowing. Someone would escort Acharya's ass to the door eventually; the journalist really shouldn't even be in the building, but Decantor and Sloan had agreed to look the other way even as they kept him in their peripheral vision. Without Carroll there to bitch about it, Acharya had a free pass to the bullpen, which should keep him occupied and alibied. And quiet.

Plus, Decantor had promised Petrosky he'd take a run at Acharya himself, see if he could pry some information out of him about the pictures, the only other person Petrosky had told—because, Kardashian-loving fuck or not, he trusted Decantor's work. Sloan too. Petrosky didn't trust that journalist asshole one bit even if he had come around to the idea of the murderer being someone else. Those photos in the oven still didn't sit right. And with the slight frame of their suspect, it wasn't impossible that their killer was working with someone else.

Dinner was a fast-food burger that coated his esophagus with grease and a chalky milkshake that was probably more chemical than cream. They ate in the car, Jackson at the wheel, Petrosky handing her napkins.

Screenwriting and drama clubs were widespread, but the three that met this evening were the most promising—they were more renowned, and larger, and for a guy looking for fame...that's where he'd go, right? He seemed to be more a writer than an actor, and the other groups were focused on things like line memorization tricks and "emoting," whatever that meant. For producers, the wannabe screenwriters, and playwrights...this was the place.

The building smelled inexplicably of oil and salt, though Petrosky could see no vendors hawking their wares to the masses—no hot dogs, no popcorn, no super-sized sodas to go with a show. Was the salt in his nose from the burger? It was almost comforting—familiar.

The auditorium itself echoed with animated voices. Petrosky and Jackson marched down the aisle, their footsteps swallowed up by the carpeting and the much louder vocal reverberations of those on the stage.

Ten chairs in a circle, seven filled. And the surround... Black curtains, just like the ones they'd found in that cellar. Unlike Brent, the goth-drama king from the university, the writers here were clothed in vibrant colors; two of them sported short pink hair. And though he'd never tell another soul, he didn't hate it. It reminded him of Billie's silver hair that somehow managed to look fresh and young despite the gray. *I should go visit the neighbors later—bring them cake. Stop being such an asshole.*

A dark-haired woman with earrings all the way up one ear turned as they climbed the steps to the stage. "Hey, guys, this is a closed group, but if you want to put your name on the waiting list..." One of the others glanced their way, a woman with spiked blonde hair, then turned back to the notebook in her hand.

Petrosky flashed his badge. "This enough to get us in for the evening?"

Everyone was looking their way now, seven pairs of wide eyes focused on the badge. The man with pink hair stood—tall, broad, definitely more fit than their suspect. In a fistfight, their perp would lose in about three seconds. "I'm Jeremy. I run this group. Is there a problem?" His face was all hard lines, chiseled like any self-respecting actor, but tight with irritation. Kids these days—they all hated cops.

"There might be a problem. We aren't sure yet." Petrosky pulled the sketch from the folder and handed it over. "Do you know this man?"

The dark-haired earringed woman peered over Mr.

Pink's shoulder, and her jaw dropped. "Yeah, that looks like Bill."

"Bill?" Their suspect's name was fucking *Bill*?

"Does Bill have a last name?" Jackson asked.

"Actually...I'm not sure he ever said." Pink ran his eyes over the other group members, but they all shook their heads. "He's usually here, but I guess I haven't seen him in..."

"Maybe three weeks," the earringed woman beside him said.

Three weeks. He'd stopped coming just before their first victim was kidnapped—that didn't feel like a coincidence. Petrosky's pulse throbbed in his temples. "Since this is a closed group, I'm sure you have ways to connect? Social media, home addresses? Phone numbers?"

Pink's gaze clouded. "I... No, not really. We mostly know one another from auditions or professional venues, and we vet members to make sure everyone's serious about the craft."

"And who vouched for our boy here?"

Pink's manicured brows rose—Jeremy, that was his name. The earringed woman glanced over her shoulder to where three of the other group members were already looking at a man with a Charlie Brown T-shirt and about the same amount of pudge as ol' Charlie around his middle. But his face was remarkably fairy-like: weak chin, dainty nose that anyone in this room could crush with one hit. Ice-blue eyes.

"We met in the coffee shop," he said. "The one over on Hill, just off campus." The coffeehouse they'd just come from. "I used to see him there all the time, writing on his laptop, running his lines. We got to talking one day, and I told him about the group. He seemed pretty serious about the work."

"Did he approach you, or did you approach him?"

"I...well, he approached me, I guess. Said he'd noticed me writing, asked if I was a playwright too."

"Did you ever see him outside of the coffeehouse, or

outside the group?" Hopefully, this guy knew where he lived, or at least details about his life that might help them find him. But the man was already shaking his head. "It wasn't really like that. I just told him to stop by here, and he did. And he kept coming."

"Did he ever show you his work?" Jackson asked.

Charlie frowned. "Well, no, I guess not. Here we talk more about the craft, how to put things together, the pieces of a play. Sometimes we act out scenes to see how it plays for an audience...like if we're stuck on something."

"And Bill never offered to share his work?"

Head shakes all around. "No," said Charlie, "but he was pretty into it. Acting his work out even in the coffee shop. It was almost like he thought his characters were there with him."

Petrosky raised an eyebrow. Was their guy delusional? Hallucinating? "And that wasn't a red flag to you?"

"I mean...why would it be? We're kind of an eccentric bunch. Characters in our stories...they speak through us sometimes. It's not that weird."

Isn't it?

Everyone went quiet. Jackson shifted, her eyes grazing one weirdo writer then the next. The earringed woman broke the silence. "Bill might have been eccentric, but he wasn't unhelpful. He was always happy to help us act out our stuff, even if he wasn't great at the acting part. But this isn't an acting class, so it didn't really matter. He did say he had written something special, though, a play he thought would make him a lot of money. Every time he came in, his stack of pages got thicker, the play got longer, so who knows what he thought he was writing—a Netflix series?"

The others chuckled, but Petrosky and Jackson exchanged a worried glance. It kept getting longer? He'd never stop unless they caught him.

Pink Man—Jeremy—nodded. "But it's ridiculous to think

you'll get rich right off. Takes a lot of practice, toiling away in the underbelly of the business before you get taken seriously. He didn't want to hear that."

I'm sure he didn't. Maybe he'd realized Jeremy was right and had gone off to make his own luck—he might not end up with money, but he'd gotten the notoriety, that sick bastard. "You said it was a longer play. Do you have any idea where the acts took place?" If someone knew the setting of the next scenes…

"No, seriously, he kept his work really quiet," Charlie said. "Almost like he thought one of us might steal it. He just said he was working on a new idea, something that would really get the audience, like Deb said. But he never told us exactly what it was."

"Well, he did say it was a romance, though." Jeremy shrugged one muscular shoulder. "Not quite a romantic comedy, I don't think, but similar. And those mostly have two basic parts: the main plot has to center on a love story, and the ending has to be optimistic."

But thus far, every one of the scenes had ended tragically. "Not all romances end well, guy."

"Well, no, but I think Bill wanted his to."

"No, he didn't." Now it was the pink-haired woman shaking her head. Her voice sounded sour somehow—nasal but sharp. "He told Laramie he was worried his story wouldn't get the ending it deserved unless he went outside the box. He wanted the introduction phase, love at first sight, but he also wanted things to move really quickly to the romance instead of the steady build you get in most stories. And he said that the end…" She frowned. "He said the end depended on who his leading lady was. And what the audience demanded."

What the audience demanded? What kind of audience did he have besides his wall of paper eyeballs? Then again, the women he took weren't just placid bystanders—they were both actor and audience. And if they didn't act right, if their bodies didn't behave the right way, if they didn't fit his costumes, if they weren't absolutely perfect... "Do any of you know where he lives? Even just a general area? His phone number?" *Anything?* How could this guy have been here every week for months on end, and no one knew anything about him?

Again, the blank faces. Irritation burbled in his chest. Close, they were so fucking close, and to hit a wall now was not an option. But one of the group members had frozen: the woman with the pink hair. Her eyes were locked on the empty seat beside her, and when Petrosky stepped closer to her, she jumped and inhaled as if she had, until that moment, forgotten how to breathe.

"Has anyone talked to Lara today?" The words burst from her lips. "She talked to him more than most of us. I mean, she humored him, even if she didn't always look excited about it."

Lara. A woman he'd happened to see regularly—who maybe had become an unrequited love interest. *Oh shit.* "We'll need you to elaborate on that, ma'am."

"I think he liked her, but she wasn't into him." Her brow furrowed. "Do you think he hurt her?"

Yes. "Do you think he's capable of that?"

Jeremy returned to his chair, shoulders slumped. Worried. He clearly believed it was possible, even if he was reluctant to say it.

"Why are you asking about Bill," Jeremy said finally. "Do you think he's done something?"

Jackson nodded. "If he is who we believe he is—"

Charlie cleared his throat. "You think he's the Measuring Man, don't you?" His voice shook.

Jackson cocked her head. "Who?" Everyone else turned their attention to Charlie.

"With the...you know. The bench. The guy who killed those women."

Jaws dropped. Eyes widened further still. Waiting for Petrosky or Jackson to confirm.

Charlie's eyes filled. "Lara...she looks like them. Like the other dead women."

The earringed woman blinked. "And he used to get so... agitated. Remember? Overacting like crazy on our work, but then when we were doing writing exercises, he'd write so hard the pen would rip his pages. And sometimes..." Her chest heaved. "Sometimes he stared at her. At Lara."

Not good. "We need Lara's last name. Where she lives. Anything you can give us."

But the pink-haired woman was already tapping on her phone, copying numbers onto the notebook in her lap, her gaze worried.

Barely breathing.

Hopefully, Lara still was.

30

"Again," he said.

Lara tried to swallow, but her tongue stuck to the roof of her mouth. The dining chair fabric was rough, a hard material like burlap, and it chafed her thighs even through her skirt. She couldn't do this again. She reached for the dining table, the wood splintered and just as rough as the chairs, and flipped the pages back to the beginning; the sheets stuck to her fingers, a dark stain near her pinky. Was that blood? The papers rustled, vibrating with the shaking of her hands. All the words were fuzzy, one page crinkled as if it had been ripped from the hand of the last person who'd held it. And maybe it had been.

Again, again, again. What did he want from her? She was trying, but how was she supposed to read when the world was spinning? *You can do it, Lara. You can.*

She inhaled deeply and started again, words she'd memorized over the last few hours, words he'd made her say over and over and over. "It's so nice to meet you. I can't believe we've never run into each other before." Every syllable tasted bitter. Like she was dry heaving them into the air.

Bill frowned. Was that really his name? She'd used the name earlier, pleading with him, and he hadn't responded. She could scarcely recall the man she'd known from their writing group, how she'd thought him timid, shy—she'd felt so bad for him. He was a little creepy, sure, but most guys were when they liked you. She hadn't suspected he was a threat.

Tears filled her bleary eyes. She'd been wrong, and now she was going to die, and her little girl was going to grow up without a mother.

"You sound like you need more water," he said.

She trembled and nodded, though she'd already had water—too much. Her bladder was on the verge of bursting, and her head, her head, too—aching, throbbing—and beneath that pain rose the hot stinging of her ankle. Rope on flesh.

He stood, his sinewy shoulders rigid as he vanished through the back wall of fabric, the floor-to-ceiling curtains black as night. Thank god he'd turned the lights off; he said he wanted to see her eyes, that he didn't want her to squint when she looked at him, but she was just glad her skin was no longer burning…even if it was cold now. She shivered. The clink of a glass rang in her ears, then the subtle whoosh of water.

Somewhere back there was a faucet. Another room. A door. Though she could not see it, her hope demanded that it exist, an opening to a world where the room was not spinning, where she was not shackled to this table, where this man was not staring at her, scrutinizing her every move, deciding what to do to her next.

Beyond those curtains lay escape.

She pushed herself to standing, the burlap scraping at the backs of her thighs, but she was dizzy, she was so, so dizzy. She collapsed back into the chair. Whatever he'd injected her with lingered in her veins like venom—she wanted to puke, to pass out, to just...lie down. But if she did, she might not get up again. And she was so weak though she'd eaten a bunch of candy, the only food he'd offered. Maybe that was part of the problem; she rarely ate sugar. Or else she'd been here longer than she thought. Was she starving to death? In her condition, she needed protein, something besides all that sugar, even if it had eased the dizziness.

Somewhere, a door creaked, or maybe it was his shoes, and then he was back, pulling the black curtain aside and stepping onto the little wooden stage, momentarily blocking out the wall of eyeballs—even if they were real, they could not have been more horrifying. They had talked about this in their screenwriter group, imagining how it would be to see their work in front of an audience, to have all those eyes watching you...but not like this.

Her skin crawled. She never wanted to be watched, ever, ever again.

He set the glass of water on the dining table. She squinted at it, trying to gauge its weight. Not heavy enough to knock him out, probably. But if he left again, and she broke the cup, she could use the shards as a blade to release her ankle and then—

"Do you remember when we used to walk down by the river?"

She startled; her stomach lurched. "I...I'm not sure." That had never happened, had it? She had gone down there a few times with her daughter when they'd had an hour between doctor's appointments, but she'd never gone with Bill.

"I used to go there to write, just sat on the bench by the water and let the words flow." He closed his eyes a beat longer than a blink. Had she ever seen him there? If she had, she did not remember. Maybe she hadn't noticed. But she couldn't tell him that. *Play along, just play along, and maybe he'll take pity on you.*

The room shimmered around her, like the air itself was

breathing. But she could tell he was smiling—his teeth gleamed like blades, shiny and sharp. Then he stooped, reaching for the chair on the side of the table, his face, shoulders out of her line of sight. *Now.* She reached for the water glass, the room wavering, but he was up and back beside her before she'd even closed her fist around the cup. Why was she moving so slowly? And why was he carrying…a dress? Where had that come from?

Yellow fabric drooped from the hanger. Little yellow straps of ribbon.

He held it up. "I need you to try it on."

Please let me go. "I'm not sure it will fit," she forced out.

"It should fit exactly." He grinned. "I made it just for you. But if it doesn't… Well, we'll cross that bridge when we get to it." He leveled his gaze at her—hot and sharp—and the hairs on the back of her neck prickled. "Get undressed."

Blackness tunneled her vision. "It's cold in here, Bill." *Think, Lara, think.* "Let's…let's wait until summer. I'll wear the dress for you, and we can go walking down by the river again."

"Let's wait?" He frowned. "That's not how a leading lady is supposed to talk."

Act, Laramie—just act. It's a script. A costume. She tried to force her voice to stay even, drawing on her deepest reserves of self-control, pretending she was in a commercial, a play, that the terror in her belly was that of her character and not of her own panicked self. But her bones vibrated, the marrow icy with dread. Maybe if the room wasn't spinning, she could focus; maybe if she wasn't woozy, she'd be able to pretend. "I'm not *just* a leading lady, not any more than you're an actor above all else. We're both people; real people. Humans who care about each other. We can talk about this, we can—"

"Take it off." He gestured to her skirt, then her top.

"No, please I don't want to, I—"

"Take it off!" he roared, and her vision pulsed, black obscuring the world before he came rushing back to her, all teeth and furious eyes.

Tears burned behind her eyelids. She pushed herself to standing, her legs unsteady as she undid the button on her skirt. It puddled to the floor at her feet. She pulled her shirt over her head, arms riddled with goose bumps, and plastered on a grin like the avid car shopper she'd pretended to be just last week in a local commercial, a grin that said, *I'm okay with whatever you want to give me.* "I'll do whatever you want. Just please don't hurt me." Her entire body trembled, but she tried to pretend it was excitement. Just another play, another scene, another ad. The air pricked like ice against her skin.

Bill moved slowly, almost reverently, as he slipped the dress from its hanger—were his hands shaking, or was that her? He raised the garment above her head and let it drop over her face, over her shoulders. Her breasts. She closed her eyes and let him tug it gently down, but it was snug, her chest trapped beneath the fabric—she couldn't breathe. And the waist was fitted. No way that would work. Two months ago, maybe, but not now.

She opened her eyes, Bill in sharp focus for one electrified heartbeat.

He clucked his tongue, and the sound made the hairs between her shoulder blades vibrate harder. "This is bad; this is very, very bad. But we can fix it."

"Fix it? How are—"

"Shh. Don't worry." He reached behind him, searching for something in…his pocket? A needle. What was he going to give her this time?

Panic stabbed at her heart.

"We will make it work, Lara. This is my masterpiece—our masterpiece. I won't let something like this get in the way."

"Please don't hurt me," she whispered. "I'm pregnant."

The world shrank around them, frost wrapping her ribs and creeping up her spine.

"Oh, that won't do." He shook his head and tapped the plunger on the hypodermic. "That won't do at all."

31

LARAMIE BAKER still hadn't been reported missing. Maybe they'd get lucky and find her eating Cheetos in her pajamas. Maybe not. Petrosky watched the street whizzing by outside the car window, the reddish-gray of the impending night already thick like the haze of brushfire. Their suspect knew this woman—this woman who looked like the other victims. How long had he watched her, wanting her to be his? How many times had he screwed up his courage to ask her out only to lose his nerve, or, worse for him, to be turned down?

How long had his rage been building?

Maybe she was the reason he'd started this bullshit to begin with. He'd sure worked awfully hard to get into her group. Had he met her there, or had he known of her before he'd approached that Charlie-Brown-looking bastard at the coffeehouse? Perhaps he had a whole list of women, women he'd stalked and planned for, the next one to be taken only if the one before failed him—perhaps it was just her turn. And what the hell was his endgame, especially with the play getting longer and longer? Practicing each scene, aiming for one perfect run-through with his leading lady? Or was the final scene a tragic type of romance, a *Romeo and Juliet* ending? Maybe he really was after death by cop. He'd certainly set himself up for that one when he took the chief, and if Petrosky got half a chance...

His cell buzzed, and he slapped it to his ear hard enough to make him wince. "Talk to me, Scott."

"Laramie Baker, twenty-four, small-time actress in local commercials and plays. She was on Broadway a few years back but moved home after she got pregnant with her first child. She's mostly living on student loans and child support. And she currently has a restraining order against her ex-boyfriend."

A violent ex? That sounded like it had potential, but he wasn't their guy—no way a dude with a restraining order would have been allowed in the same drama group as their victim. *Potential* victim. "What's the ex look like?"

"White. Bulky. Lots of tattoos; stuff any witness would notice if you're thinking he's involved."

"I'm not. Just the fact that he's a white guy gets him off the hook."

"Yeah, life imitating art imitating life."

"What?"

"Nothing."

Jackson's tires kicked up a spray of gravel as she wheeled into the apartment complex and screeched to a stop at the front curb—fuck the parking lot. He pocketed the cell as they hustled over the walk. This place was...what? Four miles from the strip where Patel and Khatri had worked? A little outside the killer's expected radius, but then again, so was Carroll. Once their killer chose a victim, he seemed willing to follow them—not great news for tracking him down.

The stairs felt steeper than they should have, the icy air biting at his lungs with each inhale. Laramie Baker's apartment, number 207, was to the left of the outdoor staircase.

The door was ajar. And from inside...screaming. *Shit, shit, shit.* He unholstered his weapon, and took the last few stairs two at a time, the shrieking intensifying with every step. But something was wrong. This wasn't the screaming of an injured or frightened woman—too shrill, too...small. *Oh god.* Scott had said she got child support. Was the baby injured? Had their suspect cut the kid and left her for dead? *Please, not a kid, not another kid.*

Jackson toed the door open and ducked inside, Petrosky at her heels. But they weren't alone. Linda? His heart shuddered to a stop.

His ex-wife stood in the living room, a small child wailing in her arms, the kid's head buried in her neck. Linda looked older than even a few months ago, but that wasn't what tugged at Petrosky's guts—she looked exhausted. Linda had been a social worker in the Ash Park system for as long as he'd been a cop, but he sure hadn't expected to see her here. She met his gaze, steady and sure—solid. As always. He wanted to say *I'm sorry*. He wanted to say *I'll try harder*. Or *you look good*. Instead, he clamped his lips shut, reholstered his weapon, and averted his eyes before she saw and understood all the things in his gaze that he didn't want anyone to know.

Jackson didn't appear fazed; she nodded to Linda like they were old friends. Maybe they'd gotten closer over the last few months while he'd been falling apart. Maybe Shannon had even dialed her up when he'd stopped taking her calls too. He really was a bastard.

"I was just about to call you," Linda said. To him or to Jackson? The little girl in her arms settled and peeked at them with her face still pressed against his wife. *Ex-wife.* "Got a call from the building manager," Linda said more quietly, her voice low, soothing, and the little girl sniffed. "Well, technically, the manager called 9-1-1, the police sent uniforms, and they called us. This sweet girl was screaming in her crib when they arrived, no sign of the mother. I'm trying to locate any other family, but it's not looking good.

We'll have to find a temporary placement until you can locate her mom." Linda shifted, one foot to the other, swaying like she had when Julie was a baby. His stomach clenched, and his chest... He rubbed at the sore spot above his breastbone, the place where he was certain every father felt the loss of a child like a piece of their heart had been extracted—a wound that would never stop bleeding.

Behind Linda, a man emerged from the galley kitchen—big cop, small hands, teeth bright white and too straight for any self-respecting officer. And behind him... "Michaelson?"

The rookie grinned, and this tugged at a tender place in his belly that he didn't want to acknowledge. *He does look like Morrison.* "Well, fancy meeting you here," the rookie said.

"Wipe that stupid look off your face, asshole."

Michaelson's smile fell as Petrosky addressed the other officer. "Any signs of forced entry?"

"No, sir. The door was open when we got here, chain lock disengaged."

She'd let the killer in then, or at least opened the door. Petrosky scanned the room. Toys on the floor, which seemed normal, but the tiny table just inside the front door had been toppled, a potted plant spilling dirt across the carpet. No evidence of a struggle in the rest of the room, so he'd probably grabbed her in the doorway—and she'd fought him. Had he not used the Etorphine, just dragged her out? That was risky; bad news for them. His pattern had been interrupted with Carroll, and now he was even more unstable, shaken, desperate, scrambling to get back to his leading man role—he'd take his rage out on the woman he had now. Laramie might not make it through the night. Petrosky narrowed his eyes at two small plastic containers on the coffee table, one prescription bottle of pink liquid, one off-the-rack container of pills. He picked up the pink stuff. "Antibiotics for the kid?"

Linda nodded. "Ear infection. That should be in the

fridge, but it was already warm when I got here, so it needs to be filled again; I can't give it to her like that."

He frowned. Petrosky was sure it was fine, but maybe there was social work protocol he didn't know about. And she was right—erring on the side of health for a kid was always a good idea. The bullet wounds in the chest of that boy he'd shot, the blood blooming against the white, blinked into his brain and vanished. He hissed an inhale through clenched teeth and rubbed at his chest again.

Linda sidled closer to him and raised her free hand like she was going to put it on his arm, but apparently thought better of it and dropped it to her side. "You okay, Ed?"

Michaelson raised an eyebrow. Petrosky scowled at him until he looked away. "Yeah, I'm fine." He swallowed hard and said: "If the antibiotic bottle was warm, it's been a couple of hours, at least."

"Car's still here too," Michaelson said. Why was he still talking? "It was the first thing the building manager looked for."

Petrosky cleared his throat and set the pink liquid back on the table beside the second container. "What's the other one?" Not a prescription bottle—

"Prenatal vitamins."

Ah fuck. Scott hadn't mentioned that Lara had a boyfriend. Then again, it didn't take having a boyfriend to get pregnant. He met Jackson's worried gaze. The stakes had just gone up—pregnancy wasn't especially forgiving, not if you were trying to squeeze someone into a custom-made dress. And Lara's friends had said she wasn't into their suspect, so the kid wasn't his. In his mind's eye, Petrosky saw Carroll's belly, LIAR carved in glaring red letters, all because of a shaper. A baby would be a far worse betrayal to a madman.

32

No cameras in the apartment building's parking lot. They still hadn't found the car used to kidnap the chief, but their perp was smart; he surely had another ride by now. The air felt colder on the way back to Jackson's Escalade.

Linda was still up in the apartment with Laramie's child, sorting out a temporary custody arrangement; he'd walked out without even waving goodbye to her. Hopefully, she'd write it off as him being worried they'd lose another woman to that goddamn park bench, which was partly true—mostly he was just a dick. Was that a required thing with ex-spouses, that he had to act like an asshole every time he saw her? Apparently.

"So, what do we know about where he keeps them?" Jackson asked, and he squinted at the dark street.

"Lots of black—walls of curtains. He creates his own stage." Petrosky had already looked at the abandoned theaters in the immediate area; all of them, not that there were a ton. But whatever location the killer had chosen was probably close by. He'd abducted all of his victims within a ten-mile radius and had to have stalked them out here too. Patel hadn't been one to travel very far, nor had the others.

Even Khatri, for all her "outgoingness" stuck near her neighborhood.

"If we had a last name, we could at least try to find his place. A car registration. Something."

"Yeah." Petrosky stared out the window. The blackness had long since stained the horizon an angry charcoal, like a dead man's pupil. A name—they needed a *real* name. And something else was bothering him: those damn pill bottles. Because Laramie might be pregnant? No, that wasn't it, though it was definitely bad news in this situation. That the kid was sick? That'd be easy to remedy, even if it was awful to be sick without your mom. Bottles. Drugs. Medication. The...barista in the coffee shop.

He sat straighter, drawing his eyes from the blackness outside and back to his partner. "What about the sugar-free thing? The sugar-free caramel he ordered in his coffee. Is that something people do?"

Jackson shrugged. "If they're trying to drop weight, it is. Might also be a ketogenic diet thing—popular with the bodybuilder folks. Which I guess...he isn't."

And their guy was already slight; he wouldn't be trying to drop more weight. "What if he's diabetic?"

Jackson frowned, but her fingers tightened on the wheel. "Carroll said the second needle he used was smaller, right? Maybe the kind you get with insulin?"

He drew his gaze back to the window. The thick black night. "Let's check the local drugstores, see if we can get any leads on a guy matching our suspect's description—someone who's purchased insulin or other diabetes-related products."

She nodded and hooked a U-turn.

The first drugstore was a dead end; no one recognized their guy, though the usual pharmacist had gone home for the night. Same with the second. But they managed to get them both on the phone after texting a photo of their sketch—nada.

Petrosky rubbed his temples where a headache had taken root; the bright lights from the street lamps along the sides of the road burned white-hot amoebas into his vision. "Where else would he go for this?"

"There are three other drug stores and two grocery stores with pharmacies within ten miles. Then there's urgent care, though I can't imagine he'd go there for insulin." Jackson's fingers tapped frantically on the steering wheel. "And there's Canada. A quick trip over the border, and you can get most non-prescription drugs at the duty-free for a fraction of the price."

"But can you get prescriptions? Insulin?" He wasn't sure. But if you could, it'd be a lot harder for them to track.

Jackson was probably thinking the same; she frowned and pulled into the next lot, a party store pharmacy with an enormous aisle of clearance Christmas decorations front and center. What had he done for Christmas? Oh yeah—stared at his bottle of Jack. With Carroll. Maybe he should call the hospital after this, see how she was doing, but Andre was taking care of her, wasn't he? Sure, the man hadn't done a bang-up job in the past, but...Petrosky hadn't either. She'd done that press conference, and he'd gone home like nothing was wrong.

He followed Jackson to the back desk: the 24-hour pharmacy itself. The man behind the counter was younger than Petrosky would have expected for a pharmacist, with wide-set eyes, deep umber skin, and the harried expression of a soldier coming off a 48-hour recon mission. The name embroidered on the chest of his white coat read: Dr. Morgan. He smiled as they approached. "Can I help you, folks?"

Jackson showed him the drawing of their suspect, and the

pharmacist's mouth tightened. "Yeah, I've seen him in the store. What's this about?"

"He ever fill prescriptions here?"

"Well, I can't tell you if he's on medications. Patient confidentiality and all."

"How about now?" Petrosky slammed his badge on the counter. "This man has killed two women, kidnapped two more, and he's currently holding a pregnant woman hostage—he will kill her, probably tonight, unless we find him first." He met the man's eyes. "Do you want to be responsible for that?"

The pharmacist's Adam's apple bobbed.

"He might go by the name Bill," Jackson said.

Now the pharmacist frowned. "Bill? No, I'm positive that isn't right. It's a strange name, like…Vivian, but not that." His shoulders sagged, and from the way his jaw had softened, he'd made up his mind that imminent danger to the public trumped the confidentiality of a killer. "Hold on," he said and retreated from the counter to the long walls of shelving in the back where they kept row upon row of filled scripts in white paper bags.

So Bill wasn't his name. "You think our guy figured we'd be on to him eventually? Used a fake name everywhere?"

Jackson's lips were set in a tight line. "If he used a fake name everywhere, including over the entire past year at the playwright group, that would mean he's been planning this for a very long time. Preemptively hiding his identity."

"No wonder he's so overambitious," Petrosky muttered. "Why he loses control." He'd probably been dreaming of slicing these women up for years.

They both drew their attention back to the counter, where Dr. Morgan had reappeared, a white paper bag in his hand. "This is his. He has a prescription set to automatically refill once a month: insulin, test strips, glucose monitoring supplies, the works."

Petrosky squinted. "How much insulin does our guy need?" He'd have to run out eventually—they'd put a watch on the pharmacy, too, in case he showed up for the refill.

Morgan shrugged one shoulder. "People with diabetes often take two to four shots a day; he has enough for four a day for a month. And it's expensive—I can't imagine he'd buy it if he wasn't using it."

Unless he was using it for something else. Most people only rationed insulin if they couldn't afford it, but their guy...he'd been planning something far more heinous. "What would insulin do to someone who didn't have diabetes?"

Morgan frowned. "Oh, that's very dangerous."

"Humor us." Petrosky leaned his elbows on the counter and stared daggers at the doc.

"Okay, um...they might go hypoglycemic."

"Which means..."

"Well, if they didn't take too much, they might get irritable or confused. Some people experience anxiety, dizziness, blurry vision, shakiness..."

Exactly the symptoms Carroll had described. He hadn't put her out, he'd needed her awake to read through his script, but he'd kept her incapacitated. Dizzy. Just hypoglycemic enough so she couldn't fight him? She had been unconscious before he drove her to the dump site, but that could just as easily have been shock. "What if they took enough to make them pass out?"

"Well, that's possible, of course, but you don't really know if someone will pass out or if they'll go into seizures. And it's not usually immediate; ten minutes I'd say." Morgan was frowning again. "The person could also die pretty quickly unless they had a way to even it out—it'd be a crapshoot."

Patel's stomach flashed in his head—the little needle marks around her belly, but not like the botched liposuction marks on Khatri. Had he spent Patel's two weeks of captivity bringing her in and out of consciousness?

"And how would he do that? Even it out?"

"Glucagon injection, maybe? If he doesn't have access to that, sugar water would do it, juice, candy—"

"Cookies." Carroll had said he gave her cookies when she woke up. Had he given her something before then? Probably. Maybe he'd poured juice down her throat or injected her with glucagon. "Does he get glucagon with his supplies?"

Morgan squinted at the bag, then looked at the ceiling. "He has in the past, but not on a regular basis."

"What about opioids?"

"No, those are controlled—he's never filled anything like that. But these days...there's always the internet. Or a street corner, if he knew the right person."

Petrosky nodded and snatched his badge off the counter. "We'll need to see that bag, Doctor."

Morgan passed it over, and they both peered at the label.

They had an address. A date of birth. And a name: Vivaan Laghari.

Petrosky headed for the door, reaching for his phone to call Decantor—backup. He wasn't going to risk Michaelson showing up, not today. "Let's go get this motherfucker."

33

DECANTOR WAS ALREADY in the parking lot when they squealed up. "How the hell did he get here so fast?"

Jackson shrugged. "Was he already out?"

"Must have been." Which meant Acharya was at home, probably jacking it to the photos in his oven—not a killer, but the guy was still an asshole journalist. Petrosky looked up at the building. Like Patel's apartment, this one was an older, renovated home: four units, tops, with outdoor stairs, and the gray skeletons of rose bushes flanking a single door on the ground level. The grass crunched beneath their shoes like the bones of tiny birds, as if every vulnerable thing in this place had already been done away with.

Were they too late? If their suspect had killed that poor woman, left Laramie's daughter an orphan... Decantor was clearly thinking the same; he was already halfway up the stairs to Vivaan Laghari's apartment.

The door was locked, but they had cause. Decantor reared back and kicked it just below the knob, splintering the wood before Petrosky even had a chance to pull out his Swiss Army knife. "Police!"

Dark inside. He hadn't even stepped over the threshold

when the smell hit him, a rotten, putrid stink. More bodies? *Please don't be that.* Petrosky raised his gun and held it steady as Decantor hit the lights in the living room. Jackson headed for the hall, her footsteps muted by the dingy beige carpet. Decantor stalked into the kitchen.

Petrosky stayed in the main living area, flinging open the door on the far living room wall, but it was only a closet—three cheap-looking jackets hung inside, a pair of boots tipped sideways on the floor. He scanned the room for other hiding places. Carroll had mentioned a sofa, that she'd been tethered to one by the ankle, but this couldn't be it. The couch here was a cheap futon, too light and breakable to hold the chief. And Carroll would have noticed the glass table in front of it. Nothing on the table, no books or lamps or coasters. Their guy clearly didn't spend a lot of time in here. *Where are you, you sick bastard?*

Decantor gagged from somewhere at his back, and Petrosky spun, his heart in his throat. The man was frowning into the garbage can he'd pulled from beneath the sink.

"What do you have?"

"Nothing, at least nothing criminal. Old meat, remnants of a salad—just trash. But it's been here for a while."

Yeah, long enough to stink up the entire apartment. But everything else in the kitchen was spotless. He must have been in a hurry to leave if he forgot to take the trash out, and more critically, he hadn't left recently...and hadn't been back since. No way their perfectionistic suspect would let his apartment reek like rotting meat. Wherever he was staging his play, he was living there for weeks at a time. He wasn't leaving those women alone.

So where was he? *Where, where, where?*

Two other doors waited down the hall off the living room: bathroom on the left, bright white tile, shiny sink, no medicine cabinet—nothing out of place. He crouched at the cupboard beneath the sink but found only clean towels, a roll of toilet paper, and…an empty box. Needles. No other supplies that he could see. Which meant the killer had taken it all with him.

Jackson was already in the bedroom across the hall, standing beside the night table. The bed was made up in a yellow material that looked like…

"Is that the same fabric from the sundresses?"

She nodded. "Weird, right?"

He touched the corner. Three of the stitches had popped, and they weren't close to even—not stitched by machine. Hand-sewn. Their guy might have tried a little home and costume design, but he sucked at it.

"So he's…wrapping himself in his lover's clothes? Surrounding himself with who he thinks she is?"

Jackson turned back to him slowly. "That's awfully poetic. Much better than the shit he writes." She lifted a notebook from the end table and read aloud: "Scene: high school hallway. She was walking across the floor. Her breasts were heaving at the sight of him. There was a tingling in his groin."

Petrosky grabbed another of the notebooks from the pile. "Lots of telling, but no showing," he muttered. "He really should work on describing the scene instead of just vomiting things he wants readers to know."

She lowered her book, eyebrow raised. "What the hell do you know about writing?"

"What? I know things." He finished flipping through the notebook and set it back on the tabletop. Lots of garbage writing, but nothing that would help them find their victim —these notebooks didn't hold their killer's masterpiece. He surely had that with him too.

One side of the closet stood ajar, a thin black line from the floor to the track above. He toed the bifold door open and squinted into the interior at… *Holy shit.* Mountains of notebooks, stacked from the floor to Petrosky's knees. While the hangers above held khakis and the occasional button-down, there was no room for a single pair of shoes on the carpeted floor, the stacks made all the more prominent by the stupid mirrored walls. "Got some surgery textbooks in here." He snatched up the top one and flipped to a dog-eared page near the middle. Liposuction. He dropped it back onto the stack. And—those mirrors. Who had mirrors like that on the *inside* of their closet? He leaned closer, squinting. There was a break in the glass just behind the open bifold. One mirrored panel was missing.

Petrosky pushed the clothing aside—pleated jeans, conservative sweaters, starched button-down shirts—and jumped, smashing his elbow on the door. Eyes stared at him from the back wall of the closet, hundreds of eyes in all sizes and shapes and colors. Some looked like they were from comics. And all of them were watching...the bed. Looked like he'd held a practice here, but there were too many neighbors to follow it up with a real kidnapping victim. This wasn't where he planned to stage the final act.

So many eyes. So many spiral notebooks, too, but there were a few books near the bottom with thicker bindings—hardcovers. Petrosky slid one out. A...yearbook?

He ran his finger over the heavily creased pages; page after page of smiling teenagers, looking like babies, but there wasn't a mark inside. "Don't yearbooks usually have signatures from classmates?"

Jackson frowned, squinting over his shoulder. "Doesn't look like our guy was very popular."

"Wait, here's one." Petrosky turned it so she could see the blue pen, badly faded. "Hey, Vivaan—best of luck! Love, Anita."

"Sounds like they had a deep relationship," she scoffed.

But it had clearly meant something to their killer; the signature was almost rubbed clean off like he'd traced it a million times.

Petrosky turned back to the student pages. Anita

Schroeder was at the bottom: dark hair, dark eyes, but lighter skin and far thinner than the victims. Whatever his type had been in high school, it had evolved since then. And now it was rigid—unwavering. Who was he trying to replicate? Or...maybe that was simply what his script called for.

Petrosky scanned the room, suddenly certain he'd see an opening in the wall, an entrance to a stage where they'd find their victim strung up. *Please don't be dead yet.* Had Laramie told him she was pregnant? If she had...that wasn't in the script.

And their killer would not improvise.

34

The eyes—they were staring at her. Laramie pretended she couldn't see them, because the moment she tried to focus on them, the room blurred, every eye swirling closer. One of them blinked. But that couldn't be real, could it?

She raised her head, tipping her chin toward the ceiling. The old rope he'd used to bind her wrists was prickly and rough—vicious against her flesh. And her arms were wet. In the mirror, she could see her reflection, the thin trails of blood trickling down toward her elbows.

Her toes were cold, colder than they'd been against the wood. Now, her feet ached against metal, a bucket that was more like an animal trough. She wanted to believe it was to catch vomit—she'd lost track of how many times she'd puked—but the way he'd looked at her, so disgusted when he found out about the baby...

I never should have told him. I should have known better.

How many shots would he give her? Two so far, straight in the gut, but the needle was smaller than a normal hypodermic; she didn't think he'd hit the baby. Still, each time, the dizziness had pulled at her so violently that she'd lost track of time—or of consciousness. Her heart wasn't beating right.

She wasn't breathing right. And she was sweating, though she was cold, cold, cold.

Was the baby okay? What if it wasn't? And had someone found Alexandra? *Please, someone, find her. Please take care of her.* Poor sweet girl was probably terrified at home without her.

I'll be back, sweetheart. I'm coming back.

She sucked a breath through her nose and pulled against the restraints, her feet slipping in the trough beneath her, toes slick with her own bile. Where had he found the trough? It hadn't been in the room when she'd arrived.

Thunk. Thunk.

He was back. She went still, letting her head hang. But in the moment before she closed her eyes, she thought she saw him in the mirror, something glittering in his hand.

Something wicked. Something sharp.

35

Petrosky shoved his cell into his pocket and stared out past the bullpen; at the blackness beyond the window.

"That was fast," Jackson said, collapsing into the seat beside him.

But Scott always was. Vivaan's mother was French-American, father American-born Indian, no convictions, no tickets, no problems. Parents, both doctors, had moved back to Europe the year Vivaan turned eighteen—they still paid his credit card bills. "And Scott managed to find a few more things online: Vivaan chatting on various US screenwriter message boards and on social media, bitching about his rejections, how he just wasn't sure what else agents could possibly want from him. He came off like a petulant child."

Jackson snorted. "I'm sure he did; he *is* a petulant child. He's twenty-two and clearly has no idea how to handle himself in the real world."

"Right. But he's smart as hell—scored a perfect 36 on his ACTs." Which was the only reason he was still out there; any other impulsive kid would have fucked up by now. Wouldn't have planned *so damn carefully*. "And Scott said the guy's father donated to the U of M medical program—Vivaan never even enrolled in premed. Never enrolled in college at all. He just hung out at that coffeehouse, probably to watch the ladies."

Jackson's brow furrowed. "So he's likely a failure in his parents' eyes."

Which explained the insecurity. Maybe even the mommy issues, though Petrosky still wasn't buying that their perp was fucking and killing his mom over and over. "They might pay so he can avoid homelessness, but they clearly aren't into the whole family thing."

"But he's not at home. So where the hell is he?" Jackson said.

Petrosky crossed his arms and leaned back in his chair, the springs screaming. This was where things got tricky. "Scott said there were no strange charges on his credit cards, nothing that we can trace to another location, and even his ATM withdrawals were from the machine near the path." No cameras. "He has taken out larger sums from his bank account in the last month, but prior to five weeks ago, he hadn't touched his debit card in a year." Not surprising—a guy with so many identities probably had yet another form of payment they hadn't discovered. But they needed to know what he'd used the money for.

"He might have been buying supplies with it," Jackson said, her eyes narrowed. "The drugs he used to knock his victims out."

"Maybe, but the withdrawals are higher than that—nearly two thousand dollars a week. No car registered in his name, no apartment or other lodging outside of the apartment we just came from—if he has another place, he's paying cash. And Mommy and Daddy are footing the bill for his insulin supplies; he doesn't have to pay out of pocket for it." All his own funds, those thousands of dollars were going to his little kidnapping-slice-em-dice-em murder hobby.

Jackson's fingers tapped nervously on the desktop. "I

pulled another list of abandoned properties while you were talking to Scott—high schools. It seems high school wasn't a good time for him, and a lot of the spiral notebooks had plays he'd written set in a high school. Now, clearly, the one he's rehearsing currently has at least one scene in a grocery store, but I couldn't find any abandoned groceries in the area, no abandoned restaurants either—nothing that would be secluded enough for our guy to keep someone prisoner."

"And the high schools?"

"Two abandoned, but they're in more densely populated areas. Decantor rode by one of them already—lots of squatters. No privacy, especially in the auditorium where our guy would probably be trying to—"

"Detectives."

They both looked up. Michaelson. "What do you want, rook?"

Jackson put up a hand. "I had him run by the other high school while I pulled the rest of the drama camps." They'd already checked abandoned theaters, but the drama camps might offer another option for their killer. In winter, many buildings where they were held went vacant—lots of kids working on their skills within their schools instead.

"What'd you find?" she asked the rookie.

"Nothing to find." Michaelson shook his blond head. "The school is abandoned like you said, but there were squatters. I pulled some of them in." He smiled as if it were somehow heroic to throw the homeless in jail for the high crime of not wanting to freeze to death.

Petrosky sighed at the sheets on the desk and turned to Jackson. "He sees himself as a real thespian, right?"

"A what?" Michaelson was still standing next to his desk —*why is he still here?* "I thought he was a dude."

"He is."

"Then how can he be a—"

"A thespian, not a lesbian. What the hell is wrong with

you?" Petrosky glanced up in time to see Michaelson's eyes widen, but looked down again before he could punch him in the jaw—maybe he could get away with tripping him. "Don't you have somewhere to be?"

The rookie's footsteps retreated from the bullpen. Jackson was shaking her head, probably at the sheer idiocy of that guy, but instead of berating Michaelson, she said, "You need to give that kid a break."

"He's a moron."

"He's trying."

He ignored her, his eyes on the list, and said: "So these drama camps...they have stages, but not theater seats?"

"Depends. Some camps are held in regular classrooms, and then they go perform at one of the local theaters. There are a couple with stages, and they're abandoned for the weeks between camps or productions. If our killer knew where to go, kept track of their schedules..." She shrugged.

But if a single person saw a light at night, or the owner walked in to set up for their next big production, he'd be fucked. "Any of the theaters rent their space?" *Follow the money.* It seemed like good advice. What better way to crush suspicion than to pay for your privacy?

"Not for long periods of time, not around here—nowhere he could sign a long-term lease. The theaters host comedy shows, Netflix specials, all kinds of shit between plays. Even the drama camps without stages host ceramics classes and art shows if they have the kind of space we're looking for—a big loft-style room."

"Right." So if he couldn't score a single location long term... "That's why he's changing locations every time he takes a new girl." They'd call every theater, every drama camp, see who had space for lease and when.

"You think he put his name on a lease agreement?"

"I doubt it. I mean, Bill? Come on. But this guy has to have a safe space—a place no one else is going to harass him."

It had to be a theater, right? A loft like Carroll described, an abandoned warehouse, both of those were more likely to have unwanted visitors, especially downtown. Their guy wouldn't tolerate the level of filth in an abandoned property, even on his best day—a playwright needed an impeccable stage. But any theater production company would be clean, and would have ways to dampen the noises; every theater, movie or otherwise, was insulated to the hilt. And he'd still added those curtains.

Maybe you could be standing right outside and never know someone was wailing behind the wall.

36

RESEARCHING theaters made Petrosky want to punch every actor that had ever existed. Several of the spaces seemed promising, but four of them were too small or too public or had numerous activities going on in the same building. No way the suspect was keeping women prisoner in one section of the building with children wandering the halls and musicians teaching tuba a few rooms over.

By the time four o'clock rolled around, Petrosky's eyes ached, his chest throbbing with exhaustion and the half-burned-out panic that still smoldered beneath the surface. Decantor had shown up with Rita's coffees, looking far too spry for the early morning hour. Michaelson had brought donuts, apparently trying to make amends for being a tool. Petrosky bit into a cruller without looking at the kid.

Jackson closed her laptop and snatched the rest of his pastry off the napkin on his desk. "Maybe you should go take a nap." She shoved the donut into her mouth.

He frowned at the sugar on her collar—same shirt as yesterday. They hadn't slept, but maybe they should at least go grab a change of clothes. He'd long since tossed his jacket over the chair, but even his T-shirt was itchy. "If I leave, who'll protect the donuts from your greedy ass?"

She stretched her arms above her head, the bags under her eyes more pronounced than even a few hours ago. "Got the last of the lease agreements here." She nodded toward the stack. They'd collected names from the drama clubs, the theaters, everywhere with available space for lease within ten miles of the dump site, and twelve miles of the killer's apartment. "So far, I'm not seeing any of the same names on the lease applications." She dropped her arms to the desk and put her head in her hands. "Where are the rest of those donuts?"

Petrosky tugged the pages from beneath her elbow and laid them side by side on the desktop. "He wouldn't use his real name. If he paid upfront in cash, they wouldn't refuse him if he said he'd forgotten his ID, and he could just as easily have a fake ID. I doubt these places are in the business of turning down money on a space that would otherwise be abandoned. They'd still have to pay to keep the heat on, or the pipes would freeze."

"There are just so many of them. How are there so many buildings that fit these criteria?"

"Motown forever, baby."

She dropped her arms and sat back, glaring at the pages like they owed her money. "We can't vet seventy buildings, each with fifty-two weeks of lease information. Even if we just look at the last four weeks, we don't have that kind of time. Laramie doesn't have that kind of time."

Their guy was impulsive with women he barely knew. What would he do to a woman he'd spent hours talking to each week, a woman he had stared at? Perhaps he'd even written scenes specifically for her. "We know the place has some theater characteristics, or at least he can quickly make it into something similar."

"And there was that chemical Scott found, too."

He frowned. "On the wood? That old lacquer stuff? That

was specific to Patel's case because of where he kept her, but we didn't find it on any of the other victims." And the killer wasn't going back to that old abandoned house.

"No, not that. The..." Jackson reached across him and fell back with the main case file in her hands. "Flavacol. Super common, from seasoned salt, right? We figured he happened to be eating it since it was only found with one vic—in the alley where he abducted Khatri. But with the constant changing of locations...maybe it came from a theater, you know? Do they use that stuff in popcorn?"

Petrosky pulled his keyboard closer and tapped it in. "Yup."

She tossed the file back on the desk and snatched his Rita's coffee cup—empty. *Joke's on you, Jackson.* "We need a place that had a working theater recently." Her hand tightened around the cup; the wax crinkled.

He gently took the cup from her and tossed it into the trash. "It might be where he kept Khatri, but we can't be certain he's keeping Laramie there too. I think Carroll was on to something when she said her room was like a cave— that it echoed like a cave. And no seats, no windows. He probably had her in a basement." They could look for two locations, one working theater, one basement, maybe narrow it that way—maybe he'd used the same fake name to rent out the place where he was keeping Laramie. Even the barista said he rarely gave the same name, but they might spot a connection.

"But...almost every place has a basement, Petrosky. We're not that far from tornado alley."

"How many lease those out, though?" Some of those theaters used basements as a space for actors to prep before going on stage, some for special-effect type stuff. Did any have smaller practice stages down below? Petrosky straightened and looked across the bullpen; Decantor apparently felt his eyes on him, and he turned their way. Petrosky raised a hand. Waved him over.

"Did you just ask Decantor to..." Jackson began, eyes wide.

"Of course, he's here to help us."

"Yeah, but you hate..." She quieted as Decantor stopped in front of the desk. Petrosky handed him a stack: a quarter of their lease agreements. "We need schematics on these places. We need to find out which of them have basements, probably a place that was a working theater in the very recent past. A place that serves popcorn...maybe." But the killer could have brought it with him. Maybe the popcorn was a prop.

Decantor smiled and reached for more—half the stack. "Sloan and I will take half. Race you to the finish." He winked and hustled back to his workspace.

Petrosky watched him go, shaking his head. "What a dork."

"A dork who's going to kick your ass at research."

But if it saved an innocent woman...

Petrosky passed her a stack. "Let's not let that happen."

DECANTOR DROPPED his pages onto Petrosky's desk and retreated to the break room, hopefully to bring them all more coffee since the big man had lost the great research race. They'd carved their initial list from seventy to twenty-six, but that was still too many to visit. And if they split up, they'd have less of a chance to actually save Laramie—assuming they were lucky enough to find her in time.

So what now? His head felt thick and fuzzy as if it had been filled with cotton.

"Any Bills or Vivaans on your lists?" Jackson asked in a voice that sounded as exhausted as he felt.

"No Bills." He stopped short. "Wait... I've got a William. William Shake."

Jackson raised her head. "As in Shakespeare?"

Petrosky straightened, his head clearing. "William..." He slumped once more. "Not sure it fits. William rented this space during the two weeks that our perp kept Patel in the cellar." Petrosky ran a finger down the pages, one after another. No other Williams. No Bills. No Shakes. No Vivaans.

Decantor returned, sliding two Styrofoam cups of coffee onto the desktop along with two more donuts.

Jackson lurched forward suddenly, her finger jabbing at a page, sloshing hot liquid onto Petrosky's arm.

"The fuck, Jackso—"

"I've got James Brooks." When Petrosky stared, Decantor said, "He wrote *Terms of Endearment*." Petrosky looked up at him, eyebrows raised, but Decantor was already reaching for the stack. "Hang on, I think I saw a Brooks, too, but that one wasn't a basement." He slipped a page from the middle and laid it beside the donuts. "Yeah, this one is a Stephen Brooks." They all squinted at the terms on the leases—the dates.

"He rented this place out during the time he kept Carroll," Petrosky said, tapping Decantor's sheet, then moved to the next page. "And then we have James Brooks at this property during the same time frame—started one week prior, overlapped this lease by two days."

Decantor was shaking his head. "What'd he do, lease two or three places at a time under different names?"

"He's a writer," Petrosky said slowly. "He knows how to do his research. Hell, he could stream one good true-crime special, and he'd know all the tricks. How to cover his tracks."

"Ah," Jackson said. "I get it now. Ernest Frost, the name from the PO Box and from the order at the fabric store—a combination of Ernest Hemingway and Jack Frost, right?"

She was already tapping manically on her laptop. "What are the other names, basements or otherwise? Let's start at the top sheet, everyone who leased space this week. See what other variations on screenwriters or playwrights we can find."

"Damon Jenkins," Petrosky said.

"Not a playwright."

"Kevin Wade?"

Jackson's fingers click-clacked on the keyboard, but Decantor said, "Wade did *Meet Joe Black*."

Petrosky made a mark on the sheet. "Doesn't sound romantic. Is it about an arranged marriage?"

Decantor smiled. "Not really."

Petrosky went back to his list. "Looks like all that time spent studying the Kardashians is finally paying off, Decantor."

Decantor opened his mouth to say something back, but Petrosky was faster. "Wait, Nicholas Sparks? Didn't you mention him before, Jackson?" Or had that been Carroll? And the location... "We went to this theater already, after Carroll's abduction, but..." Not at the right time—the killer hadn't arrived yet. He'd been smarter than they were, and now another girl was going to lose her life. His chest spasmed and settled. *Not if I can help it, dammit.*

"Yeah, Sparks writes all those gooey romance novels," Jackson said.

Petrosky made a mark on that sheet, too—was his hand shaking? He forced out: "You read that trashy stuff, do you?"

Jackson looked away.

"You read them, and then you call Acharya, and then you... Oh god, I'm going to be sick."

"Wait," Decantor said. "Acharya? The *journalist*?" He looked as shocked as Petrosky had been. "You're seeing *that* guy? Please tell me it isn't true."

Petrosky suppressed a smile.

"Both of you shut up," Jackson said. "And it's okay to like romance, Petrosky. With what we do, anything to get our minds off the blood, right?"

"That journalist does anything fucked up, I'll show you blood," Decantor muttered, and Petrosky and Jackson both looked over at him, surprised. The big man was frowning, but he sure as shit looked serious.

"I'll help you bury the asshole," Petrosky offered. "But first..." He frowned at the page. "Looks like Nicholas Sparks, Kevin Wade, and Kevin Sparks paid for three overlapping locations this week, all of which we've looked at before." But now they were on to him. He wasn't going to win.

Petrosky handed one sheet to Decantor, who was still staring at Jackson like she had a spider crawling across her cheek. Or maybe he was jealous.

Maybe there was hope for him yet.

37

Sloan and Decantor headed for the first place on the list, an above-ground playhouse complete with a stage and a concession stand. Jackson and Petrosky took the second—the basement of a smaller production house. Five miles apart. Which one? Which one? Or was he at the third location? That would be just their luck.

The theater was on the corner of a busy strip. Jackson parked a block up the street, and they hustled toward the building, scanning the surrounding cityscape, hats drawn over their ears. The theater sign rose above a sea of unassuming brown bricks—off now. Was he watching them? No, he was surely busy in his homemade version of hell, and that thought brought to mind the horrors Petrosky'd witnessed in another basement not so very long ago, the stink of iron, the chains...the cages. The dead girls still shackled to the wall with blood on their lips.

Nearby, now-closed bodegas sat crammed full of tchotchkes and plastic bottles of soda and T-shirts that usually featured whatever event was happening in the theater. He half expected to see that yellow sundress behind the barred glass, but he saw nothing but the expected rainbow of beads and travel mugs. When he'd driven by it a few days back, the shirts had featured some pop star Decantor probably knew, but those had since been replaced with images of a guy with a microphone. Paid for talking. Imagine that.

The bricks past the glass front doors of the theater faded from tan to puce as they stepped beyond the halo of the security floods. But when they approached the corner...pitch black along the side of the building. "I don't like this," Jackson muttered under her breath. In an hour, the hazy morning would lighten the sky, but now it was like walking into a void. "Not even a streetlamp?"

He drew his eyes to the more distant skyline—to the glowing ribbon of lights that slunk away from them into the early morning. But the three lights directly across the way from this side of the theater were dark. "Sure is coincidental that these ones happen to be broken." And coincidences were bullshit, they both knew it. "Text Decantor."

She nodded.

The back entry was halfway up, tucked into a little nook of brick and heavy oak. They'd woken the manager and had procured the key, but would their suspect hear the lock clanking open?

Please be in the basement, asshole. Petrosky shoved the key into the lock and turned it before he could change his mind.

Inside, the hall was just as black as the night outdoors. They dared not turn on the lights. Petrosky squinted, letting his eyes adjust, watching the shadows undulating around them as if they were underwater—and he felt as if they were. He couldn't breathe.

Slowly the room solidified in the meager emergency lights: a hallway in front of them led to another locked door that the manager hadn't given them a key to, that shithead.

But if they didn't have access, their suspect didn't either. To their left was another door, STAIRS above it in glowing white letters. Jackson nodded that direction, and they eased it open and slipped into an even thicker dark. No emergency lights here, nothing but a pathetic glow from the bottom of the steps—it seemed so far away.

They made their way by feel, stopping every few stairs to listen in case their suspect was nearby, ready to ambush them, or worse, kill the girl, but he heard nothing but the incessant whisper of their breath. Then there were no more steps, and no door at the bottom—a dim alien glow beckoned them into the hallway.

Their footfalls felt heavier here, louder, but his heart was louder still, thrumming in his temples like the beating of a drum. Black piping like giant snakes twisted over the ceiling, the bricks on either side lined with safety signs. Around them, the walls hissed, but it was surely the heat, a boiler somewhere, perhaps, or maybe running water, but the effect was eerie as if they were entering the belly of a giant, angry reptile. And where was the light coming from? Though the glow remained, he had yet to see the source—no overhead bulbs. No fluorescents winked from the baseboards.

They hurried on, Petrosky's feet aching, his legs burning, his weapon raised.

The light brightened up ahead, from the barely-there haze in the hall to a vibrant white glare that hurt his eyes. From the schematics, and the building manager, this hall was the only way into the secondary rehearsal theater their suspect had rented, but beyond the stage itself were bathrooms and a few dressing rooms complete with lighted mirrors for makeup.

They slowed as they approached the arch at the far end; curtains blocked the light up to about the seven-foot mark, but above that, theater lights blazed. Spotlights? Petrosky stepped through the opening in the curtains, but was met with another wall of fabric—two rows of thick black curtains, creating a tunnel in the center. The light seemed to wriggle out from behind the far row of cloth like a living creature. Maybe he'd find a break in the cloth that would let him see the room beyond without disturbing the material—without letting their suspect know where they were. Or that they were here at all.

It didn't take long; their guy was a perfectionistic, but he was far from actually being perfect. Petrosky lowered his eye to the slit between the curtains. Not spotlights as he'd thought, but floodlights, like those they used to illuminate a crime scene. And they *were* brightening a crime scene, all of them aimed at the woman in the middle of the room. Her head hung limply against her clavicle. Black hair shrouded her face.

Petrosky's heart caught in his throat. Was she alive? *Please be alive.* He squinted, his blood electrified, but yes, *there*, a tiny movement in her stomach—a barely-there intake of breath that he never would have seen if she'd been clothed. Her yellow dress, that goddamn yellow sundress in the same material as the bastard's comforter, was stuck at chest level, stretched tight across her breasts like a sash. Belly exposed—the tiniest of bulges. And…blood. It ran from her wrists to her shoulders in thin streams, lighter smears along her rib cage, dripping lower on her thighs, but he couldn't see her feet beyond the large brown trough she stood in. And it wasn't only blood, he could see that, too. Vomit, maybe. Who knew what other bodily fluids. And now Petrosky could see the tiny punctures along the sides of her abdomen, the swollen holes—how many times had he injected her already? The next one might put her into seizures; the next one could kill her. But though every muscle in his body ached to run to her, to free her, to carry her out of this place, their killer would not have left her strung up here and walked away.

This was his masterpiece, his epic romance. And she was his leading lady.

No, he was here, and somewhere close. But where? *Where?*

The deep black shadows that cloaked Petrosky and Jackson now were a double-edged sword—he wasn't sure exactly where the far entrance was, the one that might lead to the makeup rooms the building manager had mentioned. And with the two rows of thick curtains, the guy could essentially walk through the tunnel in the middle, in the pitch. They'd never know he was there until he shot them in the face, or, more likely, stuck them with a loaded hypodermic.

Shhhht.

Petrosky froze. The sound came again, a harsh rustle like sandpaper on wood followed by the thick clunk of boots. And...

There you are. His hackles rose.

Vivaan Laghari stalked out onto the stage, emerging like a mirage from beyond the black curtains at the far wall. His footsteps were an abomination, the heartbeat of a demon.

Jackson squeezed Petrosky's arm and shrank back into the blackness behind him. Tiptoeing. Heading around through the velvet tunnel—she'd get him from the back.

But not Petrosky. *I'll make sure you see me coming, fucker.* He wanted to look into this asshole's eyes when he brought him down.

Vivaan skirted the tub and stopped in front of Laramie's limp body, his back to Petrosky. "Are you ready, my love?"

She did not move.

Vivaan cocked his head, then brought something from behind his back—a needle, and not the smaller one he'd use for insulin. "You'll be okay," he whispered, almost to himself. "I'm here to save you." He drew it toward her flesh—toward her belly.

"Freeze!" Jackson stepped from the curtains at the far end of the room. The man startled and lowered the needle, his back still to Petrosky.

"Looks like we have an audience, my love."

Jackson sidled closer, weapon aimed. "Drop it and put your hands in the air." Her voice was low. Deadly serious.

Still, Vivaan didn't move. "I'm diabetic, I just need to take my shot."

"We'll get you insulin at the hospital."

The hospital? The only place this asshole was going was prison. Or the morgue.

"I might not make it." Vivaan lowered the needle, out to his side, and as he did, the back of his shirt lifted just enough for Petrosky to see...the knife. The butterfly knife that Carroll had told them about, the one he'd used to slice her open—to carve off her love handles. Was it still stained with her blood? Petrosky drew his eyes once more to Laramie, her belly pockmarked with needle holes. *He* might not make it? She was the one who wouldn't last much longer without a hospital.

Jackson stepped closer. Petrosky edged from behind the curtain, and Jackson shifted to the left, keeping him out of the line of fire. Petrosky kept his eyes on the knife. Inches—the man's hand was inches away from the blade, and Laramie's vulnerable form a mere foot from him. One quick movement, one slash, and—

Vivaan dropped the needle and drew his hand back, to the back of his pants. Petrosky launched himself across the room and threw himself onto the much smaller man—the guy was quick, but he was no match for Petrosky's bulk. They toppled to the floor just as Vivaan withdrew the blade.

Petrosky felt a sharp, searing pain in his side. He grabbed for the man's hands, and the pressure on his side released, but his rib cage was still on fire—the molten burning of severed flesh. Wet. The man lurched, going for the weapon again, and Petrosky brought his fist up and smashed it down into the side of his head. Vivaan grunted. The knife clattered to the wood. Then Jackson was on them, too, her cuffs out, reaching for Vivaan's wrists. Petrosky shifted back, his knee on the guy's spine as Jackson snapped the cuffs, making the man cry out.

"She loves me. Just ask her. Ask her!"

"Shut the fuck up, dickhead." Petrosky heaved himself to standing—it was hard to breathe. Jackson stood, too, her weapon once again trained on the man on the floor. She pulled her cell from her pocket but paused when she glanced his way. "Uh...Petrosky?"

"What?"

She pointed. His shirt was sticking to him, a fist-sized stain of crimson growing ever wider.

"It's a flesh wound, it's fine." But... that was a lot of blood. "Where the hell is Decantor?"

"Any second." The phone was already at her ear. "We need a bus."

As if she'd heard, Laramie groaned and raised her head, eyes wide, beseeching. Her lips moved, and though he could not hear her over the thundering of his pulse, he could read what she was trying to say: "Help." Tears streamed down her cheeks.

"Petrosky, hang on, Decantor—"

"I'm not going to let her hang here while we wait on everyone else," he said. "She's been up there long enough."

Gingerly he stepped into the tub. She was awake, openly sobbing now, convulsing as he wrapped an arm around her rib cage and whipped out his own pocket knife, drawing the blade to the rope above them. His side brightened with pain as if that one act had snapped every tendon between his shoulder and hip. She moaned. He bit his lip to avoid groaning along with her.

"It's okay, honey, just hang on. We're going to get you out

of here." His hand was burning too, everything a mess of agony. His shoulders throbbed. He sawed harder. *Come on.*

The rope gave way all at once, and she sagged against him like a sack of wet stones. But his guts no longer hurt. He stooped, threaded his arm beneath her knees, and carried her out.

38

"Looks like you healed up okay." Decantor's smile was infectious, but Petrosky plastered a scowl on his mug for good measure and dropped his coffee cup on his desk.

"No thanks to you. What were you doing again? Trying to see whether your favorite Kardashian posted something new on the internet?"

Decantor grinned more broadly. "How'd you guess?"

It was nearly a month since they'd pulled Vivaan Laghari off the streets—since they'd brought Laramie home. He still saw Vivaan's face sometimes in his sleep, but that kept the other images at bay. Feeling Vivaan's frail body beneath his fists didn't give him the slightest bit of pause—didn't make him question who he was.

Didn't keep him awake at night.

The stuff with the chief did, but he'd corrected that. Carroll wasn't his sponsor anymore. He'd cut her loose before she left the hospital, before her husband got even more upset than he was already. Petrosky wasn't about to get in the way of a potentially good thing—he'd been selfish, he could see that now. It wasn't anyone else's job to keep him clean, and no matter what McCallum had to say on the subject, he wouldn't be taking on another sponsor. No one else would do.

He turned at a squeal behind him—the door. Acharya strode in like he owned the place, grinning at Jackson in a way that made Petrosky want to remind the man that he had a gun and wasn't afraid to use it. But Jackson was smiling back at the journalist, and that should be good enough, shouldn't it? Even if it was gross. He kinda hoped Jackson had stopped giving him any; Acharya had admitted to researching that makeup stuff, that he'd had a hunch. A hunch he hadn't shared with the police, even when it might have helped them catch a killer. Shifty bastard.

Acharya set another coffee on Petrosky's desk. Rita's. "You sucking up for something?" Petrosky snapped.

"Nah, I just figured you'd be tired. Maybe in the mood to celebrate, I don't know."

"Celebrate what?"

Acharya raised an eyebrow at Jackson. "You didn't tell him?"

Fuck. If they were getting married, Petrosky was going to lose his ever-loving—

Jackson kept her nose buried in a case file. "Laramie's naming the baby Regina."

Oh, thank god. "After you?"

She finally raised her head. "Who else? You think she should name her daughter Ed?"

"Of course not, that'd be ridiculous. Edwina, though..."

She rolled her eyes. "You're a maniac, you know that?"

"It's part of my charm." And maniac or not, he'd managed to put Vivaan Laghari in jail where he belonged. They were actually making a movie about the guy, which made Petrosky want to punch Vivaan square in the nose, ruin his pretty face for the camera.

"About that movie thing..." Acharya said as if reading Petrosky's mind. "They asked me to consult."

Composed

"So you're going to help that asshole get famous like he always wanted?" *Maybe I should punch Acharya instead.*

"Nah. Well, maybe, but not in the way he wants. He's into being a leading man, but I think the guy was probably obsessed with measurements because he spent so many years obsessed with his own tiny pecker." He raised a hand, two fingers to demonstrate.

Petrosky tried to keep scowling, but his lips defied him. He chuckled. Maybe he could like the journalist a little better —at least until he screwed up again. Which he would.

Journalists always did.

Petrosky has a lot more fight in him—and Ash Park has no shortage of killers. Continue the series with *Witness*, the next novel in the Ash Park series! Addictive, fast-paced, and unforgettable, *Witness* is an electrifying ride through a maze of family secrets, desperation, and perseverance. For fans of *Criminal Minds* and *The Blacklist*.

WITNESS
CHAPTER 1

The night whispered with the thick anxiety known to criminals and cops alike; an unspoken world navigated using the hairs along your spine—where the twitching of your belly feels inexplicably linked to your trigger finger. But instead of a nasty prickling between his shoulder blades, Detective Edward Petrosky felt only the heavy weight of responsibility, its sharp edge muted by booze. Relapse had come more easily than he'd anticipated, without fanfare or preamble. One day he was sober, the next he wasn't, and he hadn't decided if he'd stop again. Maybe he didn't have to. Maybe it'd be fine. Logically, he knew that was stupid, but he wasn't sure he cared.

He narrowed his eyes at the wall where twin smears of

blood eked their way down toward the floor. Shattered glass adorned the hall table like glittering flakes of snow, though Petrosky could practically feel the heat coming off the wet edges of the wood—the blood was still fresh. It speckled the floor, smeared the baseboards in ruby, stained the wall between the hall and the kitchen.

"Front lock's been jimmied," Regina Jackson said, and Petrosky turned to see his partner kneeling by the front door, her eyes on the knob. The March wind had been mild today, but now it hissed out of the dark like a frozen blade, biting into his flesh through his sweatshirt. Jackson did not appear to notice. Her shorn black hair did not move in the breeze; even the lapels of her cream peacoat remained stiffly in place, brilliant against her dark throat. How the hell did she always manage to look like she'd just walked off the cover of *GQ Detectives Monthly*? It was four o'clock in the fucking morning; his socks didn't even match.

Footsteps to his right made him turn. Michaelson—shit, he hated that guy—strode in from the kitchen, his jacket barely missing a watch sitting on the edge of the Formica counter. A Rolex? Petrosky stepped closer, squinting. Yes, and a real one, the glass on the front magnifying the date. It didn't belong here, not in this house, not in this neighborhood. Michaelson stepped into the living room, blocking Petrosky's view of the counter, and gestured to the glass on the hallway floor. "Weird thing for a burglar to do, smashing picture frames. What'd he think, that there was money hidden behind them?"

"Maybe the intruder didn't want the family looking at him," Petrosky said. But no family, no children, smiled from the portraits behind the shards of glass; a single man appeared in all of them, sometimes with other dark-haired, broad-chested fellows, though one featured a fortysomething woman with a bouffant hairdo, her leathery skin sallow and sagging. The man was familiar, but Petrosky could not place him. *Maybe you shouldn't have had that Jack before bed, old man.* But, no, he was good, he'd just had a drink or two last night—okay, this morning—at the bar near his place. So far, he'd avoided drinking at home.

Michaelson frowned. "What's that smell?"

"Probably the garbage," Jackson said, but she wrinkled her nose. Michaelson stepped back to the sink and swung open the cabinet underneath—a trash bin. "Yup, hasn't been taken out in a while. The perp would probably have found more to steal in here than behind the picture frames, right?"

Was that asshole smiling? *Fucking idiot.* Petrosky turned back to the living room instead of looking at Michaelson any longer, but the view there was only marginally better. The couch was trashed like the pictures, the gray pillows strewn on the floor. The coffee table had been knocked over, too, its wooden legs sticking up like the stiff limbs of a roadkill corpse. "This isn't a burglary, Michaelson."

"But they jimmied the front door, and the caller said—"

"Callers lie." And so did supposed victims. The homeowner hadn't even been the one who called—a neighbor had phoned in the disturbance. Throwing picture frames was a noisy matter, as was tossing other humans into walls and over coffee tables. Burglars tended to move with a little more stealth.

"It sounded like the caller was plenty serious to me," Michaelson said, a note of whiny defensiveness in his voice. "What else would it be but a burglary? The owner wasn't even here when the break-in occurred."

"And yet there's blood all over his jacket," Petrosky snapped. Petrosky had walked past the ambulance on his way in, the homeowner inside still wearing his bloody coat—getting his hand stitched up. "Does that sound like a man who just stumbled in on his house being robbed?"

"No I mean, yes, but his hands were bleeding. He ran in

because he saw the front door open, and he cut himself on the glass. But he doesn't want to press charges."

Petrosky frowned at the hall table; all those broken frames. The only reason to ignore a home invasion, to give a "burglar" a pass, was if you didn't want the police involved. But why? Was the homeowner protecting a friend? Family? Unless he was protecting himself—a bookie, maybe. Hiding the intruder to hide his own sins, Petrosky had seen that enough times. But whatever it was, it had ended in a scuffle, and the owner of the house rubbed him the wrong way— even looking at his picture made Petrosky's shoulders tense. "Get the fuck out, Michaelson. We've got work to do."

"But I—"

"Now." Petrosky could feel the daggers in his back, the kid glaring at him, but the rookie shuffled toward the door and out onto the porch, probably with a commiserative pat on the back from Jackson. He scanned the wall again, the twin trails of blood that marred the paint—fingers and a palm, probably someone trying to grab the wall. There was way too much spatter on the floor to support this guy's claim of slicing his hand on a broken picture frame. Petrosky's eyes lit on the photo nearest him: the homeowner in a button-down dress shirt, beer in hand, dark chest hair peeking from beneath his open collar.

Who'd you fight with, fuck-o? "Did Michaelson check the bedrooms?" he asked. "The bathroom? The basement?"

"Yep. No other signs of struggle, nothing disturbed—neat."

Petrosky grunted. He'd seen a lot of home invasions, and there was a pattern to them, even when it was punk kids; thieves knew that valuables were usually kept in the bedroom so they wouldn't have started in the living room, and they sure as hell wouldn't have left that damn Rolex. So why jimmy the lock? Why break in?

Petrosky turned to see Jackson closing the front door,

pulling her phone away from her ear, though he hadn't heard her talking to anyone. Maybe he did have a little too much whiskey in his system—what time had he stopped drinking again?

"Outside isn't quite as neat, though. Looks like someone ran out the back," Jackson said. "Michaelson followed the blood to see if there was any trace of another person, but the trail petered out in the grass near the back gate."

"What's the homeowner's explanation for that?" If there hadn't been a struggle, blood in the grass was pretty weird unless their burly homeowner had sacrificed a goat to the gods of rich, luscious chest hair—that would explain a lot, actually.

"Homeowner says he ran out there in a panic after he cut himself. Wanted to see if anyone was still here." She shrugged, but her face said: *bullshit.* And whether or not it was true, a burglary, even a domestic call, wasn't their usual case—no rape, no dead people...well, probably not. There were plenty of flatfoots to take a statement on a B&E, even with a possible assault.

"Why are we on this?" He glanced once more at the living room, at the upended coffee table—one wooden leg was stained dark with blood.

She cocked her head. "The chief didn't tell you?"

Nope. He hadn't spoken to Chief Carroll in a month.

Jackson seemed to sense his confusion because she said: "This guy, the homeowner...you know him."

"I don't think so." But when his gaze dropped to the photos once more, he felt it again, that prickle of familiarity. *Why don't I remember him?*

"Piotr...something. I can't pronounce it. He's got a few priors, but nothing significant until about five years ago. His girlfriend, Louisa, said he slapped her around, raped her, and threatened to kill her if she called the police. Ring any bells? She was one of yours."

Ah, fuck. Now he knew why this guy looked familiar. Piotr Wójcik—that was his name. His victim, Louisa Parson, had stopped cooperating soon after he'd taken her statement, suddenly claimed the three-inch-long weeping gash along her eyebrow was "just a misunderstanding." Without her testimony, the prosecutor kicked it back and said there was nothing they could do, but Petrosky had felt certain Piotr had done it before—he had seen that much in the dull, unremorseful glitter in Piotr's eyes. And these assholes had a pattern; at the very least, Piotr had surely earned a few enemies besides Louisa. Had one of them come after him? That would explain why he was reluctant to tell them what had happened here. He could suddenly see Louisa's face, the dark, deep wound on her head, and was struck by an intense urge to find her—to make sure she was okay. "Need to call her," he muttered.

Jackson raised an eyebrow. "For what? It's not like she did this."

"Just...worried about her, I guess. Piotr fucked her up bad." Petrosky shifted his focus to the upended coffee table, the bloody wood, and...something was peeking from beneath it. He edged closer, grabbed the opposite leg—the clean leg—and pulled. *Uh-oh.* Beneath the table, the carpet was shiny, wet. A puddle of blood the size of his fist glared at him like an angry eye.

Someone had been hurt here. Severely. And their homeowner was still standing—no way that was his blood.

He glared at the stain, his chest tightening with unease.

What'd you do, asshole? What the fuck did you do?

**GET *WITNESS*
on https://meghanoflynn.com**

Love psychological thrillers? Try the Mind Games series! Start the series with *The Dead Don't Dream*. *A psychologist must decide whether her sleepwalking patient is a victim or a brutal serial killer in this unpredictable psychological thriller.*

THE DEAD DON'T DREAM
CHAPTER 1

MOONLIGHT FELL in harsh blades of white against the hardwood floors. It bleached the oak, but it made the filth on his hands appear black, inky and shiny and somehow heavy —tacky against his flesh. It was caked around his wrist, too, pressed into the tiny crevices of his jewelry, smashed into the circular gilded edge, smeared over the leather band. The piece was old as the dirt itself, as reliable as the ground beneath his feet, but it felt... compromised. Soiled.

He stilled, held his breath and strained his ears, but he could not hear the steady *tick, tick, tick* that usually echoed through the room like a second heartbeat—the antique clock from the night table was on the floor. Ticking away for a century, and now it was dead.

Dead. The word ate at the soft spot between his shoulder blades for reasons he could not immediately place. Though he was unable to feel his own heart throbbing in his chest, *he* wasn't dead. He was in his bedroom. A dream—just a dream. But the expanse between the area rug and the floor-to-ceiling window was covered in scattered bits of grass and pebbles. He could smell damp earth, the musk of worms. His feet were bare, cold against the rug. His toes were... wet.

Mud.

He closed his eyes, trying to force his brain to understand, but slivers of memory slipped by without offering explanation. And though he was quite sure that he was alone, he could hear the wet hiss of breath against his ear, less like air and more like the rush of some unidentifiable pent-up emotion. He could still feel the sultry damp of her lips against his earlobe, her teeth like knives, the canines of a hungry animal, tearing his throat as if she intended to sever his windpipe. His wrists hurt as if he'd been tied.

Was it really just a dream? Some of it was. The woman, her long blonde hair, her blade-sharp teeth—those couldn't possibly be real. No injuries marred his neck; no bloody ribbons of skin hung beneath his hairline. Though his wrists were sore, he could not make out any abrasions that might indicate he'd been the victim of some attack. But there were parts that felt more vital—details that stuck out in sharp contrast. He could see the moon in his mind's eye, the outdoor world gray beneath its glare. He could hear the heavy weight of silence broken only by the crackling whisper of skittering leaves. He could feel the rocks, sharp beneath the knees of his sweatpants—he could feel those abrasions even now, the enduring sting from road-rashed skin. And the dirt...

The mud was real. That was definitely real.

He opened his eyes. The dirt... it wasn't only on him, nor was it merely on the floor as if he'd tracked it inside. It was *everywhere*. A swipe of grime marred the window, obscuring the night beyond. The bedspread was crusted in fine streaks of thick black and wider smears of filthy gray.

He touched his face, his fingertips gritty and sticky—mud in his facial hair. The top edge of his cheekbone felt sharper than usual, but the dirt there was dry.

The blood was not. And though the world was a black-and-white movie in the silver gleam of the moon, he knew now that it was blood. He could smell it, woven through with the damp musk of petrichor, the metallic tang of congealing life... or recent death.

Bile rose in his throat. He gagged, his heart thundering to life, pumping furiously as if his body had only now realized that he was being pursued by some predator, his meat snared in a frenzied dance of ichor and panic. Then he was running, wobbling and lopsided, off the rug, over the dirty floor to the marble tile of the bathroom—frigid against his feet. Gooseflesh shivered along his spine. He threw himself onto his injured knees in front of the toilet.

Bile and the bitter remnants of vodka tonic poured over his tongue and dripped past his lips. But the dirt... oh, the dirt. That was far worse.

This was supposed to be over.

He retched again, again, then slumped back against the wall. He inhaled deeply, trying to steady the frantic throb in his temples, trying to ease the pulse that was turning his vision into a strobe, but he only succeeded in lodging dirt deep in his sinuses. He gagged and snorted, staring in horror at the earth still crusted beneath his fingernails and the slippery weeping chasm along the pad of his thumb. He had tried so hard to stop, but perhaps he'd only been lying to himself. The proof was here, everything he needed to know.

He'd done something terrible.

Again.

**GET *THE DEAD DON'T DREAM*
on https://meghanoflynn.com**

__The Silent Patient__ meets __You__. Every person on Ice Island has an agenda—some understandable, some convoluted, some downright sadistic. Evelyn Hawthorn is a case in point. I'll tell you about them all later... if we make it that long.

**MAD BROKE COLD
CHAPTER 1**

There's an unofficial categorization tool at psychiatric hospitals, whispered among the shrinks: Mad, Broke, Cold. If outsiders knew about it, they'd gnash their teeth and rant about the political incorrectness of it all, but they've never purposefully surrounded themselves with those who'd like to stab their eyes out. Sure, we've all met at least one person who has considered how our skin might look stretched over a fashionable armchair, but that's beside the point. Stories like this one can't go forward without transparency.

So... Mad, Broke, Cold.

Mad, so named for the Mad Hatters. Severe, persistent conditions do not respond to the kind of therapy that twentysomethings reference on social media in quips that start with "OMFG, my therapist said." The *Mad* require medications and monitoring, while dementia or schizophrenia eat holes in their gray matter. They'll leave this world as insane as the day they were admitted to Ice Island—formerly Iverson Estate, then Iverson Sanatorium, more recently Iverson Psychiatric Hospital, though they might as well call it "Nothing Left to Lose Manor." Welcome home, sick-os.

But I digress, as my father warned me I've a tendency to do. This is only one reason I spent much of my childhood locked away, where he did not need to listen to the grating tone of my voice or endure my long-winded nonsense.

Speaking of, I'd rather not prove him right.

Onward.

Broke, despite the moniker, has nothing to do with money. Trauma has severed the *Broke* from their old life, leaving them clawing at the walls as if they might unearth who they used to be before "it happened." There's help for the *Broke*—the *Broken* if you want to be pedantic about it. Pharmaceuticals, therapy, EMDR, shock treatment, oh, yes, there is hope for the *Broke*.

Of course, so long as there's hope, it's easy to believe that the problem is *you*. I always thought that if I just worked harder, I could figure out what I was doing wrong—that I could chase my demons away and be like the "normal folks" flaunting their "normal lives" like an endless parade of my own failings.

But demons don't go easy. They burrow into your soul and violently resist exorcism. So long as you have hope, you have pain. I learned to cope over the years—I'm a bit of an asshole, but a rather well-adjusted, even likable one, if I do say so myself—but most are not so lucky. I've come to believe that unrequited hope, or hope for an impossible "normal" life, is a fate worse than death. Especially for those locked up here.

On Ice Island, *Mad* and *Broke* mean the same as the terms tossed around in mainland hospitals.

Cold is a different matter.

On the mainland, the *Cold* are looking for "three hots and a cot"—psychiatric admissions that peak in early February before the ground thaws. These are the people no one notices on the street except to skirt their outstretched palms. Veterans, useless to the government once they've given up a limb to the cause; those with no access to medications or therapy until they open their wrists and force too-brief emergency room treatment; lonely chaps with no loved ones to notice when they lose touch with reality. But losing one's grasp on reality doesn't necessarily make one dangerous.

Keyword: *necessarily.*

I should clarify this up front: "psychopath" is not equivalent to "murderer." Antisocial personality disorder ups the chances for homicide, the warrior gene trips aggressive tendencies into overdrive, but it's childhood trauma that flips the—forgive me—"kill" switch. Either the *Mad, Broke,* or *Cold* might be triggered to bathe in your blood. Convince any person that they can't survive unless they do awful things, and they'll pick up a blade. If you're lucky, they'll use it on themselves.

If you're not so lucky? Well.

No one on Ice Island is literally cold, and this is for the greater good. The *Cold* want your skin stretched over that armchair, your entrails braided into a delicate pull cord, your fat used to fuel the fire in their hearth. Barring this, you're as useless to them as the homeless are to you—those you ignore because "he might spend it on liquor" or whatever moral justification helps you sleep. The *Cold* have similar justifications for the things they'd like to do to you, and neither of you is more right—or wrong—than the other. Perspective is a funny thing, is it not?

Anyway.

If you inadvertently meet someone *Cold* on the mainland, you might be fine. We all know at least one person we'd call a "psycho," and half of us are probably right. But on the mainland, most *Cold* have learned to behave. They can flip their "kill switch" off; they care about consequences. They still have things to lose.

But unlike you, clomping down the street in your snow boots, pretending no one else exists, the *Cold* on Ice Island don't skirt outstretched palms. They'll grab your hand, yank you into whatever hell they deem fit. You'll never see them coming—never see them go, either, unless they screw up.

Which is why they're here.

Make no mistake: despite whatever error got them caught, those locked up on Ice Island are viciously smart. Smart enough that the powers that be refuse to lock them in prisons due to risks to other murderers, refuse to put them anywhere they might escape. And an island off the coast of Alaska is as close as it gets to inescapable, as it was designed to be—as Alcott Iverson's family ensured it was.

But dear Alcott is a story for another time, as are the stories of the patients who reside here. Their case files, histories, police reports, hospital records—I have them all. I'll transcribe them for you, word for word, as they become relevant. It's interesting stuff, I assure you, without a single embellishment. Every person in this facility has an agenda, some understandable, some endearing, some convoluted, some downright sadistic. I'll tell you all about them later...

If we make it that long.

**SCAN THE CODE BELOW TO GET *MAD BROKE COLD*
or visit https://meghanoflynn.com**

PRAISE FOR BESTSELLING AUTHOR MEGHAN O'FLYNN

"Creepy and haunting... fully immersive thrillers. The Ash Park series should be everyone's next binge-read."
~*New York Times Bestselling Author Andra Watkins*

"Full of complex, engaging characters and evocative detail, *Wicked Sharp* is a white-knuckle thrill ride. O'Flynn is a master storyteller." ~*Paul Austin Ardoin, USA Today Bestselling Author*

"Nobody writes with such compelling and entrancing prose as O'Flynn. With perfectly executed twists, Born Bad is chilling, twisted, heart-pounding suspense. This is my new favorite thriller series." ~*Bestselling Author Emerald O'Brien*

"Visceral, fearless, and addictive, this series will keep you on the edge of your seat." ~*Bestselling Author Mandi Castle*

"Intense and suspenseful...captured me from the first chapter and held me enthralled until the final page."
~*Susan Sewell, Reader's Favorite*

"Cunning, delightfully disturbing, and addictive, the Ash Park series is an expertly written labyrinth."~*Award-winning Author Beth Teliho*

"Dark, gritty, and raw, O'Flynn's work will take your mind prisoner and keep you awake far into the morning hours." ~*Bestselling Author Kristen Mae*

"From the feverishly surreal to the downright demented,

Composed

O'Flynn takes you on a twisted journey through the deepest and darkest corners of the human mind."
~*Bestselling Author Mary Widdicks*

"With unbearable tension and gripping, thought-provoking storytelling, O'Flynn explores fear in all the best—and creepiest—ways. Masterful psychological thrillers replete with staggering, unpredictable twists." ~*Bestselling Author Wendy Heard*

LEARN MORE ON
https://meghanoflynn.com

WANT MORE FROM MEGHAN?
There are many more books to choose from!

Learn more about Meghan's novels on
https://meghanoflynn.com

ABOUT THE AUTHOR

With books deemed "visceral, haunting, and fully immersive" (*New York Times bestseller, Andra Watkins*), Meghan O'Flynn has made her mark on the thriller genre. Meghan is a clinical therapist who draws her character inspiration from her knowledge of the human psyche. She is the bestselling author of gritty crime novels and serial killer thrillers, all of which take readers on the dark, gripping, and unputdownable journey for which Meghan is notorious. Learn more at https://meghanoflynn.com! While you're there, join Meghan's reader group, and get a **FREE SHORT STORY** just for signing up.

Want to connect with Meghan?
https://meghanoflynn.com

www.ingramcontent.com/pod-product-compliance
Lightning Source LLC
LaVergne TN
LVHW040614250326
834688LV00035B/551